TERESA'S VOYAGE

TERESA'S VOYAGE

Romany Vargas

This book is a work of fiction.
In real life, make sure you practise safe sex.

First published in 1995 by
Nexus
332 Ladbroke Grove
London W10 5AH

Copyright © Romany Vargas 1995

Typeset by TW Typesetting, Plymouth, Devon
Printed and bound by
BPC Paperbacks Ltd, Aylesbury

ISBN 0 352 33034 1

One

*In recent years I, Balthazar De Fado, Journalist and Man of
Letters, have had the good fortune of being a close acquaint-
ance of Teresa Chaunce, the most renowned Lady of Pleasure in our London of Good King Charles. Both her person
and her establishment have brought great joy to many, myself included. Few, however, are aware of the many trials and
tribulations to which her life has been subject. Accordingly,
I recently persuaded Miss Chaunce to narrate to me the tale
of her eventful past, while I carried out the delightful task of
recording her words just as they were spoken, using the newly
invented system of shorthand notation.*

*Amongst her many gifts is that of storytelling, and I pass
on her words to whomsoever will read them, the fruits of
many hours spent in her enchanting company. I well remember the scene in that small oak-panelled private room in Miss
Chaunce's establishment, with its huge log fire, with the
Lady herself in a favourite walnut-wood armchair. Miss
Chaunce was now of mature years, and her tall fine figure,
her broad shoulders, magnificent bust (usually displayed to
perfection by a loose silk wrap that barely concealed her
breasts' naked glory from my eager gaze), not to mention
her majestic thick blonde hair, would capture any man's eye
and excite his passions. Imagine, then, reader, how my senses
were aroused when she spoke to me so frankly of her most
intimate adventures! For this was a tale of a woman's discovery and exploration to the farthest shores of her sensual
appetites. Imagine the fire in her lambent blue eyes and the
blushes that spread from her cheeks to the tender flesh of her
breasts and throat! Imagine the tremor of emotion in her*

1

voice when she revealed to me the most private details of her adventures and caprices!

I was born in Boston in Lincolnshire, of devout and industrious parents who were of the Puritan faith. For a young girl that meant much hard work, and many hours spent in the study of religious texts, in prayer and in the singing of hymns. I shall pass over my first years, and start my tale when I was eighteen, for until that time my life was so constrained that I had little knowledge of the world outside my home. I was already tall, with a still boyish figure, and such was the innocence of my upbringing that I was totally unaware of the nature of the physical passions which were beginning to make themselves felt within me. I wore the typical clothes of a Puritan girl, which hid from the view of the world my feminine allure: a long loose robe completely covered my body and a linen cap ensured that my flowing golden tresses were quite hidden. Did you know, though, that we did not wear underwear? Beneath that big heavy robe my virginal parts were quite naked. My breasts were already fine, although not full as they are now. They were pointed and small rather, but my most secret feminine parts, I was soon to discover, already had a delicious sensitivity to any touch that knew how to excite. In short, my body was waiting to be set alight.

For now, my sensuality was excited only by words. If at Sunday service there was a certain young and handsome preacher whose eyes sparkled with emotion when he spoke of sin and divine love, I would close my eyes, press my thighs tightly together, and experience a yearning in my lower belly that rose towards my hardening nipples until, with a start, I opened my eyes and bit my lip to stop myself from calling out. This, in my innocence, I attributed to spiritual passion.

That year my parents' business failed to prosper, and my father decided that we should move to London, relying on the offices of an honest couple there, Mr and Mrs Denver, who were fellow members of our religious group. We sailed

2

down the coast to London and took rooms near these two good people, who had a daughter, Sophie, of my own age. The contrast with my life in Boston marked me strongly, for my home town had been small and well ordered, full of devout citizens who treated me with respect. Here, however, we lived in a narrow courtyard near the Ratcliffe Highway, in the Docks of London where the streets and alleys were filled day and night with every conceivable type of humanity; drunken sailors, beggars, and rich and poor of every description. Not surprisingly, I was rarely allowed to go out, and it was not considered safe for a young girl to be seen alone by the lewd men who filled the streets.

Then the event took place that changed my life for ever. Both of my parents caught the Plague, a prevalent infection in those years, and they died within a few hours of each other. I need not remind you of the custom. When it was known that the dreaded disease had come to our rooms, the authorities came and closed us up within. For many days I sat and watched my two dear parents sicken and die amidst the smoke of the lozenges that we burnt in order to keep the sickness at bay. By a miracle I did not catch the illness. I lay weeping with their dear bodies in one room, while I was stretched out in the other. Alone, an orphan, my mind ran over my future.

Then there came into my imagination the face of the young and handsome preacher whose voice had so stirred up my senses. I saw his face near mine, I heard his words speaking of love to me. Instinctively my hands went to my thighs, pressed tight together as before, but now in my fancy it was *his* hands that pressed the soft flesh, and I began to pull up my heavy woollen clothes. I stared down at myself and the sight of my long, slender thighs emerging from the fabric awakened new feelings. I opened my legs wide, and pulled my skirts above my waist so that for the first time the secret parts of my body lay open to my gaze, for when my parents were alive I had always been overseen by someone, my mother or a maid, and was rarely alone.

3

The sight of the silky golden down on my private parts excited me in the same way I had felt in the church, and I could feel the pointed pink nipples on my still-growing breasts becoming hard and erect. But this time there were no constraints on my behaviour. One hand was inside my robe, cupping a breast, pinching the nipples, while the other pressed between my legs where my sensitivity was most aroused. To my astonishment, my hand was soon covered with the juices a woman's passions can generate so freely but which I had never before known. I carried my hand to my lips and sucked the copious honeyed emissions while my other hand continued its explorations. My sadness and horror were forgotten for a moment as I called out softly in pleasure.

A few moments later I was overcome with remorse and guilt and, putting my new-found feelings out of my mind, I took myself to the bedside of my parents, and knelt by them, hands clasped together in devotion, praying for their souls – and also for forgiveness at allowing my passions to run out of control.

I shouted to passers-by from the window that the Plague had claimed two more victims. After the bodies were removed I was allowed to enter society again, and Mr and Mrs Denver took me into their house as an adopted daughter.

One day while I was still in mourning, I was left on my own in the house; something that rarely if ever happened. Sophie, their daughter, should have been with me as a companion, but she too slipped out when they were gone. I was in the back parlour, a simple room furnished with a table, some hard chairs and a bed in one corner. I was reading some devotional book and my sadness and loneliness were almost unbearable. Then, in the alley into which the back of the house looked, there was a noise of banging and the shouting of rough voices, probably of sailors. The door opened and a youth of about twenty stood before me out of breath and sweating with fear and exhaustion. He came forward to me and stared straight into my eyes. Before I knew it his gaze set off the longings that I still tried to ignore.

'Hide me!' he begged.

Staring into my astonished blue eyes, he began pulling me across the room with him to where the bed stood in a corner. The boy quickly turned back the coverlet and climbed in.

'It's the press-gang. They're after me. If you don't let me hide, they'll take me away to sea!'

I could already hear the men knocking on doors in the alley outside and calling out to people who lived in the various rooms and chambers. I was shocked and angry at the liberties he was taking, yet powerful feelings were drawing me on. When he looked at me with a frightened and trusting expression, my heart melted. Without knowing why, I wanted to pull his body close to mine. I resolved to do whatever I could to save him from the terrible men outside. It was clear that the shape of his body under the bedclothes would give him away. So, without thinking of my reputation, I got into the bed, too. I guessed that the sailors would never molest me there. I pushed him down under the covers and opened my legs so as to hide his body under mine. I can remember it like yesterday, how I felt at that moment; the strange excitement that I had felt when he stood near me and touched me, the forbidden thrill of having the body of a man pressing against mine, the mixed curiosity, fear and guilt at what would follow. Just then the banging started at the door.

'Who calls?' I cried out. My heart was racing, and I began to perspire slightly. My passions were growing stronger; stronger than I had known before, stronger than I had imagined they could be. It felt as though a torrent were gradually gaining force as it was released from constraint.

The knocking at the door started again.

'Did any man come in?' a voice called out.

You will remember that I told you we did not wear underclothes. All I had on under my loose dress was a pair

5

of woollen stockings that came part way up my thighs, held up by a pair of garters. I called out in anger to the man outside, forbidding him to enter, while the handsome youth in the bed with me put his hand up my skirt and was slowly moving it over my leg, closer and closer to where the garter was tied. My breath came deeply and roughly, my whole body glowed with desires I did not properly understand, but the yearning in my loins and breasts told me that I wanted to share more with my secret lover before I could be calm again.

Then the door burst open and a huge sailor, brutal and with a cudgel in one hand, stood in the entrance, reeking of rum and human sweat. I can well imagine how I must have looked to him; my white skin must have been deep red, and perspiration would have stood out upon my face. My eyes would have blazed as I gasped out the words 'How dare you disturb me?' My companion's hand had by now loosened a garter, and his fingers had crept up my leg. He was caressing the knee and the inside of my thighs, moving closer and closer to the place where a woman's senses are strongest and most responsive, now waiting swollen and in a state of feverish excitation for the touch of his fingers.

Miss Chaunce at this point blushed deeply. The glow upon her cheeks spread down her body to those parts of her breasts that were open to my gaze; caused, as I guessed, not by shame, but rather by the passions which the memories kindled within her. She fixed me with eyes that no man could resist.

'My dear friend Balthazar, at this moment I was overwhelmed with the discovery of the power that passionate feelings between man and woman can have over us poor mortals! And yet the brutal man with the cudgel thought that I was showing my anger!'

'Madame,' I riposted gallantly yet truthfully, 'when I am in your company I am always aware of the power that such feelings have over me.'

6

She laughed with pleasure at the compliment, and continued her tale.

My breathing became deeper as the sailor looked around the little room, then he muttered an apology and closed the door behind him after leaving.

My secret lover pulled back the covers and crouched over me, now kneeling between my open legs and lifting them somewhat so that all my secret places were revealed to his gaze. I, too, bent over to stare in instinctive curiosity, and was astonished to see how the lips were wide open, and that the wetness had oozed out and on to my thighs. I was afraid of I knew not what, and spoke in a strangled gasping voice.

'Do not touch me there, whatever you do to me! No, not that, I beg you!'

But I did not resist. I let him pull down the bodice of my dress so that my young breasts – still small and trim against my ribs – were revealed, and I let him touch them softly, thrilling me so much that my breath rasped hoarse, making it impossible for me to speak. Then he did something that shocked and surprised me, quickening my senses more than I had imagined possible. He took my right hand in his, and guided it towards the lips of my engorged and slippery secret parts. Holding my index finger, he gently pushed it in. I stared as he slid my finger about the soft flesh and the growing wetness. The lips opened still further as the inside swelled and a tiny bump of pleasure stood out deep in the folds, erect and glistening like a baby shellfish. Still he guided my finger, down to the entrance, back up to where the organs of pleasure thrill the strongest, up and down in an accelerating motion, and simultaneously he took my right nipple in his mouth and rubbed it with his tongue and sucked. In a moment my whole body and mind were overcome. Now the waters were released from all constraint, my body flexed in ecstasy and I cried out, loud and long. He put my index finger, still sticky with the private juices, in his mouth and said,

'You see, you can still tell a future husband that no one has touched you there.'

I lay quiet for some moments, holding my nameless lover tightly in my arms. Then I was overcome with the passion of curiosity. My hand went all over his body, feeling its strength, and finally strayed between his legs, seeking to know the nature of his own secret parts. I undid his clothing and marvelled at his member's girth, firmness and the fine texture of its skin. I kissed him upon the lips, my hand moving up and down the shaft. My instincts led me to imagine it opening my body up, driving passion deep into my soul. And somehow I instinctively knew how to raise his excitement more and more. I was deeply thrilled to see how each movement of my hand, each little increase of pressure here or there, got a response from his sweating body, so much so that when he called out and my hands became covered with creamy wetness I too called out again in passion.

Then I remembered who I was and what the dangers were. 'You must go now because my guardian will return soon and you cannot be seen here,' I warned, much as I longed for him to stay with me.

When he had taken his leave, I knew there would be no going back. I had discovered a secret that had been hidden from me until now. Shame and joy, curiosity and fear struggled within my breast for supremacy. I wanted to learn all the secrets of human coupling, yet I felt shame at what I had done. These were acts that, if known about in our little community, would have ended in ostracism and severe punishment. Yet I felt proud that a man had become, for a few minutes, a plaything in my hands. I was discovering my power as a woman.

I made the bed, and rearranged my cap and robes. There was no mirror, so I peered at my reflection in a silver tray. The flush upon my cheek and the light in my eye were enough to warn me that I could easily give myself away without saying a word. Nevertheless, by the time Mr and Mrs Denver entered the chamber, I was composedly sitting upon a bench, reading my devotional book once more.

Two

Later that day I went with Mr and Mrs Denver and Sophie
to the chapel where we worshipped. As we walked through
the overcrowded streets, I was terrified as to whether I
should see my lusty young friend, who had not become my
lover yet had awakened my desires. I would look out of the
corner of my eye at each group of men as I passed, and
now my senses were stirred by the sight of a handsome
face, a bold stare or a well-turned body.

Once in the chapel, the noises of the street faded away.
Here it was bare and simple, and the pulpit reared high in
front of the altar, all dark wood and polished brass. The
minister, clad in black, stared down at us as though he
could read all our thoughts, and his voice as he addressed
us was harsh. Above the altar were inscribed the Ten Commandments, and I kept looking at the words 'Thou shalt
not commit adultery', wondering whether I had committed
this sin. I glanced around at the younger people in the
congregation, asking myself whether they shared my feelings. There was one young man of about my age in the pew
in front of me. As I stared at him I felt my passions beginning to return yet again, and I was afraid to catch the
preacher's eye in case he read my thoughts. Then I looked
at Sophie, and to my surprise I began to imagine her as a
lover, too. She was not as tall as I, but she was more developed for her age, with fuller breasts and heavier thighs.
She had black hair and brown eyes, and try as I might, I
could not stop imagining myself lying beside her on the
bed, touching and kissing in just the same way as I had
been doing earlier that day.

9

In the following weeks I fell into the usual monotonous daily routine in the Denver household, which involved getting up at dawn, saying prayers around the family table, attending the chapel to sing hymns and listen to long sermons, doing a great deal of hard work cleaning and sewing, and visiting the poor with donations of food and clothing. But now my private thoughts had changed. I still felt the loss of my dear parents keenly, but other sentiments had entered my mind. I longed for another experience like the one I had had with my unknown lover.

I spent much time with Sophie, although we had not become friends, despite being almost the same age and sharing the same tiny bed chamber. Indeed, I came to mistrust her as I was afraid of her guessing my secret feelings and giving me away to Mr and Mrs Denver. However, I began to notice that she, too, had some sort of secret life. She was very clever at finding excuses to go out on little errands, and she often took longer to finish a task than she should have done. Because I was becoming so expert in dissembling my feelings, I suppose that I had become good at reading hers, for I sometimes noticed a glow on her face and excitement in her eyes when she returned from her outings.

One night in hot midsummer I was lying in bed unable to sleep, having heard the church bells tolling three o'clock. (Because I was afraid of Sophie guessing my secret desires, and also from shame and guilt, I never went so far as to touch and explore myself in the way that my secret lover had encouraged me to do, even when alone in bed. I had never even stroked my thighs as I had on that first day.) The heavy weather made my desires unbearable, so that when I did doze off I fell into a dream of an imaginary lover.

This time my bed was surrounded by my girl companions from the Puritan chapel, but my nightclothes were pulled above my navel, my hands holding the bedhead and my legs wide apart, showing everyone how aroused my secret parts had become by the soft caresses of my male companion's hand. I was overcome by longing for him to penetrate me with his finger. Instead his tongue licked my little erect mound of pleasure and gently penetrated the moistening channel inside my slit, filling me with unsatisfied longings which frightened me with their power. While the soft gates of my femininity yielded to his imaginary caresses, and my body yearned for deeper and more abandoned pleasures, my mind was utterly ashamed that my girl companions could see me. As they watched they blushed with embarrassment, whispering scandalised comments to each other about my depraved behaviour. Ignoring them, my lover kissed my breasts while his lusty staff began to push into the tight virgin opening between my thighs and I instantly called out in delicious pleasure. My audience screamed with disgust, furiously making as if to drag my lover off me before he could fully penetrate me – and I woke up.

To my horror my sheets had been pushed down the bed, and in my sleep I had lifted up my nightdress above my waist. One hand was between my legs, where my sensations were most acute, and the other inside my nightdress, holding the nipple of one breast. In the early pre-dawn light I could clearly see Sophie, awake and looking at me with a smile on her face.

'My dearest Teresa! I've always known that you were not really a devout girl! You have a secret, I know.' She spoke severely, but a light in her eye told me that she was drawn to what she had seen.

I thought quickly, then replied, 'So have you!'

She put her finger to her lips, and got out of her bed, tiptoeing to mine, then she slipped in beside me. I was still trembling with the unsatisfied desires of my dream when I felt her full figure under her nightwear pressing against my body, and one hand was about my neck. Her body was hot like mine, and perspiration stood out on her face.

'There's a boy who works in the baker's where we buy our bread.' As she whispered into my ear I could feel her breath against my neck.

'One day when I was there with Mother she was called away for a moment and I was left alone in the back of the shop. He slipped in unnoticed and came up behind me, kissing me on the back of the neck, and when I did not resist he touched my breasts with his hands. Teresa, you can't imagine how wonderful it felt. My whole body was on fire and I wanted him to touch me more and more, but he suddenly stopped and ran away, and at that moment Mother came back in.

' "Why, what is wrong with you, child?" she cried, and I pretended to feel ill and fell on the floor. Since then I have done everything I can to make up excuses to see him secretly, but so often he is with the other men, and I am not alone.'

She stopped, as if wondering whether to go further, and I could see how her eyes were glowing with passion; as, indeed, mine must have been, for the touch of her body and the natural perfume of her hair was beginning to excite me further. I instinctively knew what to do; I could read what her desires were. I kissed her long and lingering on her red full lips, felt her skin around her neck, and gently squeezed her breasts. They were much fuller than mine at that time. I could feel her gently respond to my touch, and when I insisted she continue her story she went on.

'Often we can't do very much when we're together,' she continued, 'but once or twice he has put his hand inside my skirts, and touched me between the legs, and fondled my breasts with his hands under the dress, which I unlace for him. It was the same each time when he started to rub me I felt such excitement that I thought I would lose all control and cry out, but then his hands touched me so roughly that I began to feel pain, and I lost the sensation. Now at night I often try to do it to myself, but the passion is not the same.'

Her words excited me. I felt the sensitive flesh in my secret parts once again becoming wet, and could tell from her blushes and heat that something similar was happening to her. I told her my tale, but in much greater detail than

12

the way she had told me hers, lingering over the way my anonymous lover had moved my hand over the most intimate places of my body, and how his manhood felt to my exploring fingers. And as I spoke I began to lift up her clothes so that her full naked thighs were open to my passionate gaze. When I saw the tuft of thick black hair between her tightly closed thighs – so much more profuse than my tender growth – I wanted to explore the secrets that it guarded, but felt shame. Then she took my hand in hers and guided it to her, just as the boy had done to me.

Then my desire and curiosity became more powerful than my shyness. Her body – heavy and rounded, unlike my slender boyishness – yielded its secrets to my lips. Her breasts drew me, for they were heavy and the nipples were thick and long and dark red, the areolae bigger than a crown piece, and each time I licked them her whole body flexed in a spasm of pleasure.

All this time my hand was on her belly, stroking the strong hair below and sliding itself between her thighs, so that she slowly gave up her womanhood to me as completely as one woman can do to another. I could not resist the curiosity of exploring her melting secrets with my mouth, until eventually I lay between her legs and with my tongue extended as far as it would go, plunged my face deep into her soft entrance so that I drank her sweet copious juices, explored her honeyed essence and tasted for the first time the perfume of a woman's passion. Then, when her body began to shudder with growing delight and her moans increased in spite of her fear of discovery, I ran my tongue up the slit to where the little bud of pleasure extended, firm and erect. As I touched it gently with my tongue, I ran a finger inside her. The thrilling of her body reached a crescendo, then she relapsed into peace.

Now I had to encourage her to arouse me in order to satisfy the desires that I now felt so strongly. I discovered that, unlike me, she did not have that true understanding of where and how to touch in order to give the greatest possible pleasure. I tried to tell her what to do, but she was heavy and sleepy by now, and when we heard the sound of movement in the adjoining bedroom, she leapt out of my bed and left me still unsatisfied.

At that moment Teresa Chaunce smiled knowingly at me.

'Mr De Fado, my dearest friend, would you agree with what I say about "True understanding"?'

I smiled and bowed.

'Madame,' I said, 'what Shakespeare is for the world of literature, you are for the tender passions!'

Miss Chaunce laughed at the pretty compliment, and continued her tale.

Three

I had truly made a conquest in Sophie, but she was only the first of many lovers who were to enjoy my companionship over the years. Like me she was a passionate girl, ill suited to the rigours and abstinences of Puritan life, and she enjoyed the illicit pleasure of a woman's caresses, while still being drawn to the male sex. As neither of us had yet tasted the delicious thrill of full and uninhibited intercourse with a man, we were eager to seek out whatever pleasures we could. Yet I was pricked by twinges of conscience and guilt, wondering what my dear mother would think if she had known my thoughts.

Sophie was careful. She would not exchange as much as a look with me during the day, when other people were present. Neither word nor gesture would tell anyone that we shared a secret – that in our private life we were carrying on in a scandalous and passionate manner which would, if discovered, bring down on our heads punishments and penances, even banishment from our families. Yet neither of us could resist the pleasures that we could each take from the other, even though in chapel I often vowed to try to be a better girl.

When we were in public the two of us were indistinguishable from the other women from our church. The afternoons were long when Mrs Denver sat with all the women for sewing. Each was on a hard wooden stool, neatly ranged around the big oak table. In front of us lay needles, thread, bits of cloth and torn garments. This was our charitable work, for we would use these materials to make clothes that we later gave away to the poor.

We were not allowed to talk during these sessions. 'Idle chatter is an invitation to the devil!' warned Mrs Denver if she heard our voices raised in conversation.

But she did not want our *thoughts* to run on idly, either. One of us would sit with a book – it could be the Bible, or some devotional work – and read aloud, while the others, heads lowered to their sewing, were supposed to consider the lessons that they heard. I can remember how I would look out of the corner of my eye at Sophie when it was her turn to read aloud. I would watch her full and sensuous lips – which only the night before had passionately responded to mine, tumescent with desire, and had breathed the hot breath of her desire on to me – reading in a shy and stuttering voice the words of some divine thinker! Then my imagination would roam freely, and again and again my memories of those few moments when the young man had kindled the flames of my passion would stir my imagination. After this my desires would be thoroughly stimulated, and the strain of having to keep my features composed, as a young Puritan girl's features should be, would become almost unbearable.

Once in bed together at night, we were free! I would take the initiative after Sophie had come into my bed. She would slip in beside me in the half-light of the summer night; although her voluminous nightdress covered all of her body, the perfume of her hair and the touch of her full soft lips on mine were always enough to ignite my senses, urging me on to explore, to caress, to conjure the most exquisite passions.

First I would loosen the laces around Sophie's throat and neck, gently following up the movements of my fingers with kisses as light as the movement of a butterfly's wings. I could gauge her growing excitement by the soft blush that spread over her skin. Then I would begin to pull away at the coarse material, until her nakedness was almost complete. I would slip my hand under her lower back, just where the first swellings of her firm full buttocks lay hidden, awaiting my explorations. Lifting my hand I would

16

raise her loins a little above the mattress, and slide the confusion of clothing up her soft full thighs, throwing the whole over her shoulders, so that she was bare, plump, hot with growing desire, awaiting passively my attentions!

Even then I wanted to avoid routine. I always sought out novel embraces, new ways to delight her, and the novelty would stimulate my own senses. I would loosen my garments, and, kneeling above Sophie's recumbent form, I would take pleasure in stroking my own body. I would look down at my own small breasts with their swollen points of cherry pink, and it would arouse my fires to stare at Sophie's full, rounded, darker-nippled breasts, that were so different to mine, but so appealing. I could tell when I looked into her face how thrilled my show was making her, and I could further spur on her unsatisfied desires by touching my own buds until they hardened under my own touch.

When the entrance to the most secret nooks and crannies between my own thighs were open to Sophie's languorous looks, I would sometimes still further tease her imagination, in anticipation of future delights when we came together, by rubbing the slit with my finger until the juices flowed freely and bathed my fingers in the perfumed emissions of a virgin's desires. Then I might lubricate my nipples with these natural oils of Venus, and lower my body lightly and sensitively to hers, allowing our breasts to rub together, the cherry tips sliding and hardening in time with our approaching ecstasies.

Her breathing would become harsher, her skin would grow hot, so hot that it seemed almost to burn, and the waves of pleasure that coursed down from my breasts into the parts where sensation is at its most acute would grow stronger and stronger. The pressure of her full figure against my boyish one would raise my passion to greater and greater heights. Then she would open her legs wide, so that I could press my more slender body between her loins, and push the silky blonde hairs of my Venusian mound upon hers, gently at first. But soon we would treat each other more roughly, and I would see Sophie becoming abandoned and shameless as she held me, forcing me into caresses of greater and greater intimacy. In the heat of the nights of that summer her body would become bathed in her rank perspiration. My fingers would explore the soft wet flesh under her thick sexual hairs, and her body would flex with waves of passion as she reached the most acute summits of ecstasy. Then she would lie still. It was then that I discovered that I could bring myself to a peak of satisfaction through my own efforts, but the people that appeared in my imagination when I pleasured myself were men, not Sophie.

During the dog days of August both of us were obsessed with one thing only, and our nightly mutual caresses were not sufficient to satisfy our longings. When we went out of the house into the warm air on some errand we were both in a state of expectation, hoping that chance would throw in our way some opportunity to gain the experiences that we both so strongly desired.

Part of the problem was that when we left the house we were accompanied by a chaperone. One of Sophie's brothers often walked with us, a man in his early twenties, who was very serious and devout. Sophie assured me that it would be impossible to persuade him to allow us any freedoms. Sometimes, however, we were taken out by Aunt Sophonisba, an elderly aunt, to the home of Cousins Martha and Bathsheba, two even more elderly relatives who lived alone with only one lady's maid. Generally we walked there in the afternoon, sat with them in their front parlour until evening, chatting, reading aloud and singing hymns if the mood took us. From the street the cries and shouts of the costermongers and the voices of the sailors as they passed by would remind me of the pleasures that the outside world held; still, alas, closed to me. Little did I understand in those early, carefree yet guilt-ridden days how much I was, in the future, to enjoy both its dangers and pleasures!

As you can imagine, the hours passed by slowly when we were at Martha and Bathsheba's house. One day in that hot August, however, I saw a way to snatch a few minutes of pleasure for Sophie and myself. When a certain stage in the afternoon was reached, my elderly aunt would call her maid and instruct her to go to the end of her street to obtain a jug of fruit and wine cordial – most refreshing in the unaccustomed heat of those weeks. Accompanying the maid back to our house was the wine seller's assistant, who returned the jug to his master after it was empty.

The first time I saw him, the sight was enough to set off my passions, and from then on my imagination was alive for him. He was no older than me, tall and fair, and well-built without being gross or heavy. His skin was clear and sensitive. The fire in his eyes and the blushes that so easily covered his face were enough to tell me that a passionate nature lay hidden in his heart. I knew that only a word or a touch would be enough! In the hot afternoon weather both his jerkin and shirt would be unbuttoned, so that the fine muscles of his torso would be revealed to my surreptitious sideways glances, and in my secret thoughts I would instantly be exploring, exciting, responding to his desires. The second day he came to the house I caught his eye. Out of the corner of my glances I could see that no one else was looking in my direction; so, staring boldly at him, I winked, smiled and opened my lips to wet them provocatively with my tongue. I was surprised, yet thrilled by my own forwardness.

Immediately blushes covered his face and throat, and in a moment a tell-tale swelling between his legs revealed how quickly his desires were stimulated. Then my elderly aunt handed the empty jug to him and he was out of the room. That night when we were alone together Sophie began to ask me about him, what my feelings had been for him, whether I should like to be his lover, how I supposed he would be as a lover, and so on. For both of us, that night and the following ones, his imaginary presence would raise our mutual pleasures to higher and higher peaks.

From that day onwards we were both agog to find a way of escaping from the front room and Sophie's elderly relatives, so we could be alone with the wine merchant's assistant. It did not take me long to think of a ruse. The next day, after taking her drink, Bathsheba's eyes became heavy and she almost fell alseep. She came to herself, and saw that I had noticed her drowsiness.

She shook herself. 'My dear Teresa, you must think that I am the laziest of ladies! But I am not, you see. Not at all. These hot nights make it almost impossible for me to sleep, my dears.' She laughed, and looked at both Sophie and me when she spoke. 'Now, I sometimes take a tincture of opium on these hot nights, and then I enjoy wonderful sleep and dreams. But, of course, it is not advisable to become too accustomed to such opiates, is it my dears? So I did not take my sleeping draught last night, and you will see now that I am quite heavy!' She nodded in the direction of the oak dresser, and there I saw a big dark-brown bottle with a cork in it.

The following afternoon I was ready with my plan. When the boy accompanied our maid into the room, I flashed my usual glance at him, and he responded in just the same way as before, demonstrating how his passion was unabated. Then, when my Aunt Sophonisba stood at the oak dresser, ready to pour the cordial out into our pewter beakers, I jumped out of my chair, setting aside my sewing, and took the jug out of her hand.

'My dear Aunt Sophonisba!' I called to her. 'You must not exercise yourself so much on our part! Sit down and relax, and I shall do the honours!'

Then, placing myself where Bathsheba and Martha could not see what I was doing, I took up the bottle of tincture of opium, and poured a few drops into each of the beakers, with the exception of mine and Sophie's. I then took out, from among my clothing, where it had been secreted, a piece of paper upon which the following was written: 'Return the jug to your master, then wait by the window to the left of our front door as soon as you can – Your secret lovers, Sophie and Teresa!'

The plan worked better than I could possibly have imagined. We sat quietly, the three old ladies, Sophie and me, and drank down our cordials. 'So refreshing, isn't it?' they commented. That day was an especially hot and humid one, which for me only served to increase the fires in my blood. But it made the old ladies drowsy, and even before taking the drink they had been complaining of tiredness. Almost as soon as they had finished their opium-tinctured cordials they began to mutter to themselves as if they were half-asleep, their eyes drooped, and the sound of their heavy breathing turned to snoring. As usual Sophie followed my lead. We slipped out of the room, tiptoed across the hallway to the dining room, quietly lest the lady's maid should hear our footsteps, and closing the door with great care we went straight to the window and peered through the shutters. To our delight the boy was there. It only took a few moments to open the window wide enough for him to climb in, and the three of us were alone!

In the sullen heat of the afternoon all three of us were in a state of fiery excitement, where every touch and glance was enough to bring tormenting waves of lambent fire coursing through our nerves. My shame was becoming less powerful, my lust greater. My arms were around his waist, and my every move as I caressed his firm silken skin was taken up by Sophie who stood beside him. Each kiss that I showered upon his lips, his cheeks, his throat, his breast, was followed by Sophie who used him in much the same way. He knew not which way to turn, now inclining himself to me, now to my rival, now dividing his caresses between us, now pulling our faces together so that he could take us both at the same instant.

Even in these moments of madness, when we could have so easily been discovered by the maid, or by one of Sophie's relatives on waking up unexpectedly from her opium-induced dream, Sophie and I were in competition. With a wrench, she pulled his body round until he was facing her with his back to me. Then her arms were round him, and she pulled him firmly to her, so that, as I guessed, his manhood could press against her womanly organs, and induce sensations that so far she had only experienced under my hands. Not to be outdone, I put my hands around his waist and, pressing his belly with my fingertips, began to explore those parts of his torso that led to his private places. Now his manhood sprang free of his breeches, and my hands were on its rigid shaft, feeling its length, girth and the rounded crest of its head. Even here Sophie followed me, and her hands were beside mine, exploring too. In a moment of overwhelming passion I was on my knees before his organ, as if in prayer, and the polished end was in my mouth, the swelling bulk seeming to fill my whole being. He cried out aloud, and I pulled the dome out of my mouth in time for his masculine emissions to spray over my cheeks and lips. Sophie was kneeling beside me. The jealousy in her eyes flared up as she kissed the now slackening member, and licked hungrily at my lips and cheeks in a vain attempt to claim her place in the pleasures that I had procured for the boy – whose name we still did not know!

Four

When we returned to the front parlour, all three old ladies were fast asleep, but still upright in their chairs. This gave us time to compose ourselves, to splash water upon our faces, to settle in our accustomed places and to open up one of the devout works which were scattered everywhere in their house. After a few minutes, I took Aunt Sophonisba by the shoulder and shook her, while Sophie reached out to Bathsheba and Martha, doing the same thing. When they awoke each one exclaimed how drowsy and dull they felt, and how they must have fallen asleep without realising it, for their minds were full of such strange dreams.

The next day when the cordial arrived I followed the same routine, but perhaps I dropped rather more of the tincture into their beakers than I had used on the previous day. The boy was where he had been the day before, and the same frantic and abandoned caresses began, shared by Sophie and me. This time, for once, Sophie took the initiative, and tumbled herself backwards on to the table, lifting her skirts so that her womanly secrets were shamelessly revealed to the boy's eager gaze, while her hands took his and guided them, one to her full breasts, the other to the very lips that stand guard to the part of her sex organs that is most sensitive and intimate. While the boy abandoned himself to his pleasant task of pleasuring my friend, I held his naked manhood in one hand while the other felt every part of his manly anatomy, filled with delight at what I was discovering.

The other two were in a state of ecstasy – the boy from

the mingled thrill of Sophie's body and my skilful manipulations of his masculinity, Sophie from the boy's still inexperienced fumblings with her parts. (Sophie was so hungry to be used by a man that she was no doubt oblivious to his clumsiness.) She was trying to remain silent, in case she should attract the attentions of the maid, but the rhythmical pulsing of her loins and the noise of her raucous breathing told me that her pleasure was nearing a climax. My own organs, stimulated only by my imagination, were in a state of delicious excitation, and I could feel their emissions seeping on to my thighs. The thrill made me redouble my rubbing of the boy's member, and its tightening firmness told me that he, too, was nearing a climax of pleasure. Just at that moment there was a movement at the door and it swung open. Aunt Sophonisba appeared, and stood, staring at us with her mouth open in wordless astonishment. I stood up, rearranging my hair and clothes, hot with blushes of shame while the boy turned his back on her, trying vainly to fit his swollen member back into his breeches and tucking his shirt back under his belt. I felt momentarily deep remorse and guilt at my shamelessness.

Sophie had noticed and heard nothing, and she half raised herself to the boy, calling out to him in disappointment, 'Come back to me! Come back to me! Come and fill my womanhood with everything that you have, my dear.' Then she also saw Aunt Sophonisba, and stood up, lowering her skirts, wiping the perspiration from her face, attempting to control herself. Sophonisba said nothing, but after staring blankly at us for a few moments, she turned and went back to the parlour. In a state of terror now, we followed her, unable to imagine what form of punishment we should receive. I could hardly believe my eyes when I saw that Aunt Sophonisba, like the other two, was back in her usual chair, with her eyes closed, fast asleep. Thinking quickly, I went back into the dining room, whispered a message to the boy and helped him to make his escape.

* * *

24

At this point Miss Chaunce looked at me with a quizzical grin on her face, as though inviting me to some compliment or show of gallantry.

'I am impressed, Miss Chaunce,' I said, 'at the presence of mind that you, even at so tender an age, displayed. But Madame,' I continued, 'we have, no doubt now reached that point in your narrative when you are expelled into the world, with no protector?'

Miss Chaunce was not to be drawn, but contented herself with laughing, tapping me imperiously on the knee, 'My dearest Mr De Fado! Life as it truly is is much more complicated than we imagine it to be! There are many surprises in my tale!'

To return to our parlour. Having helped Isaac out of the window repeating my command for him to come to the house that night (his name I asked just as he was making his getaway), I returned to the parlour confident that I understood what had happened. Judging by Sophie's terrified face, she had guessed nothing of the truth. At that moment there was a terrible crash as Martha's sleeping figure fell off the chair on to the floor. Despite the noise, neither of the other two old ladies awoke, but the sound brought the maid into the room, and her cry of distress as she saw one of her mistresses in such a condition woke up both Sophonisba and Bathsheba. There was much commotion as Martha was laid down on a bench, and finally, when it had been decided that Martha was not ill, but merely overcome by the heat, Aunt Sophonisba turned to me.

'The most extraordinary thing has happened to me, my dear,' she said. 'I must have dozed off just now for I dreamt that I was walking around the house witnessing the most fantastical visions! Truly, I hardly know how to tell you what I saw!' At this she laughed and blushed, looking at Sophie out of the corner of her eye. Her mind had been so affected by the opiate I had mixed with her drink that she had not been able to distinguish reality from her own fantasies! This episode also taught me that even ladies like her, who appear to be so devout, enjoy a secret world of fantasy where little is shocking.

It was clear to me, when Sophie, her aunt and I walked back to Mr and Mrs Denver's house near Ratcliffe Highway, that my rampant passions had led both me and Sophie into the most terrible of dangers. All was not lost, however. I had, unknown to Sophie, already done what was necessary to make sure that our explorations into the nature and practice of the tender passions which draw man and woman together should continue.

Our bedroom routine started just as it did every other night, with us kneeling at the foot of the bed saying our goodnight prayers, and Mrs Denver watching us. Then we sat up in bed, each with a Bible to read, having been instructed by Mrs Denver what verse we should study. This was when Mrs Denver withdrew, leaving us alone with our thoughts, on the understanding that in a few minutes we should blow out the candle and settle down for sleep. In the high summer the single flame cast only a soft glow against the twilight, and when it was out I waited with excitement for my companion in passion to slip out of bed and come to me. The minutes passed. I could hear snoring from the next bedroom. The house was dark and asleep, and the only sounds outside were the occasional footsteps and singing of drunken revellers as they passed by our house. Still I waited, in the silence. Nothing happened. The remembrance that I was an orphan came to me, but I wanted to put it from my mind. I whispered to Sophie.

'Sophie my dear, will you come to me tonight? Or did our adventure of today fill you with such satisfaction that you do not wish any more to share caresses with me?' There was silence after I spoke these words. Then I spoke again.

'Sophie, my dear. If you do not come to me I shall come to you, for I know that you cannot resist me.' At this I slipped out of bed and came in beside her. But she lay rigid, her face turned away. I lay still, close to her, with one arm lightly touching her breast, almost as if by accident. I breathed against that part of her neck that was so soft and sensitive to even the lightest of caresses, but said not a word. Then I moved my body ever so slightly, until my lips were in contact with her perfumed hair, so that every movement of my face teased her scalp, in a way that I knew would alight her senses gently but irrevocably. I could feel her body acquire a languor, a heavy loose-limbed sensuality that was a sign that her instincts were triumphing over her shame and fear. I raised my face until my lips were in contact with her soft, small perfumed ear, and gently explored its folds with my mouth, in preparation, perhaps, for a later delightful task deep within the folds of another more secret orifice.

She turned her face to mine, and then our lips and tongues melted together as one: our hands entwined, arms hugged, and breasts, still heavily clothed, pressed together. I began to smell the perfume of her heated body, and bathe in the glow created by our passion in the course of those hot summer nights in London! Now our neck laces were unloosed, and our garments were down around our waists so that our torsos rose up out of the heavy fabric. To an observer we would have appeared white and bare in the semi-darkness like mermaids rising from the weeds of the sea, our senses animated and ready for the more intimate caresses of passion that would soon start. Yet this time for me it was different. I was awakened to passion, yet I knew that I would not find true satisfaction with her. As I lay beside her with my hands stroking the rich strong bush that grew about her maiden slit, I could tell from her languor and indifference that she too would only scale the peaks of sensual intoxication when touched with the strength and power of the opposite sex – and I was unable to give this to her.

With my lips and tongue I began to lick, nibble and explore her languid body, hoping to tease her into the sensuality that always lay waiting inside her and which I had prior to this day stirred in her more powerfully and deeply than in anyone else. Her full dark-red nipples hardened and swelled under the liquid touch of my tongue, yet when I took them between my lips and pulled, sucked and squeezed I did not feel her answering movements that spoke of her oneness with me. I lowered myself over her belly, taut with the promise of deeper pleasures. My lips brushed the silky insides of her thighs, and she opened her legs wide so as to let my eyes stare greedily in the dimness at the little crack of her mound, still tightly closed, and half-hidden by the glossy dark bush that clothed these secret parts. As I licked where her thighs adjoined these most delightful regions I waited to see the honeyed juices welling out from deep within the organ of her sex. I would lick these, tasting, sipping like a butterfly does from a flower. But today the slit remained firmly shut and sealed.

Now my tongue acted as the key to her sex and its gentle journey up and down the dark folds sought to stimulate the flow that would open the gates to the ardour that waited within. Yet still Sophie's sensuality lay buried beneath her languor, and my eager tongue failed for once in its pleasurable task.

Now we lay together again, bodies entwined, arms tightly holding each other, our rich tresses lying tangled in profusion – my gold and Sophie's ebony mixing as shamelessly as our bodies had done in moments of mutual delight. I watched her full red lips moving as she whispered in my ear, in response to my question.

'The way that Isaac touched me was not at all like your caresses, my dear Teresa. You seem to understand my passion better than I know it myself, my dearest; you unlock my secrets and yet I am not ashamed! Or rather, not until the act is complete. Isaac did not understand me in that way. He was clumsy compared to you. When he thrust his fingers into me he hurt me at first! And yet the feel of his hand on me, so masculine, so strong, has given me a foretaste of what might be to come. To see the size of his . . . manhood . . .' When Sophie said this word to me she blushed, and I could feel the heat of her body as she went on, 'It made me long to be opened, to be penetrated, filled by such an organ, so now that I have come so close, my dear, to such a terrifying pleasure . . .' She blushed again, and ran her hand over my boyish figure for some moments, as though comparing me in her imagination with him. Her hand strayed on to my silken bush and pressed into that region which in a man is thrusting and swollen.

The effect of her words upon my own heated senses, and the thrill that a touch on such a region naturally creates, was enough to release those sticky yet creamy virgin emissions with which my maidenhood was still so copiously endowed. When Sophie removed her hand, her fingers were quite wet!

Her eyes were sad as she put one finger in her mouth, then a wicked gleam came into her eye as she tasted the end. It was as though she were a child sucking a stick of Spanish liquorice, which was to be used as an ingredient in a medicinal potion. I took her hand in mine, thrusting both into my own, yearning slit, in the hope that I could ignite fires in her, having failed by my own unaided efforts. For me it was easier to achieve a wave of passion than it appeared to be for Sophie, yet even as I enjoyed such moments, I too felt dissatisfied. While I forgot myself for some moments in a wave of delight, even as the fire of joy was beginning to recede I could sense in myself an unstaunched yearning, a lust for further joys that would thrust deeper in me in a way that Sophie's girlish hands could never do, be they ever so sensitive and understanding.

I turned my face to Sophie's again, and cupped her full swelling breast in my palms as I replied. 'Yes, Sophie dear, I understand. I, too, need to feel the power of the male part, now that I have broken my milk teeth with your dear person! But I have not told you, my dearest,' here I kissed her gently on the mouth, on her cheek, on the soft flesh under her chin, 'I have already made it possible for us to experience these masculine joys. For while you, my simple friend, were covered in confusion, thinking that all was lost between us and Aunt Sophonisba, I was thinking of you and your pleasure!'

29

At this I arose, and with my night attire unlaced, stood boldly by the casement window. Sophie stared up at me in astonishment.

'Now, my dear friend Balthazar,' said Miss Chaunce, *'you must understand my situation as it was then.'*

Teresa's brilliant blue eyes stared at me in a manner so well known to those many men who have lost their heads and hearts to her – amongst whom I would include myself!

'Madame,' I replied, my heart beating faster, *'please enlighten me! I am entirely at your disposal!'*

Teresa's eyes burnt brighter and a faint blush spread over her cheeks, made deeper by the flickering red of the flames from the fire warming our dark chamber so comfortably. So comfortably, indeed, that I could well imagine myself back in the sultry heat of that August all those years ago in which Teresa's tale was now taking place.

She laughed and stretched out her hand from her silken wrap – a fine hand, yet strong, and her arm was bare beneath the loose fabrics.

'Come, my dear friend! Embrace me: you seem quite overcome with feeling.'

Now I was kneeling by her chair, my head in her perfumed lap, her hands caressing my chin and lips.

'Compose yourself, Balthazar. There is much more tale to be told. Calm yourself!'

In obedience I stood up, and returned to my seat, fixing my mind on the task of holding my pen steady. I sharpened the goose quill in readiness for my transcription.

As long as our nocturnal adventures took place in absolute silence, we were safe from the attentions of Mr and Mrs Denver, or, indeed, of any other members of the household. For Sophie or I, even when we were abandoned to the raptures of the womanly passions, never uttered any sound louder than a soft moan. Likewise, when we moved, it was with care not to make noises which might draw attention to ourselves, for Mr and Mrs Denver were asleep only a thin withe and plaster wall away from us.

As soon as I stood at the casement shutter, my hand on the catch, I remembered how we opened it in the morning – with a push, a release, a click and a squeak. Now, in the semi-darkness of the summer night, I strove to turn it slowly smoothly and silently. The thin wrap fell from my shoulders, yet the heat, the anticipation that thrilled through my nerves, the labour of pressing and moving with infinite slowness, made the perspiration stand out until it ran down the valley between my breasts, dropped into my eyes, and oozed over my belly into the hairs that stood guardian to my secret parts.

Now I stood almost bare-breasted at the casement and, through the leaded panes of glass, I saw clearly down into the deserted street below. There, bathed in the gleaming rays of the full moon, stood Isaac! He had obeyed my whispered instructions! He was now ready and impatient in the street, waiting for the window to be opened so that he could climb in.

I turned to Sophie, and signalled to her. In a moment she was beside me, her blanket over her nightdress, out of modesty, perhaps, and she gave a tiny gasp of joy when she saw Isaac. But his eyes were on my nearly naked breasts and not on her. In a thoughtless movement Sophie took the catch of the casement window in her hand, and turned it, to bring forward the moment when he could be united with us. The noise of the catch springing free echoed around the silent house. I heard a movement in the next room, of Mrs or Mr Denver sitting up in bed. Then the voice of Sophie's mother rang out.

'Who goes there? Sophie! Teresa! Are you both well? What a noise there was just now!'

I strove to be calm, and called back with a sleepy voice, 'Sorry, dear Aunt, for disturbing you. I have knocked the candle over in the course of some nightmare. I pray forgiveness for awakening you. Go back to sleep, there is no cause for alarm.'

I signalled to Isaac to go away, and with silent mimes and gestures told him that he should return the following evening. Then we stood silent many minutes until I judged it safe to pull the casement shutter to, and creep back into bed.

Five

The following morning Sophie and I were getting ready to walk out in the street in the company of Sophie's brother, in order to buy provisions from the local chandler's shop. As I said before, neither Sophie nor I ever paid any particular attentions to each other when others were with us, as we wanted to lessen the possibility of our secret being discovered or even suspected. However, when we were together on that day in the entrance hall of our house, putting on our caps and overgarments and taking baskets for carrying provisions, I guessed that she was displeased with me, judging by the expression in her eyes and the proud way she held herself. What had I done to deserve her resentment? I asked myself.

If at that time I had been able to see into her secret thoughts, none of my subsequent adventures, both for good and for ill, would have taken place, and I should, perhaps, still be a Puritan lady, by now married for many years with a great many children and weighed down by all the labour and tribulations of running a home! On the other hand, with my gifts and proclivities, I should no doubt have been discovered on another occasion, with another chain of punishments and adventures attendant upon my disgrace!

As we set off, my senses as well as my mind were in a turmoil of longings and lusts, happy anticipation and fears, mingled with moments of remorse. I was careful not to raise my eyes to the many handsome young men who shouldered past me in the narrow crowded streets; rather, I kept my eyes fixed to the ground in front of me, my shopping basket tight in both hands in front of my body, my view on one side bounded by the walking figure of Sophie and on the other by her brother.

Once in the chandler's shop with my two companions I tried to keep my eyes to myself, and my thoughts calm and measured, only thinking of the purchases that we were to make – butter, flour and cheese from Cheshire – purchases to be wrapped by a young apprentice, whom I would gladly have eyed boldly.

Then I felt my face turning crimson, and stared at Sophie's brother as he paid for the goods. The apprentice's hands caught my fancy. They were white hands, soft and yet masculine, and in a moment, despite my best intentions, my imagination saw them lifting up and loosening my clothing, touching my flesh, exploring, stirring up my female passions.

Now Sophie was before me, looking into my eyes. She laughed scornfully and turned to her brother, who was just completing payment to the chandler's apprentice. 'Why, my dearest Teresa, you astonish me! You are quite overcome with enthusiasm! You embarrass me! Since you feasted your eyes upon that young apprentice you seem to have quite forgotten yourself!'

Sophie's brother was at her side, staring at me with distrust and astonishment, then frowning darkly with suspicion. I composed myself and made light of what Sophie had just said.

The rest of that day I avoided Sophie's company as much as I could, afraid of her hostility, ready to abandon the adventure with Isaac that lay ahead, promising delights and dangers in equal measure. Even when we lay in our chamber that night after Mrs Denver had taken leave of us, the single candle still burning on the table between our beds, the Bible held in my hands as if for reading, my fears led me to feel remorse, and I resolved to reform and to try to become a good girl once again. I would ignore my past adventures with Sophie, and not refer to my plans and adventures again.

34

'Shall I extinguish the light now, Sophie dear?' I asked.

'Not yet, Teresa. I am not ready.' At that, I laid my Bible on my side of the candle, turned away from my companion and tried to compose myself for sleep. Although it seemed that sleep would not come, I must have dozed off, for Sophie was at the casement shutter when I was next conscious, and she was slowly and silently releasing the catch. She was intent on her task, which she performed with maddening deliberation. Then the hasp was free from both shutter and window, and Sophie stood by the open window. I saw the light in her features that the excitement of her passions was arousing, and I knew that Isaac was in waiting again, as he had been the previous night.

Then she took the laces around the neck of her night attire and loosened them, taking off her nightcap, so that her long black tresses fell free. Then her throat, her shoulders, rose free above the ugly garments, which fell to her waist so that her heavy yet upright breasts and broad shoulders were naked for the gaze of anyone who cared to look. I was on fire once again at the vision of loveliness that she presented to me, standing erect and shameless for the first time. Previous to that night I had only known her lying, generally shyly, amongst tumbled garments and bedclothes. My good resolutions fled.

The cold light of the moon and the red glow of the candle played across her body – such a paradise of swelling breasts and slender waist and fullness of arm. My heated imagination conjured up the secret chinks hidden yet ornamented by her hairy thicket and my eyes lit upon the nipples, each pointing upwards like small dark-red fingers, inviting the touch of hands, of lips, of tongues. I smelt the sharpness of her perspiration as she tumbled her hair, stroked her womanly parts, licked her lips and pinched the tips of her breasts that now rose and fell in time to her rapid breathing, calling out to Isaac's lust.

Even as my own parts melted into a yearning sensuality, my mind told me with dismay that Sophie had been jealous of me the previous night. I had shown my uncovered charms to Isaac while standing at the window, while she had not done so, and he had stared at *me* alone. Now she was attempting to redress the balance of his affections and curiosity; when he entered the chamber, he should go to her, and not to me, and she should be able to finish off the pleasant task that she had commenced in her mother's house, yet had not taken through to its delicious conclusion!

Now Sophie was leaning out of the casement, no doubt looking down at Isaac, who now would be climbing up to our window. The whole of her upper torso leaned out and her body strained as she took the boy by the hand in order to pull him upwards, to assist his passage into our sleeping chamber. Then with a start she was upright again, with Isaac beside her, ready for the strenuous task ahead of him, and now fully understanding the absolute necessity for total silence.

Oh what delights Isaac's person promised us, as he rapidly divested himself of his breeches, and stood before us wearing only his shirt. He was slender, yet with masculine power, as smooth and delicate of skin as a woman, yet strongly muscled. Already, before either of us had been able to commence intimate relations, his masculine organ was engorged and erect, as smooth and shiny as if it were made of polished ivory, yet hot too, with lambent fires of pink upon its dome and pulsing in time with his racing heartbeats.

Now the two were together, and Sophie's hand stroked his naked parts, and there was wonderment in her eyes as they feasted upon this source of boundless future delights and joys. I too was almost swept away by desires that were all the more powerful for being stirred up by that on which I gazed, and by the action of my involuntary imagination.

My secret orifice, my thighs, my lips and breasts were in a state of fevered excitation. Even the movement of my own body against the clothes and sheets was enough to raise my passion to levels where my conscious control would be lost. Sophie lifted Isaac's hands to the firm ripeness of her breasts, and as she moved her body, pressing in response to his touch, I was able to admire with my conscious mind the contrast between their bodies. His torso was pale and muscled, hers full and darker of complexion. His ivory shaft shamelessly pointed upwards, from the sparse golden thicket from which it sprung, already wet at its tip, and vibrated with each movement of his body, so close to Sophie's rounded belly and tangled maiden hairs that it would have required only a bending of his knees and a thrust upwards for its pink glossy dome to commence stretching and opening her inner maiden parts. Now Sophie was looking down at his organ, and was moving her wet expectant orifice towards the sticky male tip. Suddenly with each little twitch of her body he groaned and his shaft spread its copious masculine emissions all over her belly, so that it trickled into the black silken shadow that covered her mound of Venus. She grunted with frustration and grasped his glistening member in her hands, sliding them up and down in an effort to retain his excitement.

But I was not to witness what I had thought would be the inevitable outcome of their conjunction. Isaac's eyes were not fixed on Sophie's, nor did they wander over the delights of her maiden person. Rather they were on my face, and his hands dropped from their exploration of Sophie's paps; with one arm loosely around her waist he moved close to my bed, stood over me so that his ivory staff, which had lost none of its trim erectness, thrust near my face, close enough for me to reach up and grasp it, for me to reach over and explore its size and firmness with my mouth. But I stayed still, afraid to displease Sophie, pent up with desires that needed only the lightest caresses on my parts to bring me to total abandon.

Isaac slipped the bedclothes off my body, and he knelt between my now wide-stretched thighs, loosening the laces around my breasts and throwing up my nightgown until my secret parts lay open to him, uncovered, aroused to the point of the keenest passion even before his exploring body

37

pressed down on mine. My every nerve thrilled in anticipation of what was to come. Then his hands were on me, stroking, exploring, clumsy yet insistent, commanding yet shy to enter those parts where contact with his hands would release surge after surge of boundless feeling. And he spoke to me, whispering with his hot breath in my ear, 'Dearest, dearest, let me take you, Teresa. Let me possess you, you angel, you image of all that is beautiful.'

But Sophie's face expressed her resentment, and she would not be left out. She was beside me, and her hands touched my body; hers were gentle and soft, his rougher and harsher. Hers entered into the most secret places shamelessly, his were shyer. Yet I desired *him*, not her. She kissed my breasts – boyish, pointed, so different from the heavy globes that brushed my belly and silken gold bush, while her free hand took Isaac's staff and drew it to where her busy mouth was on my nipples, wanting to excite both of us simultaneously.

'Isaac', she whispered, 'me, take me dearest. Teresa loves only women. Take me, thrust yourself in me, let me take you in my mouth . . .' As she spoke, my deepest crevice exploded with flames of nervous sensual fires, and my body flexed again and again. At that very moment Isaac's staff again discharged its masculine passion, twitching again and again, soaking Sophie's hands, spraying its thick creamy emissions over my rapturous body, wetting my breasts, cheeks, thighs and belly in a seemingly endless rain of masculinity.

The fires in my blood had driven out my guilt, and I desired that Isaac should become a regular visitor, but I also wanted the rivalry between Sophie and myself to cease. When he left I whispered in his ear, 'Come again tomorrow, but with a trusted friend!'

The following day passed in much the same way as the others, and I managed to avoid all communication with Sophie. I hoped, if that night each of us could content ourselves with the joys and raptures that we both so ardently sought – each with our own clandestine lover – she would no longer feel the bitterness towards me which made me so fearful for my future in the household of Mr and Mrs Denver.

Now in my sleeping chamber it was Sophie who took the initiative again, opening the window silently and stealthily, and helping Isaac through. Then he too was leaning out, and in a moment a companion was in our little chamber beside him, and both were clearly ready and willing to sample our delights, with neither of them showing any bashfulness. But while Isaac was no older than we were, and almost feminine in the grace and softness of his body, his companion, whose name he refused to reveal, was some years older, taller, heavier, stronger, of swarthy complexion, with thick black hair and a moustache.

At a gesture from him – for the older man took the lead in all things that evening – Sophie and I loosened our night attire, revealing our naked breasts to them. Then, at another gesture, we both lay on the bed and at a further command pulled our skirts up high, so that they hardly covered our maiden parts. Imagine my astonishment to observe the two men standing together quite unashamed, clad only in their shirts, the older man's arm around the younger one, observing our charms and discussing our respective merits quite openly. The older man then commanded us to lie on the same bed, turn our bodies this way and that way, to embrace, to kiss each other, to open our limbs to his admiring stare, to show each hidden zone in turn for their evaluation and consideration. It was clear that Isaac had little experience of witnessing uninhibited womanly play, for our display soon caused his manhood to rise up as hard and faultless as on the previous day but with no touch of another's hand, while the other man, so heavily muscled, became only distended but not upright. However, I could see he promised weightier fruits when his machine was fully empowered. No doubt he was reserving such joys for when more intimate contact did occur.

He kept up a bantering commentary as he watched us, and observed the growth and distension of Isaac's member with curiosity. 'So, my little friend Isaac. Your passions are aroused beyond measure at the sights you see on the bed before you. Which do you most desire? The voluptuousness of the dark-haired girl, all heaviness and sensuality, full heavy thighs hiding her secret depths from our probing eyes, so tightly pressed together, and the perfumed ebony bush, through which even now I see the honeyed essence oozing? Or, on the other hand, the slender sinuosity of the other, as lean as a boy, whose narrow thighs and golden down reveals all the rosy delights of her unopened maidenhood to anyone who cares to sup at the source of her lighter juices? But I see there is no doubt in your own mind as to the font of the greater pleasures. Your eyes are fixed on the slender lady – her pink lips, delicate breasts, tiny waist and coral upright zone of pleasure have caused your shaft to display its youthful virility to the full – and no doubt the sight enflames that lady's lust.'

Here he laughed and took the end of Isaac's shaft in one hand, as though testing it for hardness and resistance. Pulling my hand with his other, he put it where his had been, so that Isaac's oozing masculine juices covered the inside of my palm with much promise of what joy was to come.

Then we were together upon the bed. Ah, my dear friend, who can describe one's first experience of almost totally uninhibited rapture with the partner of one's preference! The delights of enjoying his kisses on lips, on legs, on ears, on breasts, on the private lips for which my thighs were opened wide. Ah! The rapture of his manhood between my hands, possessed by me, pressing on to my breasts, in my mouth. The joy of feeling my womanly orifice being opened and plumbed by strong soft masculine fingers, of feeling wave after wave of joy burst inside my loins, of sensing his body flex with ecstasy at each squeeze, and each throbbing of my instinctively skilful hands upon the organ of his pleasure.

But then came the momentary anticlimax when his body was over mine, and his manhood felt larger than I had ever imagined it would be as it moved onward, slow but firm, into me, opening my virgin lips wider and still wider, with no end to his capacity to stretch me. I was bathed in perspiration from the heat of my passion as well as from the warmth of the night, and so was my first lover, Isaac. I bit my lip to stop myself calling out in pain, to keep back the cries that welled up from within me spontaneously, and my hands grasped him fitfully. One moment I was urging him deeper, the next pushing him away as the pain became unbearable. I was intoxicated with the rank odour of his perspiration that ran off his cheek and trickled down the sheerness of his pulsating belly. Then a greater wave of pain shook me, and the huge staff within me reached a wall against which it seemed folly to attempt to thrust. Without thinking more I pushed him away, and then the member fell out of me. At the same moment I held its end in my hand, tight, pressing; I felt it twitch over me like a live fish and my hands filled with a flood of his masculinity.

I aimed with one hand to point the hot jet on to my breasts, nipples, lips and face, and the thrill of his delirium sent my body into a climax of joy so vast that I felt I was falling in ecstasy through darkness.

When I came to myself I saw a very different scene on the bed beside me, for Sophie had failed to arouse her companion. While the man lay back on the bed, staring at me, she attempted with her mouth and hand to raise his manhood to that point where it would find joy within her own feminine orifice. But now I knew that, delightfully luscious though her body was, she lacked the natural gifts (that I so abundantly possessed) of bringing delight to lovers.

At a gesture from him I knelt beside her and used my hands on his heavier and thicker shaft to complete the task that she had commenced so badly. But he would not do me the honour of completing within me the job that Isaac had failed to finish; for, as he said, 'I cannot enter into what another man has used so recently.'

Six

The first light of the summer dawn was grey behind the shutters in our sleeping chamber. The coolness that came on at the end of the night was already showing promise of the oppressive heat that would come with sunrise, for these were the dog days of August, and the burning weather had followed Sophie and myself through all our adventures together. Just now we were lying in our respective beds, modestly clothed and capped, arms clasped in front of our bodies, outside the bedclothes, as we had always been instructed to do.

'Secret hands lead young girls to the devil's work!' Mrs Denver would say after praying with us at the end of the beds.

The close chamber was austere and bare. The whitewashed walls and plain deal furniture spoke of simplicity and calm, of the regulated rounds of a Puritan family's life. The table that stood between our beds held the two black-bound Bibles that we read every night – their words of faith and wisdom had become truly a witness to the illicit pleasures that we had now become used to. A pewter candlestick stood between the holy books, and the street outside was silent and calm, waiting for the break of day to fill up with the lewd and riotous throng. I looked at Sophie's face on her pillow, so innocent and girlish, and wondered whether I appeared as untouched to an observer by my exploits as she did.

My mind went back to the state of shameless lust to which I had abandoned myself only a short time before, and I wondered at myself, for I had never imagined that

43

the carnal act between men and women could be carried out with such openness. Yet I felt less shame than I had expected. I remembered how Isaac's body had been above mine, pressing me into the bedclothes, his staff thrusting, opening, rubbing relentlessly. I remembered, too, how at moments in my delirium my half-opened glances would note the eyes of Sophie and her male companion upon me, and how I found that the pleasure and curiosity they felt at my public display of pleasure only served to stimulate the sensations I felt.

Sophie was lustful like me but she was also jealous. Her humiliation of the night before, her failure to bring to her partner the delights I had shared with mine, would have stirred up even a saint, let alone someone who was deceitful and hypocritical.

I was now in a state of great trepidation and fear. What was I to do? The very next night both Isaac and his friend would be waiting outside the chamber, in the street, expecting to come into our beds once again, and taste once more the fruits that they had been introduced to by us. But the next time the older man would certainly wish to be with me, and even as my mind worried about the future and tried to find a way to escape from the predicament in which I found myself, my imagination was at work, picturing the other man. What would it be like with his stronger and rougher masculinity? Would his strength and power be too much for my inexperience? Or would his superior knowledge and understanding of the female sex – for so I imagined it to be – be such that he would carry out the deflowering in a manner in which joy would triumph over pain?

These thoughts, and many other similar speculations, oppressed my consciousness as I later entered the parlour of our house in order to take the morning repast. The family was, as usual, ranged around the oaken table, waiting on my arrival. As demurely as I could, with my eyes lowered, I took my place in front of the wooden plate and pewter bowl. Out of the corner of my eye I saw the faces, and they all seemed to be staring at me. Mr Denver and his sons, all with the same long, bony angular face and close-together pale eyes; Mrs Denver, so like Sophie, but coarsened and heavy with age, hands worn from the constant work she did for the family and for charity, eyes quiet and kind, yet submissive, too. And Sophie was there. When I caught her eye for a moment I was taken aback, and avoided looking at her again: she was pallid and exhausted-looking, eyes reddened as if from crying, her hand shaking as she dabbed her eyes, her lip trembling from suppressed emotion – or so it seemed. I knew better!

The kitchen maids stood obediently by the vat of oatmeal porridge on the kitchen range as Mr Denver at the head of the table rose to pray. Tall in his black clothes, he seemed to stare me out as he prayed. And when he spoke of sin and repentance in his prayer, I was sure that his thoughts were on me!

Then in silence I partook of our simple repast, for it was the custom of the household never to speak during mealtimes. But on this day, again and again the usual silence was broken by the sighs that Sophie uttered; sounds not so much of grief, but rather of shame or reproach, and I knew that each moan, each dabbing of the eyes, was an arrow aimed at my emotion-filled breast!

After the morning's fare was consumed I went away as quickly as I could in order to carry out my tasks for that day. And while I was alone in the parlour, my hands busily working, my mind was vainly striving to find some way out of my predicament. But everywhere I looked I saw only blank high walls, closed doors and barred windows. Then Mrs Denver was standing beside me. She placed a hand on my shoulder.

'Teresa, Mr Denver has heard the gravest reports concerning your behaviour. I pray that they are quite untrue! You must go to him at once and answer his questions.' She appeared strongly moved, for she was truly a most soft-hearted and sentimental creature, unlike, as I was soon to know for certain, her daughter. 'I hope for your sake,

45

Teresa – for you have become a very fond daughter to me, even though you are not of the family – I hope . . .' She paused, and her mind appeared confused. Then she continued, picking up once again the thread of what she wished to say, '. . . that what I hear is totally without foundation.'

At this she brushed away a tear, before leading me to Mr Denver's office where he carried on his business. I had never been into his room before, and when I saw the great black oak table piled high with documents, and the bookcases against the wall gleaming with leather bindings and gold lettering, I felt a chill in my heart, even before I saw the expression on his face, the eyes hard, the complexion pale with anger. His right hand was on his Bible, his high-crowned black hat stood by his left side, and on a low stool Sophie sat, weeping dry-eyed. It was in this court that my fate was decided.

At this point Miss Chaunce seemed overcome with her emotions.

'Madame,' I said, with what I hoped was both tenderness and respect. 'Please do not allow your feelings of regret to run away with you. A woman such as you, with your fine parts, rare talents and extraordinary accomplishments, should have no cause for sorrow at past sufferings and youthful errors.'

I shall never forget her features when she turned her face to mine. They were both brilliant with the fires of her ardent nature and soft with the griefs with which memory can pierce the stoutest of hearts. My senses had been stirred by the piquancy of the tale that she had been narrating. The vivid manner in which she called up to the eye of my imagination the scenes of her first explorations had stimulated my appetites. Furthermore, dear reader, I beg you to remember that I was in the presence of the lady herself, who was the source of all these delightful and affecting adventures and anecdotes!

Teresa no doubt was conscious of the effect her words were having upon my passions, yet I believe that she, too, had been affected by the force of her own words.

'*My dear friend, Mr De Fado,*' she said, dabbing her forehead with a linen handkerchief, '*I feel quite exhausted with the emotions and scenes that I am reliving after all these years, and I observe in you a certain distraction of the features. I suggest that we should continue our conversation for the immediate future in more relaxing surroundings.*'

When Teresa rose up out of her chair, her loose wraps and kerchiefs drew attention to the beauties of her figure in the most titillating manner possible. The graceful movements of her hair and arms, of her legs and loins, wafted to my masculine senses the sweetest perfumes of body, hair and lips, rose water and musk, and I began to feel embarrassment at standing up in her presence, lest my evident physical excitement were to attract her attention. But she saw my condition and laughed.

'*Ah, Mr De Fado, what I see there promises shared delights for both of us! I am glad that my words to you have had the effect that nature intends!*'

At this, she drew me towards her, pressing my engorged masculine organ shamelessly against the yielding femininity of her loins. The beauties of her breasts were now rising out of the loose fabrics almost totally unencumbered, and wave after wave of perfumed airs teased and tantalised my eager nostrils so I enjoyed that delightful state of expectation before the senses are blunted by satiation.

Her hands were strong as she drew me to the far end of the chamber. Pulling a hanging back from what I had previously thought to be a wall, she revealed a four-poster bed, rich with velvets and silks and waiting on our pleasure! Soon Miss Chaunce sank back amongst the fabrics, and her practised hands soon divested me of my overgarments. For my part my hands, lips, arms, my entire male form resisted no longer the tasks to which she invited me – to touch, to press, to stroke, to explore. With gentle tugs at the satins that hid the beauties of her upper body from my eager eyes, the mature luxuriance of her womanly breasts was mine for the taking. I buried my face in their white and perfumed silkiness, excited the rosy pink tips with my lips, while her soft *but strong hands were busy with my parts, until my under-shirt fell from me and my organ, gorged and aching for her attentions, rose free.*

With a toss of her remaining wrap, her legs, her thighs, her most private nakedness now lay open to my gaze. Her hands were on that organ of delight which would impale her womanhood, and my fingers grasped the silken bush that or-namented her crevasse of joy. As the satin lips loosened and liberally coated my fingers with her honeyed juices, for a moment my mind reflected on her mature womanly attrac-tions – the fullness and softness of her form, the stately poise of her neck and shoulders, the profusion of gold that anointed her secret parts and the proud fire of her eyes. And I asked myself how she would have been as a Puritan maid – more slender, less developed in form, tighter to open and enter.

The perfumes of her womanhood intoxicated me. My fin-gers plunged deeper, her hands were in my hair and I was drawn on to the ultimate source of her mature joys. Like a flower giving up its honey to the bee, her womanhood opened to my busy lips and tongue, which thrust further and further with each straining push against her body, and with each lick new reserves of honey welled up. Now we could wait no lon-ger and her hands were on my shaft, exciting, guiding. Her mouth was pressed to mine, as my organ slid gently into the silken gates of her womanhood. And the portals opened to my thickness, yet held firm. Its juices lubricated, yet each thrust was resisted by a friction that brought my peaks of sensation higher and higher.

Now Teresa was calling out to me in joy, again and again, each time her body flexing with more and more abandon-ment. It seemed that my masculine organ grew harder and harder, bigger and bigger, until she shrieked with utter aban-don, my whole body seemed to explode within her, and Miss Chaunce and I embarked on that gentle downhill run that ended with us lying unashamed in each other's arms, at peace with each other.

After some time spent in this state of blissful calm, Miss Chaunce spoke once again about her past life. Clasped in my arms as she lay, I was unable to transcribe her words with the exactitude that I would have wished. However, my professional work as a journalist has developed my powers of memory to a remarkable degree. Consequently, I believe I can truthfully claim that the following section of her narrative is a fair and accurate account of what I was told by Mis. Teresa Chaunce.

I do not wish to dwell on the events that followed in that painful scene where Sophie proved herself to be truly evil-minded and vindictive. Neither do I want to stir up too much grief in remembering the scene itself in more detail than is necessary for my tale to proceed.

Mr Denver stared at me for a few moments, speechless. I lowered my eyes meekly, and waited, not knowing what was to come, but fearing the worst. Then he arose, his face dark with emotion. He stood straight, and pointed at me, slowly and with the greatest dignity. His voice shook, but it was as deep as the voice of thunder. 'I accuse you. You have been accused! Your devilish crimes will bring shame and corruption upon all of us if not corrected, if not justly punished. I know not what action to take, but with prayer and steadfastness I will be guided still. Speak, and answer your accuser!'

I stood dumbfounded, not knowing what to say. I was afraid to incite his wrath any further by questioning him. I stayed silent, and after some moments, Mr Denver continued.

'I brought you into our house as our daughter out of pure kindness and pity. But my true daughter', here Sophie groaned quietly, 'tells me that you have tried to lead her into evil ways! It is painful to me to speak of what I have heard from the mouth of my pure and innocent daughter. But I must speak. You have devoted yourself to the pursuit of sensual pleasures when we trusted you to carry out the tasks that we set you! You have taken every opportunity to corrupt young men who came into our house. You have used every excuse to make assignations with those who pander to your depraved tastes! Sophie saw with her own eyes these assignations take place, but out of a misplaced loyalty to you, and a wish to ignore the shocking truths in front of her very eyes, she said nothing until now. No doubt my dear daughter's innocence is to blame for her inaction in the face of the many evidences against you. But the ultimate insult – not only to dear Sophie, but also to me, and to my faithful and devout wife – occurred last night when men, your paramours, congregated outside your chamber window in the night, asking to gain admittance to the house!'

I did not know what to say to these accusations, for in reality the depravity and abandon had gone much further than Mr Denver knew, and involved Sophie as much as me. I contented myself with weeping, for I truly felt ready to weep, with my future looking so dark.

'You do not attempt to deny what I have said. That only means that you admit your guilt. But we must investigate further. Sophie tells me that two depraved villains will be waiting for you outside our house tonight. Further to this, she has given me a ring belonging to one of these rascals, which you were given, for services rendered.' At this he held up a silver band, from which he read off three initials – no doubt those of the older man, from whom she had somehow obtained this token.

There is little point in prolonging this part of the narrative. I was condemned by Mr Denver. A watch was kept outside the house that very night, and Isaac and his friend were accosted by the Denver men, and my guilt was established. Unfortunately for me, the two of them made off before they could be properly questioned, which meant that Sophie's innocence was still assumed. It is a strange fact, however, that it was through the good nature of Mrs Denver that I was launched on the strange adventures that characterised my later life.

It was Sophie's good-hearted mother who persuaded her husband not to punish me severely in the normal fashion, but rather to return me to Lincolnshire, where I had grown up, on board a coastal sailing ship, destined for an institution for the reform of young girls who had gone astray. As none of the family were willing to accompany me on this ship, I was forced to go alone. Mrs Denver was horrified and, despite the reputation that I now possessed, decided that it would not only be scandalous for a young girl to travel alone on a ship full of sailors and ruffianly merchants, but also that my virtue would be compromised – after all I was being sent North to restore it! Consequently, I was sent out alone into the world with my hair shorn and wearing a pair of breeches so that I should be able safely to pass myself off as a boy. All I carried were a few shillings concealed about my person and a letter of introduction.

The episode that followed taught me what unexpected effects can flow from the most well-meaning actions. In this case, when I was at the Dockside, ready to board my vessel, I was seized by a group of ruffianly seamen, and knocked unconscious. I had been taken by a press-gang, and I was to be a sailor!

Miss Chaunce, when she was speaking these words, had her eyes closed, as if her emotions and exhaustion had led her to the verge of sleep. Taking this hint I rose from the bed, dressed myself, and, gathering up the copious notes of our conversation of that day, took my leave. The following days were spent in copying and editing this wonderful narration, and also in waiting impatiently for a summons to return, in order to hear more.

Seven

And come the summons did! I sat in the same chair, in the same chamber, listening to a tale of new places, new and strange adventures while my busy pen laboured to keep up with the flow of words.

At first I was in darkness, my head ached from the blow that I had suffered in the street, and my stomach was sick from the rolling of the ship. The sound of the waters, the creaking of the ship's timbers, and the cries and chants of the mariners told me that I must be deep down in the bilges of a ship that was already at sea. I cannot say how long I remained here, lamenting my fate. Little did I know that this was to be the pattern of my life for many years!

But even here, in one of my blackest hours, sleep and imagination gave me a temporary release from my sorrows. Suddenly in my dreaming fancy I was in a richly furnished sleeping chamber and the curtains of the four-poster bed were drawn back, revealing Sophie, as naked as the day she was born, displaying her heavy sensuality shamelessly in a way that she never had done while I had known her. You will note that it had never been our custom to show ourselves to each other entirely unclothed. Sophie lay back, her hands behind her neck, lifting the curve of her heavy breasts high, opening her thighs as if inviting exploration. Beside her stood Isaac, clad only in an undergarment and even in the dream I felt a stab of anger and jealousy, for he had been mine, not Sophie's. The two looked at me and smiled their welcome. Isaac undid a drawstring, and his lower garment fell away, revealing his aroused nakedness to the two of us without shame. Then he walked to me, drew my body to his for a moment, and commenced loosening my heavy garment so that in a few moments I, too, was as my companions, bare and unashamed.

Now all three of us were on the bed, Isaac lay beside us dividing his kisses and caresses equally, and my passions were soon unleashed. Now he was holding me from behind, and his hands were on all the places of my body where the sensitivity was the greatest, while Sophie was before me, legs open, offering her womanly parts, begging me to treat her as a lover, as I had done before. Her familiar juices were on my lips and my tongue sought out the hard little bud of pleasure that was hidden deep in her honeyed folds; the bud, which, if sucked would bring her to a peak of passion. And at the same time Isaac's hands were on me from behind, his strong arms lifted my thighs so that I had only to be lowered to be impaled on his manhood, and I was scaling the peaks of pleasure at just the same moment as my two companions. Then the grinding sound of a key in the lock woke me to my current reality, and I wished I was still dreaming.

My dark chamber was flooded with light that dazzled my eyes, and silhouetted in the doorway was the tall figure of a man. He came to me, and pulled me towards the doorway roughly, looking me up and down keenly. He was a lascar, and his golden brown body was stripped down to the waist. He was barefoot, and his only garments were a baggy pair of blue and white striped pantaloons that came down to his mid-calves and a red cap round which his long straight black hair tumbled down to his shoulders. His body was broad and muscled, yet lithe and supple, too, and it glistened with oil and perspiration. Despite my fear at my situation, in one part of my mind I pictured the man's body responding to my touch, for my mind was still partly in my dream, and I could imagine deep within my secret parts the rigidity of his manhood. I wondered how passionately he would return my sensual caresses.

His hand ran through my short hair and he chucked me under the chin and laughed as he led me into the open air.

Around me on the lower deck the mariners stood staring at me. Some had fine bodies like the lascar, some were skinny and hollow-chested, some were fat, some had deformed limbs. There were many missing teeth, eye-patches, livid scars and missing fingers and toes. All around them was the tackle and gear of the sea – coils of rope, iron tools, boxes of cargo lashed to iron rings in the deck. Every part of the ship was in motion to the stiff breeze, creaking, swaying, singing to the rhythm of water. The open air began to take my seasickness away. Then my gaze went up beyond the mast, as huge as a single giant tree, to the upper deck. There by the rail and observing us closely was a group of men and women in Puritan dress: tall black hats and black coats with plain white linen for the men, and the shapeless woollen dresses and linen caps that I knew all too well from my past life for the women.

I almost laughed aloud in my surprise, for I then knew that I must be on a ship bound for Virginia, carrying some of the members of our faith there bound for a new life; an enterprise much favoured by the people I had grown up with, and one much discussed. For a moment my eyes met those of one of the men on that upper passenger deck. I saw a look that I knew from some of my father's companions. The memory of my dear parents brought a moment of grief as I speculated what my mother would have felt if she knew where I was now, and anger took hold of me as I thought of Sophie and Mr Denver. The intensity of the man's blue eyes, close together and deep-set, and the tense muscles of his long bony jaw, the turned-down mouth, the lean stiff unbending strength of his body, as his hands gripped the oaken railings, all spoke of repressed passions. I wondered for a second if Mr Denver might not have secretly shared his daughter's lustful nature. The man's eyes followed mine as I was dragged along the deck to the Captain's cabin.

* * *

Teresa sighed, and a faraway look came into her eye. She looked into my face with an expression of sadness and regret. 'There now follow times in my life which it now gives me much pain to recollect, my dear friend.'

I knelt beside her, and took her delicate fingers in mine. 'Madame, you need not continue if it pains you.'

Teresa gestured at a small brass bell on a dresser. In obedience to her wishes I picked it up and rang it. A moment later a maid appeared and at a word from Teresa she brought a dark-green glass bottle and two pewter goblets. I filled the goblets and we drank together. She allowed me to loosen the lace kerchief that she had tied around her paps, until the famously beautiful organs were once again revealed in their bare magnificence. Now in the full weighty fruitfulness of a woman's maturity, she allowed, even encouraged, me to explore them, first with my hands, then as passion led to the casting away of restraints, with my mouth and lips. My hands lifted perfumed petticoats and explored the silken softness beyond the tightness of her garters. The organ that now rose hard and rigid as a column out of my breeches she excited with skilful pressure of her hands until it was ready to explode with passion. But her practised hands held back that moment until it buried itself deep within her own pink crevasse, both my companion and I tearing aside all modesty in the shared need to open and be opened, to penetrate, to goad the mutual pleasures to their highest peak.

After many words of affection, Teresa and I composed ourselves again, and her tale continued.

The harshness of life on board that ship was evident from the first moments, and coming as I did from such a sheltered background, I was quite unprepared for the depravity of the sailors whom I now had to share my life with, pretending all the while to be a boy. I do not wish to tell you in detail of the routine on the ship, and the menial work that I was forced to do from the very moment that I was released from captivity, but rather to pick out those parts of my life in those weeks that bear upon the present theme.

The communal sleeping quarters were all below deck, in the hold, and the sole illumination came through small portholes, and from one or two oil lamps. The first nights it was a full moon, and as I lay in my hammock, still dressed in my doublet and breeches, all around me in the dimness would lie the sailors in all states of dress and undress. Everywhere I looked there were men's bodies. I remember on one of the first nights near to me and slightly below, a boy of my own age was already asleep, his nakedness only covered by a sort of loincloth. I stared in fascination at his body, so appealing and mysterious in the half-light. In his sleep he turned so that he lay on his back, arms and legs wide open, his pale skin almost luminous in the dimness. Then his body moved restlessly, as if he were dreaming, and he muttered to himself. His organ began to swell and harden until it was straining against the thin material of his sole covering, the shape of its head outlined against the cotton. What dreams must have been going through his mind!

Then he spoke in his sleep some more, and his hand went down inside the garment and held the member, pulling it until it poked out of the scanty piece of cloth. It was thicker than Isaac's organ had been, and its head was wide, like the head of a mushroom. He held it tight, and wetness began to stand out from its tip, so that, as he moved his hand up and down its length, it began to glisten with the juices that were now smeared all over it. Now the hand was rubbing up and down more rapidly, and I longed to be beside that member, holding, touching, exciting and being excited, so as to be able to satisfy the longings that we both shared. Then in a moment the movements stopped, and the organ seemed to take on a life of its own, pumping as if it were a thing alive and not part of someone's body, spurting its discharge again and again over the boy's chest, over his hand, on to the hammock.

Then the thought came to me that in these crew quarters there were many men who yearned for the touch of a woman, and many men, like this one, who were quite open and unrestrained in their behaviour. I wondered if it would be possible for me to keep my secrets without the help of a protector.

That night I fell asleep amidst many unhappy reflections of this sort. The next day there was no respite for me, and I spent my time in hard labour, pulling at ropes heavy with sea water, that chafed my hands, scrubbing decks with sand, learning to climb the rigging and being told the names of the various sails.

It was then that the lascar who had taken me out of my prison – his name was Dunga – began to play a part in my life. Ignorant and brutalised though he was, he appeared to have taken a liking to me. When the boatswain gave me an order that I did not understand, for example, he would be behind me to explain what was expected of me, and to help me to carry it out. I saw, too, that his strength had earned him a certain amount of respect amongst the crew. I decided to take him partially into my confidence, and use him as a protector. Accordingly, I explained to him how sheltered my life had been up to that time, how I was not able to adjust myself to the life of the crew straight away, and how I hoped that he would for the time being act as a friend to me and protect me from the brutal crew members as much as possible.

Then, quite instinctively, for I was as yet an apprentice in the world of sensual variations, I said what I imagined might keep his loyalty. 'If you wish to use me in the manner of a woman, you may do so.'

It was night, and the crew were mostly in their hammocks, asleep. We were on the decks and in the midsummer weather the soft airs were delightful. I encouraged him to go with me to an unfrequented corner of the ship, where we should not be disturbed. Alone with him, strangely excited at the prospect of a clandestine and illusory adventure with such a man, I gazed admiringly at his body, so hard and poised.

'Come!' I said, gesturing to a twist of rope for him to lie on beside me, touching his body so as to tease his senses into passion. Soon I had his member in my hand, astonished at the hardness, smoothness and girth of the well-oiled shaft. I excited the tip with my tongue and lips, hardly able to take the whole width in my mouth, and held the base tight lest he should discharge the vital juices before the time was ready.

'If you wish to enter me in the manner of a woman I shall submit to your desires. Would you find satisfaction from taking me as if I were a woman, and not a boy?'

I could tell from the light of lustful anticipation that came into his eyes that the prospect pleased him, and I half-turned away from the lascar, pulling my pantaloons down and bending over so as to let him see the beauties of my snowy buttocks, but not the glories of my womanhood, so near but still hidden from him. I reached back at his body, and pulled him towards me, all the time rubbing, pressing and teasing to bring him up to higher and higher levels of excitement.

Now his hand went to my tight and virgin fundament, and his finger commenced teasing it, encouraging it to loosen. This must have brought him great pleasure, for I could feel the first male liquids beginning to seep out of the end of his member, and his body sweated more heavily than ever. I led him to open my tiny hole up with first one finger, then two, then I egged him on to approach with his member. The touching and the excitement had made my private parts as swollen and aroused as I had ever known them, yet I could not permit him to explore me there, for my womanhood was to remain a secret. To my satisfaction, his hands were on my back, and made no attempt to go down my front where my shapely, if still small, breasts grew. His manhood was pressing on my hole. The pain grew, and I bit my lip to stop myself from crying out. Afraid to let him go any further, I held the organ tight in order to make him discharge before the act was consummated. To my excitement as well as his, he began to groan and gasp, and I felt the tip tautening in my hand when suddenly my nether parts were doused in his sprayed fluids, and the member twitched as if alive. When Dunga reached the point of climax, I too called out softly. Just then, I thought I glimpsed a face momentarily in the darkness, watching us, but when I looked again it had gone.

Later that night I was in my hammock and I awoke to see two sailors advancing upon me. One was large-bellied, toothless, with a scarred cheek. The other was his opposite: hollow-chested and slight, with rheumy eyes and an imbecilic expression on his face, wearing soiled rags round his loins. As they approached I closed my eyes in feigned sleep. I felt their hot breath upon my face, and hands pulling at my breeches, as if to loosen them. Then there was the sound of two mighty blows, and I opened my eyes to see both ruffians unconscious on the floor and Dunga standing by me. The whole sleeping quarter was roused from its slumbers by what had occurred, and Dunga called out to them, threatening death to anyone who so much as touched me!

My relief that night as I drifted back into sleep was mixed with fear, for I knew that, while I had found a temporary way out of my danger, my secret would certainly be discovered very quickly. I remembered the Puritan man who stared at me so hard when I was dragged out of my prison. I wondered whether he might become a more secure protector than the lascar!

Eight

As days lengthened into weeks on board the ship, I began
to fail under the burden of the hard work that was my lot.
The weather changed, and we suffered from unseasonable
gales that, reportedly, blew our vessel off course and forced
us southward, far from our normal route to New England.
Like many others, I was constantly seasick. The back-
breaking labour was wearing me down, and I would lie on
my hammock at night in a state of nausea and aching exhaustion. The ropes cut my hands and the salt water made
my wounds sting. I was forced to climb rope-ladders in
winds that made the ship heave in the most dizzying manner, showered with salt spray. My lascar lover did what he
could to keep from me the hardest jobs of all, but I could
not rely on him to protect me from everything. Luckily his
sensual needs were of the simplest kind, and, having satisfied him beyond his expectations on the first night we spent
together, he showed no inclination to experiment further,
and my nether hole soon became accustomed to its novel
use.

I soon found out that the Puritan man whose stare had
so drawn me the first day I was allowed on deck was one
John Barebones, the leader of the Puritans, and indeed he
was taking his group to Virginia. He insisted that all the
crew should attend the divine service he led every day on
the top deck. I managed on most days to find a place at
the front of the crowd of crew members, and, being familiar with the customs of people of this sort, I knew what
behaviour would please him. So while most of the seamen
maintained a sullen silence when John Barebones

preached, I made it appear that I was overcome with religious fervour.

The first day I tried to draw his attention to me he took as his text 'He gave to the sea his decree, that the waters should pass his commandments'. His voice and manner were harsh as he warned all of us that God's vengeance would follow us wherever we tried to flee, yet there was at times a passion in his eyes that I was able to recognise. It was the same passion I used to feel when the words of the preacher aroused my secret emotions. Hidden behind his rough and cold exterior there was a heart susceptible to the softer emotions – I was sure.

At first I confined myself to sighing sadly and covering my face as if to hide tears, staring deep into his eyes as if wordlessly seeking his help. He was aware of me, for on the second day his eyes sought me out from the very moment that I arrived at the service. He spoke of 'For I am a jealous God' and at the climaxes of his speaking, when his emotion was at its warmest, I fixed him in the eye, raised my hands to heaven and cried out in despair. He noticed immediately, as I knew he would, for it was in this way that our people behaved when, worshipping together, the spirit took them. He stood in silence for a moment, staring at me. Then he recovered himself and continued his address.

That night something occurred that made me all the more eager to escape from Dunga's protection. He came to me as usual, as many other recognised pairs of men did, but when I tried to force him into going up on deck to carry out the act, he took me in his arms, turned me to him and tore open my doublet. Now my secret feminine charms were uncovered in all their glory. He was speechless as he stared at my body. I pulled his face to me and whispered in his ear, 'You must help me to keep my secret. Do not betray me and we shall enjoy pleasures together that you will never find elsewhere!'

Soon we were on deck again, and in a redoubled frenzy he pushed me down on to a pile of rope. The rough material cut into my rear as he pulled off my lower garments, and stared at my female form with an expression of wonder and hunger. He took my ankles and opened my legs as wide as he could, staring all the time at the furry blonde down and the folds of flesh that concealed the seat of my womanhood.

After so many weeks of dissemblance, and submission to a perverse form of love, my body ached for the normal relation of man with woman. I had lost my feelings of guilt and shame. I was careless of my future, heedless of what might happen to me if my secret were known to the crew. I reached out to my lascar's body, oiled and smooth, and drew out the great member. I placed my hands around it and drew him to me with all my strength. It stood out harder and thicker than I had ever known it, and it glistened with the first of his emissions.

But suddenly he tore himself away from me and knelt between my legs, pushing up and apart, frantically licking, sucking and biting at the wetness between my legs, thrusting, opening and exploring with a tongue that was seeking out my innermost juices and secrets. My body was on fire, and I held his head in my hands, pulling him tighter to me, until he was up again and in, gently and tentatively at first as he stretched the opening further than it had been stretched before by Isaac's slimmer organ. Then it slowly explored deeper until it came to that part where the tightness had pained me before. But the slow power drove it relentlessly past this point and a moment's pain dissolved into joy. I felt my thighs wettening with shared juices as he filled me deeper and deeper, onwards and inwards, until I was full of him in his entirety. Our bodies thrilled together and I felt him overflowing far within me. Then he went slack, his body pressed heavily on to mine, so that the ropes cut into me. I ignored the pain and ran my hands up and down his back, and let his full lips kiss mine, perfumed as his were with my own female emissions – while the creaking of the ship and the motion of the waves lulled us.

Then he pulled me up and rearranged my clothes,

looking around furtively. He gabbled in my ear, words of passion mingling with expressions of threat, telling me never to reveal my secret until we were both away from the ship, and warning me that the slightest hint of unfaithfulness would be rewarded with punishment. My moment of supreme pleasure was succeeded with the most terrible dangers.

The time had come to escape from him, and the next day at the service of addresses and prayers I was ready. John Barebones again became terrible with passion when he spoke with deep feeling of death and repentance, and of how contrition was necessary to achieve divine life. I stared into his face and managed to make tears start in my eyes. He saw, and his voice faltered for a moment. I covered my face with my hands and shook my head as though overcome with sorrow and repentance. Once again I sensed his eyes on me, and I peeped out from between my fingers. He was staring at me, as I had hoped, and his voice told me that he had lost the thread of what he was saying. I knew I had succeeded! Soon the final prayer had been intoned and the final blessing requested from God, and everyone was beginning to disperse. John Barebones fixed me with his piercing gaze and came up to me, putting his hand on my shoulder to stop me from leaving, asking me my name.

I humbly replied with 'Terence', the pseudonym I had employed while on board ship.

'How came you to be a sailor at such a young age, young man?' he asked, in a kinder voice. 'You are no doubt sodden with sin, truly depraved, like so many of these villains who snigger and ridicule the word of God when I preach to them daily. Yet I have on occasion sensed that you have been moved by my words, and wonder whether Divine Providence has not placed you here amongst this blasphemous crew in order for me to help you to find your salvation.'

I looked him in the eye again, with my most pathetic expression and replied. 'Yes indeed, I have many sins that weigh on my conscience. Until I heard you speak I did not know that I could find salvation. But, Sir, if you have any pity, please help a poor sinner like me.'

He stared back at me for a moment. Then he told me to present myself at his cabin early the following morning after prayers. The Captain would be informed of the special favours that would be due to me as long as I was willing to receive instruction from him.

That night I lay in my hammock, hoping that Dunga my lascar companion would be too tired to come to me. But as usual he was at my side, signalling for me to go up on deck as I had done the previous night. I had to obey, and indeed part of me was eager to take pleasure in what he had to offer. But fear of what would happen to me if anyone else on the crew found out my true identity made it impossible for me to extract my full portion of joy.

So when I was back in my hammock amongst the sleeping sailors, my senses were still unsatisfied, and when I fell asleep my drowsiness was interrupted by a dream that came back again and again. I was lying on a very large bed in a small room, panelled in wood, in semi-darkness, lit only by the candles at the side of the bed.

I had only a thin silk shift over my nakedness, and Sophie was standing over me clad in the same way. I gazed with desire at her full figure, so voluptuous, with such broad shoulders, such strong arms, such heavy thighs. Then she was beside me, and my nostrils were filled with the musky scent of the natural perfume of her womanly parts, and her kisses were on my face, my neck, my shoulders. I became aware through my rising desire that our breasts were now quite naked of the silken shifts that had somehow fallen back. Her body was above mine. She supported herself with one arm on either side of me and as she lowered herself the hard pointed crests of her breasts brushed my own softer, smaller pink buds, which in my case tipped globes that were dainty and tight against my ribs when I was on my back. Then her breasts and mine touched firmly, just where the points of pleasure are most powerful, and I felt my body overwhelmed with a sweet longing.

Now her soft furry mound, in which her most secret lips hid, was pressed gently against mine and it moved with a firm rhythmical pressure that pushed me closer and closer towards the moment of complete abandonment. My arms were round her body, and I pressed my fingers into the delightful cranny between her full buttocks, my hands encouraging her movements against me. Her skin was hot to the touch and was becoming damp with the perspiration that was now running out of both of us as we both sighed and gasped in our ecstasy.

'Oh my darling!'

'My sweetest love, you will kill me with pleasure!'

Then she was half-lying, half-kneeling between my legs, and her hand encouraged me to explore her body, to hold her nipples tight for a moment between fingers, to feel the weight of her breasts, the tautness of her belly, the silky luxuriance of her private hairs. Then, suddenly to my amazement, in my dream it seemed as if I were holding a male member in my hand, hot, yet as smooth as ivory, rigid, yet as soft as velvet, and my passion soared yet higher when I knew what was to come. Its head presented itself to my soft pink and fleshy lips, and by tiny gentle movements it loosened the gates, and gently and slowly eased itself into my passage – for I was still inexperienced, and needed to be used carefully, before I was fully opened up to all that a manhood could present to me. We were both triumphantly in tune, the staff rigid, me wet and open, and I called out again and again in ecstasy, with boundless pleasure, and for the first time – only in my dream, alas – I experienced what the farthest shores of passion could bring.

But I was awoken by the ringing of the bell that announced the new day, and I knew that soon I must visit the cabin of John Barebones.

Nine

I went up the companionway onto the upper deck that morning with my dream of the night before still stirring in my mind. I tried to compose myself in readiness for my conversation with John Barebones. If I were to continue with my present disguise I knew that I must convince him that I had become a convert; then no doubt I should fall under their protection, and so be invited to join their party in the New World. The prospect of having to return to the ways of the Denvers filled me with dismay. Even though life was now full of risks and dangers, I now had freedom, and I wanted to be able to do those things I was best at!

At this I involuntarily gave a low laugh. Teresa ceased her story, coloured slightly with anger and reached out to slap my wrists with her fan.

'My dear friend!' exclaimed she. 'I do not expect you, of all people, to ridicule me! Yes indeed, it is in the tender passions that draw man and woman together where I excel, and I aim only to please and to be pleased. I should not have become the acknowledged champion of all ladies of pleasure without the apprenticeship I served in the years of adventure that I now recount for the delectation of the world!'

I was embarrassed at my indiscretion, and remorseful at having offended Miss Chaunce. I stammered my apologies and begged her to continue. She bowed, accepting my regrets, and continued her tale.

I was now on the upper deck, and one of the petty officers was waiting, looking at me mistrustfully.

'John Barebones has chartered this ship, so his wishes must be followed. Make sure you don't take advantage of him. He seems a most worthy man!'

At this he knocked at the oaken door of a small cabin that stood on its own, with narrow windows and thick leaded glass in them. There was a moment's silence, then a voice within called to us to enter.

John Barebones was sitting at a small deal table upon which lay an open church Bible. The room was all panelled in oak, and the dim light from the small thickly glassed windows was shining on the open pages. Behind him was a bunk with a single bed made up in it, and between the door and the deal table was just enough room for a stool. I stood quietly, alone with him. His eyes were on the pages of his Bible. After a moment's silence he turned his head to me and stared, his eyes taking in every detail of my person – my hands, my face, my figure, my legs. Was it my imagination that I thought I saw again the look that had so impressed me before – a look of repressed passion, of powerful, obsessive sensuality? This was my greatest test yet. Would I be able to tame that powerful spirit for my own ends?

He continued looking at me. I stared at the floor and made myself burst into tears. I knew what I had to say. I talked through my tears of my remorse at my previous existence. I told him that I had been a miserable sinner all my life, and my present misfortune at being press-ganged into the navy was only the result of my wasted past. I reiterated that I wanted to receive instruction from him.

I could see that my words had pleased him, and he motioned to me to sit. That day he began to teach me the things that I already knew, about the beliefs that Mr and Mrs Denver had shared, and I managed to respond to him in just the right way: appearing to be ignorant of what he was telling me, yet also eager to learn. At the appropriate moments I expressed much joy at the promises he made of future happiness and freedom from guilt. After an hour or two's talk along these lines, John Barebones ordered me to return to my post as a member of the crew, and commanded me to see him at the same time the following day, if I wished to save my soul, as he put it.

So now I was still a member of the crew, while spending time in John Barebones' cabin pretending to learn about his beliefs, while really waiting for the right moment to make him into my own instrument. Whenever we met I hinted to him of terrible secrets that tormented me, for which I believed it would be quite impossible for anyone to forgive me. Each time I told him that, he swore that anything could be forgiven to true repentance. As time went on I also spoke more and more about sins of the flesh, hinting that I had lived a disorderly life of the senses already, and that I was now eager to slough off the burden, if only I could bring myself to speak frankly about my experiences. The more that I talked the more his curiosity was aroused. I began to notice how he would stare at me with that level stare, with a slight reddening of his cheeks and forehead and a bulging of the small veins of the temples, which so often signals suppressed passion.

Soon the day came in his cabin when I decided to launch into the first confession of my sexual adventures, with the intention of arousing his desires to such a pitch that he would be willing to accept me for what I was. By this stage of our voyage, the tempestuous weather had abated, and we were far off course in warm southern waters, with such light breezes that we made but little headway. The clemency of the climate no doubt quickened Dunga's appetites, and I feared more and more the consequences of discovery.

John Barebones was reading to me a passage from the New Testament, and when he came to the words, 'Let he who is without sin cast the first stone', I spoke out to him, seeing the moment had come.

'If I confess fully the nature of the sins of the flesh that I have committed, would you truly not cast the first stone?' I spoke vehemently.

The stare came into his eyes, the same that the Old Adam must have had in the Garden of Eden when the sweet savour of the apple was still between his teeth. I resolved to confess my relations with Sophie, without letting him know yet that I was a woman, not a man, and for effect exaggerating events somewhat in order to strengthen the effect of the tale.

'When I lived in the house of my adoptive parents there was a daughter of the family, Sophie, eighteen years of age, who had a maid of the same age. Sophie was tall and slender, with a white skin, and long black hair, while her maid Antonietta, was darker than her, of mixed race, shorter and much more voluptuous of body. I soon began to harbour secret desires for both of them, and after only a few moments' dalliance with Sophie in a dark and unfrequented corner of the house, I resolved to enter her room at night and throw myself upon her reciprocated passions. Her room was small, and illuminated during the hours of darkness by one dim night-light. I remember she was sleeping soundly but restlessly. I sat beside her on the bed, and admired her beauty from close quarters and at my leisure. Her long black hair fell loose all over the pillow, and in her sleeping movements she pushed down the bedclothes so that I could see that her body was unclothed under her nightdress. I gently loosened the laces about her bust, and gradually her fine shoulders and cleavage appeared, stirring my desire to possess her wholely. Pulling back the sheets so that all of her body lay uncovered, I raised up her skirts a little and touched her full white thighs gently with my hands, astonished at the fineness of her skin.

'The sweetness of the perfume that came from her body began to excite me to the utmost, so that my whole being became animated with lust. I pulled the last coverings away from her breasts so that they lay exposed, totally naked to my gaze and my wandering hands. Following my instincts my lips also began to touch and explore the red summits of those still small but oh so voluptuous mounts! It seemed as though she was so deeply asleep that no matter what I did she would not awake, so I raised my own garments above my waist and slipped into the bed beside her, trembling with passion. My hand had returned to the sweet exploration of her thighs, and at a whim I began with my mouth and tongue to lick those softest and most secret areas which lay at the juncture of her thighs. Here I finally found the warmest and most sensitive crevice of all open and waiting for me. Marvelling at the fineness and silkiness of the black hairs that stood guardians around the flower-like organ, as pink as any rose, I was about to plunge my tongue in and seek out the very bud of pleasure when a momentary sound made me look up towards the door, and there standing watching us was Antonietta, dressed only in a short petticoat and a satin vest.

'We stared at each other, and I was ready for her to go off and raise the alarm, therefore leading me to suffer terrible punishments and no doubt Sophie, too. But she simply put her finger to her lips, smiled at me, and sat by the bed, as if to invite me to continue, and encouraged me to continue her delightful task by touching her mistress's body herself. While she was doing this, I was able to admire Antonietta's fuller figure, for her body was only covered enough to tease my senses and curiosity, but not enough to lessen the force of her own individual charms. The nipples of her full breasts pressing hard against her shift raised the thin material into outline. In a moment I followed temptation and pulled at this garment too, and was excited to distraction by the sight of her firm golden body now entering into such intimate contact with her mistress's slimmer, whiter form.

'Sophie still appeared to be sleeping, but now she muttered words of passion in an undertone to both me and her servant, and with each arm encouraged Antonietta and me to kiss and caress, each kneeling on either side of her, while her hands touched each of our bodies in the most shameless manner. This nearly brought me to a peak of excitement there and then. I tried to draw myself back, for I wished to complete this business with Sophie. But this she would not yet allow, performing sleepy movements to brush me away from where I touched. Instead Antonietta offered herself in front of her mistress and lay between her white and heavenly thighs, caressed by her while letting me enjoy her firmer, stouter, darker body, with her pit of pleasure liberally covered in thicker and harder hairs, while her stronger fingers searched and pressed me into a state of ecstatic abandonment. Then, to my unspeakable joy, when we had both satisfied our needs for passion, the girl turned on her mistress – who opened her eyes for the first time – and carried out such love games as satisfied her needs, too!'

While I was recounting this tale to John Barebones I must have been so carried away with the concentration required to tell a lascivious tale – so extracting pleasure to the utmost – that I took little notice of the effect that it had upon him. I now ceased my narration, and looked up at him with what I hoped would be a humble expression of sorrow and repentance.

John Barebones was staring at me astonished and transfixed. I should remind you that it was the custom of Puritan men to wear their tall black hats indoors as well as out, and his black tunic and breeches were only relieved by his starched, high white collar. But his face was suffused with red, as of someone who is repressing a strong passion, and I saw that his hand shook as it played with the pages of his Bible. Then my eye came to rest on his breeches – as you will know, the Puritans wore their breeches loose in those days. There, between his legs, was the unmistakable swelling that told me that my tale had had the hoped-for effect: exciting his passions beyond the stage at which he could suppress them. I did not wish to make obvious what I had seen, but I looked again out of the corner of my eye. To my surprise, the swelling was such as to indicate that John Barebones' male member was truly of huge dimensions, even greater in length and girth than that of Dunga, my lascar lover.

'John Barebones, I have now confided in you just one example of my past depravity and sinfulness, offences which I truly wish to put behind me. But I have even greater offences to confide to you, and I must now extract from you a promise – nay, a solemn oath – that whatever I tell you from now on will be shared only with you and with God!'

When John Barebones finally spoke, it was from between dry lips, and his voice had lost the ringing tones of conviction that was its chief characteristic.

'Yes, indeed, I am most surprised at your frankness, Terence Chaunce, yet I believe that your willingness to speak so plainly to me shows a degree of trust which has perhaps been sent by Providence. Shocking though such depraved behaviour must be to anyone who has enjoyed the benefits of a moral upbringing, I do not, nevertheless, admonish you. In someone like you, lacking so completely the least elements of moral education, repellent and unnatural acts cannot be condemned.'

Here he stopped for a moment, and a different expression flitted over his face – lasciviousness, curiosity – that told me that on the morrow he would be eager for more tales of lust and depravation.

Ten

At the service the next morning John Barebones was even more histrionic. He cried aloud to Heaven. He abused the sailors for being depraved rascals. He begged everyone who was not saved to look for salvation. But all the way through the service his eyes kept returning to me, and I knew what was truly in his mind.

Late that night in the sailors' quarters I looked around at the sleeping figures and resolved that the next day would bring me escape. When I went up the companionway for my conclave with John Barebones I had well prepared what I was to say.

'John Barebones!' I cried as I came in to his cabin. 'Your words moved me today. I must beg a favour from you. A very great favour. I wish to free myself from the burden of wrongdoing which I carry around with me. But, forgive me, I am still afraid that if I tell you openly the nature of my secret, you will betray me both to the rascals in the crew, not to mention to those of your own people, who unlike the seamen are so seemly in their comportment.'

The gleam of passion lit up his eyes again, and I was sure that he wished to hear more at all costs.

'No, no!' He spoke impatiently. 'You may depend on me, I shall not betray any confidence that you give, provided that I am ensured that you are truly sincere in wanting to reform your life.'

At this point I burst into tears. 'Yet my wrongdoing is so scandalous that I cannot believe that you will listen to what I recount without becoming so wrathful that you will in the end betray the confidence that we have between ourselves.'

He was becoming impatient, and was longing to hear more lascivious tales. 'My word is my word, Terence Chaunce, you may rely upon it totally and without reservation. Speak. Indeed, not to speak would indicate a lack of openness which would not be in accordance with the workings of Divine Providence whose presence I have observed in our meetings.'

'Please, then. Swear to me on the Bible,' I said boldly, taking his hand and placing it upon the black book that lay in its usual place upon the desk. He looked at me in surprise, but did what I asked of him. I then started my next tale, which I hoped would finally lure him on into my power.

'After this scandalous episode with Sophie and her servant I took to consorting with both, but they did not permit me to visit them every night, and while sometimes I took my pleasure with them together, at other times I went with Antonietta alone. This episode occurred on one such night. She slept in a tiny room at the top of the house, no larger than an alcove, just big enough for one bed, which was, however, of sufficient size to allow the two of us to sport together. It was, I remember, a warm night, and we were both lying upon the bed with only the scantiest of shifts to cover us, those so rumpled and disordered as to scarcely cover any part of us. The single candle nearby cast a delightful glow upon my friend's body, for her breasts were very full, and tipped with the plumpest and darkest nipples imaginable, surrounded as they were by swollen and silky areolae.

'I was exciting them with my fingers and lips, and in return her hands were on me, exploring those parts where the organs of sensation are most responsive to the touch of another. That indescribable delight of yearning was goading us, leading us to more passionate caresses. My companion was uttering little cries and whimpers of pleasure when there came a light tapping at the door.

' "Who is it?" cried out my companion, and after a whispered exchange of words, the door opened. There stood one of the other servants of the house, a page who was usually in attendance upon Sophie's mother. Little more than one-and-twenty years old, he was of such a delicate and almost feminine beauty that I must confess, John Barebones, I had already many times desired his touch upon my body.'

At this point I looked up, and I was not surprised to see his anger and shock at what I was now saying – for, of course, he still believed that I was a man. I raised my hand and begged him to let me continue my tale, reminding him that he had sworn never to betray me, whatever I recounted. So I continued, describing how I had lain beside the maid and the page while I watched them engaged in the most passionately amorous play, how she had reached the extremes of abandoned pleasure while I too shared in their caresses, and how, after she had attained a sweet satiation, the page then turned his attentions to me.

At this point I paused in my story, and looked at John Barebones again. As had happened on the day before, his face was red with a blush of excitement, and I could see out of the corner of my eye how his manhood was distended with the lusts that my story had lit up in him. As before, the light in his eye was that of any man of lewd nature bent on the pleasures of the flesh, and not at all that of the leader of a party of serious, religious pilgrims. But now he was wrathful, and he called out to me in a loud voice.

'Corrupt youth, trying to lead righteous men like me astray who wish only to help you!'

I begged him to be silent for a few more moments, reminding him once more of his promise to me. 'John Barebones, I am not what you think I am. But remember that you have vowed to help me. So now I must tell you the truth.' Here I loosened the buttons of my jerkin around the throat, so as to reveal the upper parts of my breasts. 'The Terence Chaunce that you see before you is Teresa Chaunce, a woman who has by a most unhappy fortune become a sailor on this ship, and who throws herself on your mercy, John Barebones.'

At this I threw off my jerkin and, unbuttoning the light cotton shirt that was my only other undergarment, experienced the intense sensuality that only a woman can feel when her femininity is bared after having been confined for a period of time, for my love-making with the lascar had always been hurried and clandestine. I had never been able to enjoy the physical pleasure of baring my parts in private, of enjoying the sensation of watching one's body excite the passions of another.

I looked down at myself freely for the first time since having been abducted on board this ship, and enjoyed the sight of my breasts standing out tight and lightly pointed, the little pale rosy tips pointing up sharp upon the raised domes of the areolae, and without thinking I brushed my fingers against the tips and teased them into swollen erection. I looked shyly at John Barebones, and he was staring enraptured at the same delightful points, and I knew that I had him in my power! With a toss of my arm the shirt fell to the floor, and I rubbed my hands over my womanly form, feeling the silky skin, the firm resistance to the pressure of my palms and the thrilling of my nerves, that ran down my belly into my loins, which caused my secret lips to swell, to melt, to loosen in readiness for the touch of a lover.

I came round the table to John Barebones, held his hair in my fingers, and drew his head to my breasts; but teasingly, for I did not yet allow his lips to touch the tips. Rather, I pulled his face on to my belly, letting it explore and arouse that place between breasts and loins, as if we were in the gateway to more intimate joys. At the same time, I loosened my breeches.

So step by step I permitted him more and more liberties with my person, but I was determined not to yield myself to him totally without a show of resistance, for I guessed that it would be advantageous to me to make a show of virtue to him. For his part, John Barebones said nothing, but appeared to have lost all sense of his position and of how unfitting our behaviour was on board a ship of this sort.

Now we were enjoying close embraces, and his body had become hot, his breathing hurried and hoarse, as though his instincts were winning the battle against his inhibitions and morals. I could feel his swelling manhood thrusting against the fabric of his breeches, and my hands were upon his body, holding and arousing, until I knelt in front of him. More confident, now that he had not resisted my advances, I began to speak to him.

'John Barebones! I have longed for the touch of your body ever since I first saw you upon the deck when I was taken out of my prison! While I have been sitting with you here in your cabin, learning from you about sin and repentance, I have been overcome with passion, passion for you, for your mind, for your body.'

At this he merely growled with the harshness of some ravening animal and buried his head between my breasts, licking and biting as though he were ready to devour me. I spoke again.

'I beg you, John Barebones, to remember our trust! I came to you demanding succour, spiritual counselling. You have sworn never to betray me. Yet now we have both embarked on that journey that leads to more and greater joys of the flesh, and you have forgotten yourself so much that no one would now recognise the John Barebones who preaches righteousness to the crew every morning!'

At this I stood again, and thrust him down into his chair so that my womanhood was only two hands' breadth from his eyes. I bared it by opening my breeches, then drew him towards it, raising one leg to his shoulder and pulling his torso until his face brushed me where the softest flesh falls away into the silky bush of hairs that hide the organs so special to every woman. I then guided his hand to the inner parts of my thighs.

In a moment he was upon me, like a mad animal, his passions bursting forth after being suppressed for so long, unwasted in their intensity. I was on his bunk, his body over mine, and his manhood, huge and of a girth I had never experienced with my other lovers reared shamelessly from out of his black Puritan clothes. Once revealed in its full primitive power it brooked no restraint, but immediately plunged into my female parts, opening, stretching, burrowing deeper and ever deeper, and for both of us all restraint was thrown aside. Again he came at me, and yet again, and each time was as the first time, rough stretching, pleasure so intense as to be indistinguishable from pain. Relentlessly and repeatedly his male fluids flooded my deepest recesses, yet his senses were so inflamed that these climaxes brought him and me no peaceful satiation, as is usual between man and woman. Rather, each *coup de grâce* once achieved seemed to inflame him the more, and after a few moments' respite he would return to the fray.

John Barebones' passion was mine too, and I shared his every ecstasy. But each time that I was constrained to call out, his hands would be upon my mouth, and his hot breath whispering in my ear would warn me not to utter a sound, otherwise we should be discovered and both of us ruined.

I have no recollection of how much time passed in this way. Gradually, however, the tide of passion turned, and we lay together in his bunk, he on me. Meanwhile, my eyes explored the closely confined cabin, with its oaken beams and planking, and we listened to the sound of the waters, the shouts and singing of the mariners, and the creaking as the timbers flexed together.

Now John Barebones was whispering in my ear. There were words of passion, words of love, words of jealousy, but also those of hatred and reproach. Reproach for having awoken within him a part of his nature which he knew intimately, and which through self-discipline and willpower he had kept buried in chains, like the serpent, Satan himself. Hatred for my possessing, like him, a lustful and lascivious nature, for being the very image of what had been hidden in himself for so long.

Then, with a sudden movement of his body, he was standing, and once he had rearranged his clothing he placed his tall black hat on his head. He was once more the Puritan leader.

'Duties call me elsewhere. I must go. I shall give you further orders. In the meantime you must go about your duties. Dress yourself and leave my cabin.' It only took me a few minutes to transform myself into a sailor once again. But as I opened the door of the cabin in order to leave, I turned to him.

'John Barebones, you are sending your lover back to sleep amongst ruffians and scoundrels!' His features flushed red and were contorted with jealousy. Then I was on the ladder down to the lower decks, and my hard duties returned. I was a man again. Yet, while I scaled the rope-ladders, scrubbed decks, pulled and carried, a man amongst men, my inner female organs were still in such a state of excitement that they served to keep my secret in the forefront of my mind the whole time.

At the end of that day I was sitting with the rest of the crew upon the lower deck, taking the gruel that was our evening repast out of a wooden bowl. The weather was still warm and the winds calm. There were only a few pink clouds in the evening sky, and the sun burnt low and red on the horizon. Then the Captain's first mate came up to me and gestured with his thumb to the upper decks. 'Captain wants you. Wants to talk to you.' And he led the way to the poop deck, and there, through a carved and gilded door-frame, was the Captain's cabin.

I was full of expectation as I knocked on the heavy door, for good or ill I knew not. His gruff voice called out to me, I pushed at the wood and entered. The room was candlelit, and at the desk opposite the Captain sat John Barebones. The candlelight flickered over the mass of charts, navigational instruments, sextants and compasses and his features were grim and unbending, as his public face always had been. I wondered at his ability to look at me as though nothing of what had passed between us earlier in the day had actually happened. The Captain looked at him questioningly, and with a gesture from John Barebones, he started to speak.

'Terence Chaunce, I find myself in the most unusual

position of being asked by the leader of the group of the good people who have chartered this ship to release you from your obligations to me and the owners of the vessel. John Barebones assures me that the conversations which you have participated in with him have led him to believe that you would, given the right guidance, become a most useful member of society. In addition to this,' and here he gave a short laugh, as though telling us that this was his main consideration, 'John Barebones, this good man, has assured me that he has consulted with the other responsible members of the group and offered to buy your freedom with a generous sum of money which will be entirely at my disposal. In order to free you in the future from any obligations to the ship-owners, you will be entered in the ship's log as having fallen overboard.'

John Barebones looked deep into my eyes, and although no outsider could have guessed the nature of our bond, the fire in his eyes reminded me yet again what sort of man he really was. 'Terence Chaunce, what have you to say for yourself? Do you wish to enjoy the advantages of becoming a useful member of our society? Do you wish to live a devout life, of work, of prayer, of service to others? Or would you rather continue as before, wasting what God has given? Speak. You must choose for yourself!'

Eleven

I ended that day a different person from the one I had
started it as! I was once again a Puritan, and because of
my background, which none on the ship suspected, I knew
how to behave in order to gain their respect and admiration. Yet only two people – the lascar and John Barebones – were aware that I was in another type of disguise.
Dunga was distraught at losing me, I could tell from the
glances he threw at me whenever he had the chance, but he
was unable to say what he knew, for fear of being punished
for speaking against the Captain.

But I was happy to be free of the back-breaking toil and
harsh conditions that had made my life miserable, and I
strove to appear carefree, although my moods of sadness
and apprehension for my future occasioned appearances of
grief and sorrow. However, my Puritan companions and
mentors took them to be the workings of my conscience.

That very first evening, after I had been taken into their
group, and after I had been given a suit of clothes – black,
with a tall black hat, and simple white linen; the uniform that
all the men wore – John Barebones called a meeting of the
company upon one of the upper decks that had been set apart
for their use. John Barebones was in an exultant mood. He led
the company in prayers of thanksgiving for the gift of Providence. By this he meant me! The night was calm and moonlit,
and the prayers, hymns and exhortations seemed to echo up
to Heaven in the most impressive manner, making me almost
believe that John Barebones was doing a great deed for me
and that he was not just a hypocrite, misusing his power and
influence over these good people in order to gratify his lusts.

I was given a rota of duties quite different from those that I had had whilst with Mr and Mrs Denver. These were the duties of a young man, and involved preparing and maintaining the equipment that was stored in the hold of the ship, in readiness for use when we landed in Virginia. But this was light work compared to what I had been used to. The truly hard work was in my atonement. I was given a plan of Biblical readings that required many hours a day to fulfil. I would sit with my group of young fellows listening to the teachings of those men who were most learned in theology. And then, each afternoon, came my private meeting with John Barebones himself. He had told the company that my salvation still required much private discussion with him, or, as he put it, 'Our dear brother in Christ, Terence Chaunce, has sinned very greatly, my friends, and the nature of his faults is such that he can talk freely only to me. Once we have rooted out each last vice, once we have received assurances both from his words and his deeds that his past sins maintain no more hold over him, then our private meetings will cease. But I must warn you, my dear friends in Christ, that until Terence Chaunce has freed himself from the bonds of his past, that you must make no enquiry as to who he is, where he is from, and, most importantly, what those sins were from which he is so eager to liberate himself.' Such was the hold that John Barebones held over his company that none at first questioned this strange injunction.

In the mid part of the afternoon I went to his cabin. As soon as the oaken door closed behind me, a different John Barebones made his appearance. During those first days our meetings were almost light-hearted. I would commence by baring the womanly parts of my body, and walking about the cabin half-naked.

John Barebones, with all of his Biblical learning, would return again and again to the idea that I was his Eve and that he was Adam, waiting to be initiated into the sins and delights of the flesh by me. I would parade my charms in front of him, rubbing my dainty breasts with my fingers, in order to excite my own passions, then I would invite him to accompany me in my joyous task. At first he would refuse, calling me a lascivious woman, only to be despised and rejected. But I knew by the swelling in his breeches that my actions had already aroused his lusts, and that he was merely feigning indifference.

Then he would fall on me as though he were mad – which I truly think he was, for he was maddened with lust. His male member would tear me open as if it were a creature that had a mind of its own, a hog greedily seeking out the juices and perfumes of my female parts, parting the orifice with its blunt head, taking itself into where the tightness would be overcome, widening, lubricating with his masculine fluids, raising my sexual feelings to such a pitch that I hardly knew any longer who I was, nor whether John Barebones was really he, or in truth, Adam himself.

Only when the first flames of his passion had burnt themselves out would he treat me as a lover usually does, taking delight in the body of the partner – although he would never remove any of his outdoor garments, so that in our love-making my skin would always be rubbed and scratched by his black coat and breeches. I would guide his lips to my silken nipples, which he would fall upon with a sort of hunger that would reignite the fires waiting in my belly ready to flare up. I would open my loins to him, and the roughness of his head as it rasped against my soft white thighs, the tongue seeking out my honey, would make the fires burst out with gathering strength. Knowing that his eyes would be fixed upon my open slit, liquid and swollen from the effects of his passion within me, I would draw attention to the beauties within the pink lips by using my fingers to open them further to his visual exploration. Then, by teasing the most sensitive parts, I would maintain them in that erect and damp condition that most excites a lover, by giving promise of the delights that only await the partner's arousal to be taken and enjoyed. And for John Barebones he achieved that excitation of his satiated member by taking those inner parts in his mouth, by sucking, nibbling, licking the juices as though they were an ambrosia that carried with it the secret ingredient of a love potion!

His lips would cause wave after wave of bliss to break over me – waves that were more thrilling than any that I had experienced with Sophie, who as a woman had not the power to arouse me, more forceful than the lascar's lovemaking, for he had the simplest needs and never varied his desires, nor the way he satisfied them. It was then that I had to cover my mouth with my hands, in case my cries of delight should draw attention to what was being enacted in this small and private cabin. Then his head would break away from my secret parts, and his masculine form would rear up above me, and his staff would be ready for the fray again. I would perhaps be so carried away by the sight of its size and strength that I could not resist taking it into my mouth, and with my tongue raise it further towards that point of bliss which we would share yet again.

In those first days he was at his most gentle after we had exhausted each other's desires. Then he would talk about the future he saw for the two of us. He promised that when we landed in Virginia we should escape from the rest of the company. He alone had unfettered access to the gold and silver coin that, while of less value in the colonists' state than it was in England, would allow us to acquire the goods we needed to start a new life upon the inland frontier where we might live relatively undisturbed. There, he imagined, we should build our future through our own labours, amass capital, and in time return to a comfortable life in England. When he sketched out this dream he seemed to think it would be a great joy for both of us to be together, alone and living only for each other. I must confess, however, that even then the prospect of an existence of this sort held little appeal for me. But as the saying goes, beggars cannot be choosers, and my first need was to escape from the predicament into which I had fallen.

Both he and I were great dissemblers, and thus we both were able to comport ourselves in public as though the

86

relationship between us were purely on the spiritual plane. In reality I had chained him to me by the power of my sensuality, by arousing his hidden lusts to such a pitch that he was ready to throw all away. But he was unable to renounce his position, and the battle that took place within his nature between the two mutually hostile persons that inhabited the same soul was such that his behaviour became by degrees more violent, more irrational and more highly charged with strong emotion.

He began to rant at both the company and the crew during the daily services on deck. His voice would call out aloud so that it seemed to ring out to the very horizon, calling again and again on us all to admit to our secret lusts, to confess, to repent.

'For the Devil comes to us secretly and in disguise,' he would call out, and for those who had the key to his thoughts, everything he said had a secret double meaning. 'He comes as a harlot, disguised as a sailor, he comes as a pious man, whose sober clothing can scarcely cover the tempting parts that will drag even the most righteous of us to our destruction. I say this to you as one who has watched the nakedness of temptation daily, for it moves and lives amongst us all. The Evil One comes to us as naked as Eve herself in the Garden of Eden, luscious with the sweetest honeys, with cherry lips and breasts of coral. The Evil One will light your lusts and unchain the hidden serpent, so that it will rise up, powerful beyond measure.'

When he began to speak like this on the first days I would peer at my male companions and wonder whether they would discover what was in John Barebones' hidden mind, or whether these would simply be moved by a colourful metaphor that urged them back to the straight and narrow path. I soon discovered to my surprise that John Barebones' dark influence was strong over these good people and that his terrible warnings affected them deeply.

I should say here that I slept in a cabin in which were many bunks close-packed together, and my companions were all men of the company, devout and serious young

87

fellows for the most part, some robust and hale, others more bookish in their habits, paler and more sedentary. Sometimes the pressure of the monotonous life on board the ship was too much for them, and they would engage in horseplay, indulging in mock fights, joking punishments and brutal practical jokes. But hidden under their simplicity there was much dissembling lust. For example, often when two of the young men were in close contact, in a sporting struggle one or both of them would experience a strong physical arousal and I could see their erect manhood straining against their breeches. Even dressed as a man, I suppose I must have appeared extremely effeminate, and I noticed many clearly prurient glances thrown in my direction, particularly when we were in the sleeping chamber, getting ready for rest.

Knowing that I slept in the presence of many men fired the anger that lurked in John Barebones' imagination. He was jealous to think of me in such close proximity to many who could so easily be tempted, and yet he was also convulsed with a dark joy to think that he alone possessed me, that he alone had penetrated my secret, that I was totally in his power. He would instruct me to confess that I had had sexual relations with one or other of the young men, and to describe to him in graphic detail how it had been and what services I had been forced to perform for them.

At this point Miss Chaunce laughed sadly. 'John Barebones was a strange man, my dear Balthazar, and his demands were not like those of other men. But I must confess, my friend, that there were times when I shared with him very great joys. The closeness of his cabin, the fear of discovery, made more acute by the sounds of passing footsteps, the voices of people familiar to us both, served to raise our peaks of sensation to a higher, more piquant degree, and his obvious guilt at the nature of our liaison, coupled with a gift that I discovered at this time for storytelling, made this time of my life a not unpleasant memory.'

I bowed, and paused in my scribbling long enough to reply

to Miss Chaunce. 'Indeed, Miss Chaunce. Pleasure and pain are often mingled so closely that it is not easy to know when one leaves off and the other begins. I have heard that there are habitués of your establishment who gain much pleasure from confounding pain and pleasure, especially when the pain is administered by a peasant girl with strong arms and ample endowments!'

Miss Chaunce laughed, and shook her head, for she was the soul of discretion.

'That is as may be, my dear Balthazar, but my contention is in relation to mental pain, not physical. When I have completed this part of my narrative I may demonstrate that to which I refer.'

At this she smiled meaningfully at me, and I fell silent, wondering what adventures she had in store for me on that next day of her narrative. She continued her tale.

One day remains in my mind. When I came to John Barebones' cabin at the appointed time he was seated in his chair, a little away from his desk, at an angle. The Bible was open in front of him, and his finger was on the page as though he were fully occupied in whatever text he was reading. He did not look up when I stood in front of him, but with a gesture of his hand he indicated that I should divest myself of my tunic, shoes and breeches, so that I was clad only in my shirt, which revealed the beauties of my thighs and breasts to his gaze, without, however, baring my pit of joy. John Barebones still feigned absorption in the text of his choice. Then he looked up at me, and read out from the holy book. 'Thou shalt not commit adultery.'

Then he looked me in the eye. 'Have you committed adultery, Teresa Chaunce?' I knew what was expected of me. I covered my face with my hands, and pretended to show regret for what he supposed I had done, and at the same time, as though by accident, pushed the fabric of my shirt back so that my shoulders were bared.

I pretended to be overcome with grief, holding my head between my hands in despair, I threw myself down on the

89

floor of the cabin, and, again, apparently accidentally, loosened a button or two upon my shirt, so that my torso was bared to his eyes. Kneeling on the floor at his feet, my part-nakedness aroused my own senses, as it did his. He was still staring down at me, pretending to feel wrath, when he truly was maddened with desire.

'Who was it with this time, you incorrigible young woman? Which of my companions have you corrupted to-day?'

Now my shirt had fallen about my waist, and my breasts rose up sharp, with the tips apparently pointing up to him, inviting his lust to proceed. At this invitation I mentioned two names – two of my companions in the sleeping quarters. One of them was a stout young fellow, the other slim, pale and studious.

The effect on John Barebones was immediate. His breathing became hoarse with anger. 'If you wish forgiveness,' he stammered, 'you must confess all. Tell me exactly what occurred. How did you meet, where and when. How did they use you, how did you entrap them in your sensual wiles? Tell me all, all!' His voice rose high, and I was afraid that he would excite attention and that we should be discovered.

I fell back on the floor, with the shirt covering only the skimpy zone about my loins, and raised my arms behind my head in order to fan his senses with my pose. Then I commenced my fictitious narration.

'I was in the hold of the ship carrying out my work on the inventory of the goods that we have in store. I was alone for some moments, and the unaccustomed heat, the loneliness, made my thoughts stray to lascivious imaginings of past loves. Imperceptibly and unconsciously, my hand followed the inclinations of my thought, and in a trice my jerkin was open, one hand feeling the soft flesh of one breast, touching its soft resistance, exploring its roundness.

'It was at just that moment the Devil's messenger came to me in the form of' – and here I used the name of the sturdy youth – who stood in the entrance to the hold unknown to me, staring. He came up, taking hold of both wrists and laughing. "So you are found out, my dear! I have known since the first time that I met you that you were a woman, not a man, and that you would bring delight to me some day." '

At this I stared into John Barebones' eyes saying, 'I held myself thus,' cupping my naked breast in one hand, pressing and squeezing lightly, and placing the other hand under the folds of the shirt, moving my hips and thighs against it in a sinuous and suggestive manner.

But now I had excited my own senses, and the melting in my womanly parts, the rigidity of my nipples and the desire for his body to take mine, became unbearable. I continued talking. 'My companion's senses were inflamed by the sight of my body, and his hands followed mine to where I was touching myself. His masculine power stirred up waves of sensations, irresistible sensations that chased through my nerves, so that every part of me thrilled in anticipation of rougher pleasures to come.

'Now my hands were on his body, strong yet sensitive, powerful with the strength of his unslaked lust. He tore my breeches from me, and lifted me in his arms ready to throw me on to a pile of cotton and woollen fabrics that lay in one corner of the hold. I felt small and defenceless in his arms. He lifted my body upwards and his lips came into contact with the soft skin where my belly meets my bush. Almost involuntarily I opened my thighs. At the same moment he threw me down on the soft padding, and my secrets as a woman were open to his excited glances.'

John Barebones was in a paroxysm of fury. 'Wicked woman! How dare you talk so shamelessly about your exploits in such a way! You should be full of guilt, full of regrets, ready to repent!'

At this I laughed and, with my fingers, I opened the lips of my womanly parts, bringing myself to the point at which merely a touch by my lover would have brought about those spasms of pleasure that cause our conscious minds to be quite powerless. I continued with my narration for John Barebones' sake.

'Now my violator tore off his clothes before me. He was naked, powerful, built like a god, ready to take my womanhood at his pleasure, his staff ready for the fray. Yet the staff, I knew, longed for the touch of my fingers, the stronger clasp of my hands, the teasing butterfly grazings of my lips, or the lickings of my tongue, to bring it to its greatest peak of excitement.'

At this John Barebones took me up and thrust my body upon the table in front of him, my legs twisted around his waist, capturing me to him. I pulled him into me, ready to extinguish his lust in mine. His ram's head was pressing the lips, and it pushed into me again and again, until we reached satiation.

Twelve

It was becoming clear that John Barebones' mind was gradually growing unhinged as a result of the confusing and contradictory emotions that tormented him. Much as he demanded fantastical tales from me concerning my imaginary exploits with the men of the ship, he became unable to distinguish truth from fiction, and soon seemed to believe that I had truly dallied with many on the vessel.

The first hint that the ship's company had of his mental confusion occurred during a daily act of worship. He intimated that in future the company should take pains to become more vigilant, for the tedium into which the days had fallen in the recent spell of heat and calm was leading certain members of the company to evil thoughts.

'There are men in our band who think to take advantage of the seeming innocence and good nature of young boys who almost appear to us as women!' His face was twisted with fury, his voice echoed to the very horizon. 'Beware of the wiles of such depraved young seducers, and be vigilant against the prickings of the Evil One!'

These words disconcerted many, and even before John Barebones had ceased talking, there was some animated discussion under way, carried on in undertones – something that had never occurred before, for usually his words were heard in respectful silence.

In our tryst in his cabin that afternoon he was more perverse than he had ever been before, demanding the most minute descriptions of lewd perversions supposedly taking place on board the ship.

* * *

Miss Chaunce was thoughtful for some moments.

'As you know, my skills as a player are considerable. John Barebones was taken in by the illusions that I created for his sake, to the extent that his eye saw the protagonists and not me alone.' She reflected sadly at the recollection. *'I can even say that it was my gifts as a player of dramas that led John Barebones to his destruction. But it was the hand of fate alone that allowed me to survive the strange voyage.'*

I bowed, and begged Miss Chaunce to continue.

'You are the child of the Evil One,' cried John Barebones with terror. 'You have been sent by the Devil himself to corrupt this expedition, through the agency of me, the spotless leader.'

'Yes!' I cried in reply. 'I come to you hot with the fire of my lust, burning with flames that no single man can extinguish, nor none of your companions dampen. Come to me, satisfy me! Penetrate to my deepest parts!'

John Barebones' face was dark with terror as he sank down on his knees in an attitude of prayer. 'Why, oh God, why have I been chained to this temptation? Is it Your will that my spirit should be used for such dark purposes?'

I slipped my breeches off and loosened the tunic, and my secret parts, although bare of clothing, were veiled from view by the tails of my undershirt. I rubbed the soft white insides to my thighs, the parts that abut on the pit of pleasure itself, drawing attention to the hidden beauties by pulling some of the golden hairs that ornament my womanly parts so prettily, to remind John Barebones of what lay in wait for him.

As I pulled and stroked I spoke again. 'John Barebones, what you see is like a flower whose honey is sucked by many bees and butterflies, accepting all that come to sip its perfumes. Those with whom I share my quarters have become so enamoured of it that they cannot pass a night without alighting in my bunk to drink!'

John Barebones held his hands over his ears, as though unwilling to listen to what I had to say. I lifted them away as I talked, and pulled his face nearer to my person, rubbing his cheeks against my loins, where the promise of fulfilment was strongest. Then I backed against his table. He buried his face in my pretty purse, now so aroused that the lips stood open and swollen with desire, ready for the thrust of John Barebones' shaft. But before he was ready, he licked at the juices which were now flowing copiously between my thighs.

But even now he would break off wildly and call aloud to his Maker.

'Help me, oh Lord, to defeat the evil that is lodged in this place. Let my male staff extinguish it, for it can enter deep into Teresa's parts, and destroy the devils within her.'

Then his staff thrust into me, and waves of pleasure coursed through my body, stimulating my breasts, churning my belly. He would pause in his task time and again, and would call out, 'There oh Lord, it is nearly done. Let it be extinguished!' At this he returned, and went to it again and again. His passion seemed unquenchable. As for me I was already beginning to tire of the adventure, but I found that my pleasure was heightened by picturing in my imagination one or other of the young fellows from my cabin coming to me.

The next day brought about the downfall of John Barebones, leading to my liberation by the strangest fate. In the course of the rest of that day it became clear to me that John Barebones' company were beginning to harbour doubts about me, and I saw suspicion in the eyes of many as they passed me upon the decks. I noticed whispered conversations stopped suddenly upon my proximity being observed, and comments with hidden meanings were thrown my way behind my back.

John Barebones again commenced speaking, as he invariably did nowadays, about the sins of the flesh. He became even more agitated than he had ever been, and called out to the company at large.

'There are even those amongst you who have led our dear sister in God, Teresa Chaunce . . .' and here he paused and stammered, then recollected himself, 'Terence Chaunce. There are those who have led him to enjoy sensuous delights in cabins . . .' but even as he spoke there was a murmuring throughout the group, as though in astonishment at seeing the truth for the first time. Then, on what seemed a prearranged signal, two or three of the older men, who possessed some authority with the others, went up to where John Barebones stood and, taking his arms respectfully yet firmly, led him away to his cabin.

It is not necessary for the purposes of this narrative to go into any detail about events that followed, although they would form an interesting tale in themselves. I was indeed unmasked as a woman, and both I and John Barebones were tried for adultery. But the greater suffering was John Barebones' lot, for he was branded a cheat, a hypocrite and a liar. My treatment, in contrast, at the hands of the Puritans, was more generous than I had anticipated. They did not know my true background, and I gained sympathy for my condition, claiming to be an ignorant girl who had been harshly treated by fate. It was promised that, upon my arrival in Virginia, I should be free to go on my way. But until that time I was to submit to the required punishment, which was to stand all day by the foremast, hands tied in front of me, and head bowed, exhibiting my shame to whomsoever chose to come by and stare, and a red letter W was to be sewn on to my dress as a reminder that in their eyes I was a whore.

John Barebones, meanwhile, was to suffer graver castigation, for he was bound to the mainmast, legs and arms manacled like a common thief, clad only in loose shirt and breeches, hatless, awaiting his flogging and subsequent expulsion from the group upon the arrival of the vessel in Virginia.

The weather remained still and hot, and the sun hung blazing in a reddened and cloudless sky so that the crew members and the company became lethargic from the heavy airs that the broiling sun created. But so much more so myself, for I was condemned to stand all day uncovered and without water.

Miss Chaunce paused at this point. She stared thoughtfully into the roaring log fire for several minutes, as though in her mind far away from me. Then she seemed to come to herself again.
   'Mr De Fado, I cannot talk any more today. I beg you, do not importune me, but I look forward to your company at the same hour tomorrow!'

Thirteen

The following day I was at the residence of Miss Chaunce at the appointed hour. She was awaiting me. 'I am glad you are here. There is much that is new and interesting for you today, my friend,' she said, winking at me and smiling her same smile.

As that day progressed, the heat became more oppressive, and what little movement of air there was fell away. We were caught in a dead calm, in which the sea stood leaden about us and the sky became dark with heavy clouds. In the oppressive silence everyone suffered from a strange slackness of spirit. Then an air swept over the ship, bringing a breath of coolness, and the smell of rain. A moment later the glassy sea gave a heave, and on the far horizon there commenced a continuous flicker of lightning. From behind this light a profounder darkness grew which soon reared above the ship, and a wind came out of the darkness, growing in its force until the ship was tossed about in a frenzy of great waves and spray. People were thrown in all directions about the decks. At one moment it seemed as though we should sink into the depths and at the next we were lifted up to the heavens themselves. Then finally a wave greater than any other towered above us. Then I remembered nothing more.

I became conscious, still tied by the hands, and floating by the mast. Around me in the water a few pieces of wreckage moved about in the swell. In a state of terror I pulled myself up on to the mast, as far out of the water as I could get. By working my wrists together and ignoring the pain

of the chafing, I loosened the cords and threw them off me.
I saw no other living creature in the immensity of the
ocean. I called out in fear, and after my cries faded into the
sound of the waters, a faint voice responded.

'The Lord has punished all the evil-doers!'

*'My dear friend Balthazar, there were no survivors of that
shipwreck, except for John Barebones and me! I shall leave
it to wiser heads than mine to speculate about why it was that
fate, the gods or whatever else it may be chose to favour us
and not more worthy people. The fact is that we were condemned to stay together in that great emptiness alone without food or water.'*

We manoeuvred our floating masts until they were together in the water. Then, using ropes and other pieces of
debris, we succeeded in constructing a crude raft. I lay
back in the hot evening sun, the rough timbers cutting into
my body, thinking of little but my sad fate. As the evening
drew on, I began to suffer the discomfort attendant upon
wearing a heavy garment soaked in the sea water, and,
tormented by the itching and scratching that it occasioned,
I doffed it and lay back quite devoid of clothes, something
that I had never done before in John Barebones' presence,
nor, indeed, in the presence of anyone else. During all of
this time, John Barebones had lain silent on the raft, in a
state of apparent trance, unconscious of what was going on
around him.

My nakedness gave me a feeling of innocence, no doubt
how I felt when I came out of my mother's womb, and I
rejoiced in the delightful physical sensation of the sun's
rays upon my skin. I was full of pleasure at being able, for
the very first time in my life, to expose my body to the light
of the sun, the breezes, to the very horizon itself, with no
one in view to cause me shame, no one to restrict my caprices; in short, I was for the first time in my eventful life
quite free. Perhaps because it seemed that John Barebones
and I would have only a short time to live, unless a chance

vessel came by and rescued us, I felt a great desire to celebrate life. Both my body and mind became suffused with a great wave of passion in which every organ, every part of my body, yearned with desires that were all the greater for being totally unconstrained by society.

Now John Barebones was staring at me, his eyes glittering with lust. I knelt by him, for he was still lying down, and without saying a word, loosened his clothing, like mine still damp from the sea water. He continued to lie passively, and made no attempt to stay my hands. I wanted my companion to be as naked as I was, and he did not hinder me as I pulled his garments away from his nakedness, and, indeed, appeared to be aroused by the touch of my fingers upon his pale skin, burnished bronze by the colour of the evening light. I lifted his hands to my breasts, and the touch of the palms upon me brought on an urgent passion. I pulled down his breeches, removed his shirt, pulled at his undergarments, so that we were, for the first time ever in our strange relationship, together as two bodies only, without any of the trappings of the civilisation we had left behind.

Having abandoned his Puritan clothes, he was merely a man, and the power of his masculinity led me onwards to touch and explore, feel, kiss and excite by gentle pressure that grew more violent by the moment. I was more alive to our physical nature than I had ever been before, aware of the salt upon his skin that lent a savour when I touched his body with my mouth. I saw the salt upon my own skin, and, lifting my arm, smelt the natural perfume of my body mingling with the pungency of the sea. Now my igniting passions burnt brighter still, even before I had placed my hand on his manhood, or my lips or tongue had alit upon it, like a butterfly upon an upstanding flower.

My fingers ran through the hairs that guarded that softer, more yielding flower perfuming my womanly loins, and as I raised my hand to my mouth I marvelled how naturally the ancient perfumes of the ocean blended with the liquids of my womanhood. John took my hand in his, and kissed and licked each finger, and as his caresses travelled up my arm I saw his manhood swell and stiffen, quite without any touch on my part. Then his lips were in the hairs that nestled under my arm, and the nerves that ran down to my breasts, to my loins, deep within my scented flower itself – all these nerves I say were in a state of excitation, thrilled yet unsatisfied.

The light of late afternoon cast a soft romantic glow over our love-making, and I was oblivious to the roughness of the wooden spars under my body as we lay side by side. With his hands on my thighs, his lips sought out those pink tips that for me on that day carried such a sensitivity that my secret flower was on fire, and I cried out again and again with the ecstasies that coursed through my entire body. It had become a fiery organ, and upon it John's fingers, more tender than they had ever been before, and his lips, busy upon my bare skin, lit fires with each touch. Wave after wave of joy wracked my body, and at each wave I called out to the sea, the sky, the setting sun, rejoicing that in my last days I was able to experience such unconstrained passions.

My caprice enjoined me to seize the initiative from John, and to mount above him, so that I could, in the midst of my lust, raise myself up in the open space, and, clasping his masculine part in my hands, guide it into my secret flower, now fully aroused and honeyed from the effects of my partner's explorations of it. His hands grasped my waist and pulled me downwards, so that I was filled, fuller and fuller, deeper and deeper, and the forces of passion that coursed through my whole physical being swept away my everyday thoughts, worries, hopes and fears, and for some minutes I floated upon a cloud of joy.

But joys are fleeting, and are so often succeeded by suffering. Night on the raft was cold, and when we garbed ourselves with our damp clothes again, the discomfort was great. Day, when it came, brought relief from the cold, but then hunger, thirst and fear began to prey on our minds. I cannot say exactly how long we drifted upon that makeshift craft, for my mind soon relapsed into a kind of feverish delirium in which I was unable to distinguish between reality and the fumes of my disordered senses. As time went on I was tormented by thirst. I was assailed by images of creatures rising out of the sea carrying casks of water, which they applied to my lips, only to vanish before the first drops of liquid could enter my parched and swollen throat.

The agonies of our drought affected John Barebones' mind most severely. After our earlier moments of joy, his mental condition deteriorated, so that he spent much of his time lying on his back crying aloud to his Maker, to Christ, to me, to the supposed crew members, who, in his confused condition, he thought to be with him on the raft, begging assistance and forgiveness for his own transgressions. And he returned to the theme that had obsessed him from the beginning – namely that I had been a corrupter, an emissary of the Evil One, and that my mission had been to ensnare his company into my meshes.

The nightmarish hours, days, nights of blackness and of terror – I know not how many – continued. My hallucinations and John Barebones' ravings mingled in a web of illusion.

Then a great shape rose up above me, a range of mountains that looked like a ship, or a ship masquerading as a floating mountain. Creatures reached out at me, coming down from out of it, and I drew away, not wishing to let myself be pulled into another illusory dream-play. Yet they persisted, and I was lifted up, and water was in my mouth, and strong spirits. Then I slept much.

I awoke, and a dark-gold-complexioned face looked down at me, smiling. The full sensuous mouth moved and spoke words, in a strange tongue of which I understood not a word. She passed a glass to me, and in it there was white wine. I sipped the golden liquid, and the warmth of the drink suffused strength and goodwill through my body. I spoke some words, asking where I was, who the speaker was and where my companion was. My helper merely smiled, shook her head to indicate that she understood nothing. Then she placed a finger on my lips, by which I understood that she was telling me that I should not talk. She put the flat of her hand on my forehead, and lifted it hurriedly, miming pain, as though to tell me that I was suffering from fever. The touch of her hand was light and cool, and her laugh, so wide, so deep and musical, brought comfort to my mind. Then I looked around the cabin, and listened to the creaking of the ship's timbers. Although plainly built, the furnishings in the cabin in which I had found myself were rich, finer than I had ever seen before in my short life. The bed coverings were luxuriously brocaded, the sheets were of what I took to be fine linen, and the glass from which I had drunk was of some intricate design that indicated great cost and fine taste.

Then I was carried away by a great wave of fear, and wished not to be in that close cabin. I threw my bedclothes to one side, and stood up, as if leaving the room in order to enter, as I supposed, on deck. The effort was too much, the floor rose to meet me, and blackness descended upon me again.

When I awoke again it was night, and a lamp of brass, richly wrought like everything else in this cabin, was burning beside me. I was alone. I cried out in fear, and in a few moments my companion was at my side, speaking words, as before, touching me with her soft cool hand, and helping me to drink cooling draughts of water. Then followed bowl after bowl of nourishing soup, which, however, caused me to cough, for it was hotly spiced in a way that was new to me, coming as I did from such a Puritan background.

The following day I had still not stirred outside my cabin, or, indeed, out of my bed, for I had been offered assistance for the most intimate necessities of life. I still had not seen anyone other than my helper, who seemed to be of African origin. My solitariness, and her grace and kindness caused me to become strongly attached to her, and her many smiles and simple caresses brought me much joy. She came in at the late part of the afternoon, and as

104

she bent over me to touch my forehead I noted with pleasure that she was finely perfumed and very cleanly, as though she had but recently bathed and the shampoos and oils that she had used had been the most costly.

Indeed, up to that time I had mixed only with people whose tastes had been most simple. As my sanguine nature led to my senses being aroused easily, I need hardly say what effect the sensuous bodily perfumes of my new and nameless friend had upon me. She made gestures indicating washing. Then, leaving the room for a few moments, she returned with a large bowl, and a pitcher of hot water. A further journey brought a tray of perfumes, unguents and washing implements.

Now she pulled the sheets away from the bed and with gestures and movements of her hands bade me to sit up. For the first time I looked down at myself and appreciated the nightdress that I was wearing – simple, yet made of linen and silk. She gestured to the washing implements, and started to loosen the laces that tied my clothing around my neck. Now I appreciated for the first time that my companion was a finely made woman, maybe a few years older than me, with a proud upstanding body and stately carriage, broadly shouldered, strongly limbed, with a lustrous skin of a dark golden hue. Imagine my surprise and delight when such a delightful person took upon herself to divest me of the one garment I wore! Yet such was the artless nature of what she did that I accepted my unaccustomed nakedness as natural.

Once the nightdress, with the aid of her soft hands, had been lifted from my body, she encouraged me to look at myself. What a ruin my gaze encountered! I was burnt red by the sun, and in many places my fine skin was peeling, creating a very ugly effect to the eye. There were bruises, cuts and grazes all over me, and dirt and salt had caused each scratch to suppurate.

What a contrast my poor body must have made with that of my helper, with her soft and faultless golden skin! Yet as she inspected me she showed no distaste. Rather, in the most natural way possible, she touched my finest features, such as my pretty breasts, their pink upstanding nipples, long fine legs, even the silky bush of hair between my legs, in each case expressing her approbation, and she brushed each one of them with her cool hand, in admiration, but with no sign of lust.

Soon I was standing with my feet in the bowl, and her hands rubbed healing oils, carried sponges filled with perfumed soaps and poured lotions over me. Without the slightest trace of lasciviousness on her part, or any feigned shame, every part of my body, even the most intimate cracks, folds and caresses, received their share of her attentions and their ration of scented lotions. I say she carried out her task without any lasciviousness, but for me each touch of her hands, each caress of the sponge, each application of oil teased my entire body into a state of delight that I fought to keep hidden from her. Even though my heart was beating too fast, and the heaviness of my breathing would have told anyone what sensations my body was enjoying, even without the copious emissions that were seeping out of my secret womanly parts, and, I had no doubt, coating the insides of my thighs with honeyed juices, she continued. Then she touched my nipples fleetingly with a sponge, languorous with warm scents, a touch so light as to be like the brushing of a butterfly's wing as it flutters past on a summer's day. But in my excited state, that momentary contact was enough to set off in me a spasm of pleasure from my melting loins, and I uttered an involuntary gasp of passion, such as I would have uttered while sharing my bed with some lover.

My companion and helper saw what desire she had aroused in me, and laughingly, without any embarrassment, she held a rosy nipple in her fingers. With the other hand, she pressed me between my legs where my female lips had opened out, and, quickly and expertly feeling my hidden bud of pleasure, she set off more and more waves of joy that were all the more ecstatic for being so unexpected. Then she washed my body clean with fresh water, dried me, laid me on the top of the bed and commenced to rub more healing balms into my sores, chafings, burns and bruises, rubbing unguents into the rest of my body with strong movements of her hands that relaxed me to such an extent that I fell asleep, only to wake up the next day with the sun high in the sky and myself in a state of such well-being as I had never before experienced.

Thus I stayed in that cabin for several more days, eating heartily, being washed, perfumed, having my body cared for in a way it never had been previous to this strange adventure, until I was fully healed, and, if the truth were told, somewhat plumped out from the lack of exercise, the relaxation and fine rich food. The wonder of it was that I was experiencing such pleasures on board ship, an environment not usually associated with such luxurious living.

Then one day my companion entered the cabin – until now I had not seen any other person upon this ship but the one woman servant – carrying clothes, very richly made, of cotton and lace, with fine embroidery upon them, and silk stockings and soft leather shoes, all new, with a type of high heel that I had never had the opportunity to wear before that day.

I must mention that, after that first day of pleasure with my companion, I had been able to carry out my own offices, and was unable to repeat the sensual delights that she had wrought upon my body. Perhaps as a consequence, when I began to draw on to myself these beautiful clothes, with the silken undergarments, diaphanous stockings, garters, and such like, the sensuality of the fabrics against my skin, now scented and pampered like never before, created in me a yearning for the touch of another body, a desire to experience fully once more the joys of love. My companion's eyes were upon me as I dressed, and she stared in open curiosity at me in my nakedness, speaking low insinuating words as she helped me into the garments. My hair, which had now grown and fell to my shoulders, she helped me to arrange, brushing it for me, putting lotions into it to perfume it and soften it. Then she plaited and arranged and each touch, each pull, each pressure, was enough to stir me up for what I hoped was to come. Finally, she gestured to me to wait for her, and, leaving the cabin for a minute, returned with a looking-glass, something which I had not seen for many a long day, for there had been nothing of that sort on board my other ship.

When I looked I could hardly believe what I saw, for the many effects of the many attentions I had received, following upon hardships, had seemingly changed me into another person. My face was fuller, rounder, my lips heavier, with a curve to my smile that seemed to promise pleasure to anyone who wished to take it. My eyes had become more beautiful, or so it seemed, being brighter and a more brilliant blue, and beneath my proud carriage the *décolletage* of my dress revealed a glimpse of bust that was fuller, more womanly, and yet firm and upstanding in its allure. I blushed, and at this my companion laughed, and, taking the glass from my hand, embraced me, closely and frankly, touching my female curves with admiration.

Then she led me out of the cabin into the light. The world was brilliant with sun and the balmy warmth of the fresh breezes that blew across the decks made delightful airs to bathe my senses. The ship was bigger than the one on which I had commenced my journey. My cabin had been in the corner of the middle deck, and as I followed behind my companion I stared over the railings. All about on the lower deck the faces of seamen were turned up, staring back at me, everyone frozen in a moment of astonishment at seeing me. And then I looked up, and there was but one figure standing by the railings above me – this was a majestic person, a man of great distinction. Tall and well-built, he was clean-shaven, with thick black hair, dark brown eyes, and a pale olive skin. He was dressed in the finest clothing, a velvet doublet, slashed and lined in silk, high boots of fine glossy leather, and a velvet hat, soft and light, to keep the tropical sun from his eyes.

My companion led me to the steep ladder that led up to this deck, leading the way. When I reached the upper deck she backed away from me, the man came forward, and as he moved I caught the scent of musk and sandalwood. He bowed low, and his voice was deep and husky, his English clear, if heavily accented.

'So the beautiful stranger is fully recovered from her ordeal. She came to us like Venus rising from the waves!' He held up a hand, as though to stem a flow of words. 'But no, do not speak. Mystery is more alluring than the clear light of reason, do you not think?'

And so, my dearest Balthazar, commenced a period of my life that lasted for many years, in some ways the happiest time of my exciting but ill-fated career.

Fourteen

He gestured with one arm to a corner of the upper deck where an awning made of embroidered white cotton had been erected. Under it, in the cool shade stood two couches of basketwork and ebony, and a table, upon which were set liquid refreshments in glasses and dark bottles. His hand was strong as he took mine, and I felt clumsy and awkward in the presence of someone so stately as he. He bowed again as I settled on one of the couches, and at a gesture from him Leonie (for that was the name of my companion, who now assumed the role of servant) stood by me, and, taking a pitcher jug, poured a fruit cordial into a glass for my refreshment.

He sat in the couch opposite me, and taking off his hat, bowed his head before speaking again.

'But allow me to introduce myself to you. My name is Fernando dos Mattos, Count of Braganza, nobleman of the court of King Afonso, Emperor of Portugal, en route to Brazil, returning to my post of Governor of San Cristován. And may I take the liberty of asking by what name I am permitted to address you?'

I responded, and Fernando laughed. 'Such a suitable name, do you not think? It was chance that brought such a beautiful woman as you', he bowed again in his seat, 'to be drifting alone in these tropical seas in the company of a madman. And it was chance, again, that brought our vessel to you in your hour of need. And for me it was chance that has given me such a delightful companion to lighten the tedium of a lengthy voyage.' His eyes were upon me now, admiring my body, my features. I had no doubt his mind was full of curiosity, and maybe even desire to take possession of my freshly restored charms. I felt a flush upon my throat and cheeks, testimony to my social unease, and I involuntarily raised my hand, in a vain attempt to hide my more personal beauties from his gaze.

'Such charming signs of embarrassment serve only to increase your allure, Miss Chaunce. I have observed before today that blonde, pale-complexioned women's skins are so sensitive as to change colour with the slightest sign of discomfiture, anger or any of the intimate emotions.' The breeze from the deck blew gently past us, and a combination of its heat and the teasing that his words set up in my passionate emotions caused my whole body to transpire, as surely as if he had touched me with his lips, while that organ of joy hidden deep below my tightly pressed thighs had already commenced to yearn for the pleasures that I knew he longed to share with me. I had no doubt it was mixing its wet and fragrant secretions with the perfumes that Leonie had rubbed into my body.

'You no doubt will wish to know more of the port to which you are now accompanying me as – how shall I put it?' He paused, and laughed. 'Shall I say, as a companion? Let me tell you something about San Cristován. It is a city in the Brazils, also known as the Land of the True Cross. Of relatively small size now, it is unparalleled in its wealth, in the valour of its gentlemen and the beauty of its, what word should I use, its females?' He laughed again. 'But I digress. San Cristován is destined for future greatness. As a small settlement it is on the very edge of a continent filled with all manner of savagery. There are forests where a man can be lost for ever only a few steps from his companions; there are wild animals, poisonous insects, trackless deserts, barbarous people whose nakedness is untouched by any sense of shame and cruelty or by any feelings of human sympathy. You must not expect to find the grace and sophistication of court life in our European capitals –' here he bowed in deference, as though he supposed that I was familiar with such a way of living '– but you will, as I have

112

already indicated to you, meet with many gallant gentle-men, and, while great ladies are only rarely to be met with as yet in such a new land, you will do much to remedy that lack by your presence.'

Here Fernando – for that was how I was to call him – stood up and came to my side. The perfume of his toilet water again assailed my nostrils, and as he stood with the pitcher of cordial in his hand he was in a position to look down into the fine curve of my breasts, for the dress in which I was done out seemed designed to draw attention to those feminine delights. Instinctively, I threw my body forward a little as I raised my glass, causing my curves to move gently in their loose coverings, and no doubt giving my companion a foretaste of the beauties that awaited him.

When I held the glass my hand must have shaken some-what, and he put forward a hand to steady it, firm, strong, sensuous. He bent down as he poured so that his face was on a level with mine, and stared frankly into my face. 'Your perfume combines with your natural exhalations. Leonie has chosen well. Now that your body has become heated, the transpiration brings the scents strongly to my senses. I understand from the reports she brought to me that she carried out her duties with grace and diligence? For one whose company since entering this vessel has not been with such a finely made female as yourself – or should I say lady? – such an assault upon my senses is, to say the very least, marked and very powerful.'

I turned my eyes to his, and my rapidly growing passions must have been most evident from my features, for he seemed discomfited at our physical proximity, and took my hands between his, raising them to his lips, and bestowed a lingering kiss. The feel of his lips, as soft as a woman's, warm, bringing fires to my passionate nature, created in my mind the fantasy of his hands tearing the fabrics from my body. I had to bite my lips to stop them opening in sensuous invitation.

He sat on his couch again, and began talking once more. 'You may find it surprising that I live in such fine circumstances here on board this vessel, when most ships are bywords for bad food – starvation even – brutality at least, and all sorts of crudity. For myself, I see no need to suffer, and being possessed of a very considerable fortune, I have chosen to make this ocean voyage a time of pleasure, rather than what it is for most people: a punishment. I would like to speak to you with total frankness, Miss Chaunce. In my life at the Court of the Emperor of Portugal I am accustomed to the company of the finest flower of the race of Lusitanian womanhood. On board this ship, delightful though it be,' and here he cast his hand lazily around the horizon, at the blue sky and deep blue sea, 'the company of servants does not wholly satisfy my needs. It is a truly extraordinary chance that has brought to me a woman of brilliant charms, the whiteness of whose flesh transpires blushes and perfumes that I long to bury myself in. It is not that I lack female company, Miss Chaunce. Rather, the brilliance of your beauty has quite taken me by surprise. When my servant Leonie reported to me how she found your naked charms I scarcely believed her, for she praised you almost beyond measure. But now I see you dressed in fine stuffs I only think she did not do you justice.'

At this moment the force of his words, spoken with such power and feeling, served to fan my passions to still greater heat, and I am sure that if then he had come to me the merest touch of his body would have turned the dull ache of yearning that my entire lower parts were feeling into fires in which my passions were brought to a peak of sensation.

Rather, he gestured with one hand and Leonie came up to us, having been watching from I know not where. He spoke quietly to her in their language. She took me by the hand and led me to a carved and gilded oaken door, opened it and gestured to me to enter. The cabin was larger than the one that had been home to me on this vessel, and it was furnished with woven wall hangings, fine gilded and carved chests, and an oriental screen that hid one corner.

114

But the main item was a bed, wide and low, with scented candles set into the wall on both sides, adding their illumination to the light that came through the blinds of the open window and scattering a dappled brilliance over the interior.

Leonie made me to understand that I was to sit on the bed while she prepared herself for her task. She hid herself behind the screen, and as I could guess by her movements, bare arms and noise of slithering fabrics, divested herself of much of her clothes. I knew not what would happen to me – how I was to enjoy the sensual charms that lay in wait all around me, and with which of these two people. Then she came out from where she had been. She was clad only in a single cotton cloth tied around her loins, not wide enough at the back to cover the cleavage between her high, tight and ample buttocks, but just enough at the front to hide from my curious gaze her secret parts. For the rest her lustrous skin, brown and unblemished, was bare, and her high-set breasts were tipped by swollen areolae of black that held their crowning nipples proudly pointing upwards, as if in invitation to physical exploration. She laughed at me, for my face must have expressed surprise and sensuality, and, coming close to me, so close that every pore on her skin was visible, she put her arms behind my body and loosed my overgarment, indicating that it was her task to prepare me for bed.

At this point in her narrative Miss Chaunce broke off for a few moments, calling for a draught of wine to restore her spirits. Then she turned to me, her senses excited, her complexion ruddy with her fiery nature.

'*Ah, my friend Balthazar, the memory of that day is with me still! How can I explain to you my sensations in that magnificently furnished cabin, with my still youthful senses on fire, in intimately close proximity to a lady whose charms were displayed to me afresh with each new move that she made. Now her breasts brushed close to my face, bringing the perfume of musk to my nostrils; a moment later the upper,*

115

inner reaches of her thighs opened up momentarily, giving me a glimpse of further, more secret charms that I longed to explore. Then her fingers were on my own bare thighs; I could no longer hide from her the secrets hidden between my legs, for she slipped off my diaphanous stockings and undid my garters. Balthazar, Balthazar, can you not agree that this would have been for me a truly worthy opening to a new chapter in my life, a life devoted to the pleasures of Venus?'

I nodded agreement and continued writing my shorthand notes, unwilling to let even a single one of her carefully chosen words to slip by unheard.

Finally I was lying on the freshly opened sheets, while Leonie knelt beside me. All my most intimate physical secrets as a woman had been bared by her soft hands, and now with low words she told me that her master would wish me to be freshly perfumed before he would enter this bed with me. Bringing a bottle of crystal to the bedside – I kept my hands clasped behind my neck lest I should be tempted to touch myself involuntarily – she poured a small quantity on her fingers and let some drops on to the end of her breasts, allowing the musky liquid to run down her. Then she repeated the action on each of my own rose-coloured, softer, smaller ornaments, and rubbed a similar quantity under my arms. Turning my body over, she ordered me to part my legs, and with a single swift action, rubbed a little inside the cheeks of my derrière, and finally, turning me to the front again, made me open myself entirely by widening my legs, whereupon she gently perfumed the soft entrance to my slit.

At the very moment that Leonie's fingers, wet and musky with the perfume, entered my female parts, I noticed that Fernando was standing in the doorway to the chamber, staring, smiling admiringly at me. The sensation of Leonie's female hands on me mingled with my desire to please him, to be pleased, and I called out with a single cry of pleasure, thrilled, but not satiated, with the little shock that lit my female parts at that moment when her finger brushed against the bud of pleasure lying in wait deep in my folds.

Then he was beside the bed, and with an unashamed movement of his body, he stood beside Leonie. She brought a stool from a corner, upon which he sat while she carried out on him a similar task, undressing him, pulling off one fine piece of material after another, until only a pair of light white cotton breeches stood between my lustful melting gaze and his uncovered masculinity. He watched me approving my body and I let my legs lie open, unashamed of the wetness that I knew had been oozing out of my aroused sweet crevice, making it look like a pink tropical sea anemone, to be sucked and enjoyed. Leonie was kneeling in front of him, and her body was between his legs, unashamedly clasped between his thighs as she loosened the cords that held up his breeches, sliding the material down his flanks, pulling it away from his staff that now stood up bare and strong, a column of manhood, a bringer of joy to me! Once Fernando was quite naked too, Leonie leaned forward a little so that the points of her breasts swayed only a very short distance from the tip of Fernando's staff, and she seemed to be awaiting orders from him, perhaps to pleasure him in a way that was familiar from much practice.

But his eyes were still on me, and with only a gesture from him Leonie was dismissed. Her final duty was to hold open the sheets for her master, waiting until he was in the bed before covering his body, and retreating behind the screen. In a few moments she was gone, and the door was shut behind her.

I had lain, aching and passive, luxuriating in the feel of the fine sheets, enjoying fires that ran through my flesh from my secret parts, all of me aching for the touches and caresses that were to be mine; and now, as he came near, my expectations were further aroused by the fine masculine perfumes that he brought with him into our bed.

Miss Chaunce sighed deeply, and fell silent once more. Rarely had I seen her so moved by the effects of her narrative.

117

Her hand shook, and perspiration stood out upon her upper lip.

'Madame, may I be of assistance to you? I believe that you are discomfited.'

She sighed deeply, and appeared saddened. 'No, my good friend,' she replied, with sadness in her voice. 'It is only a fit of nostalgia for someone who became very dear to me, and the memory of that first meeting with him will always fill a privileged place in my recollections.'

'Yes Madame, I fully understand,' I said.

I cannot describe what happened that afternoon and evening in detail. Each hour seemed endless. Every moment of passion contained the experience of months of everyday pleasure, and yet the hours passed with such rapidity that when we were disturbed I felt I had been with my lover no longer than it takes to breathe in and out again.

Fernando lay by me some time without talking, then touch by touch, caress by caress my body and his spoke together, at first tentatively, shyly almost, as my hands touched in response and I came to understand his body, and how it answered, how it returned my gentle slow caresses. At each moment my body thrilled to his feel, yet each thrill left me hungry for more, and each tiny pang he perceived, and his body was on mine, taking me deeper into the torrent of passion that flowed nearby, waiting for the moment to sweep us away.

Now his lips, his hands, his staff were upon me, and every part of my body was on fire. His lips became more insistent, more pressing in their demands, and my secret flower ached for deeper and harder caresses, and still his body waited until I had ascended to a higher and yet higher empyrean of desire. Our bed of joy was fanned by hot airs from the world outside that kept the shutters in constant motion, and caused our bodies to perspire heavily, so that wherever they were in contact was wet with the mutual distillation, my perfume sharp, acrid, his sweeter, heavier, more musky. As my skin blushed deeper and ran with my own sweat, Fernando hungrily licked my body dry, biting and sucking, until, at the junction of my thighs, his mouth met the honeyed juices that my secret flower had emitted in shameless profusion. The novelty and the intimacy ignited his forces beyond measure until my whole being was filled with his passion, my flower was plucked again and again, and his juices overflowed in me endlessly in a rhythm of delirium and repletion. The light faded and the cool of darkness replaced the heat of the dying day. Then we lay together, melting into each other's arms, and we rested.

Some time later I awoke from a doze, and I found that I was alone. Not knowing what to do in this new situation, I lay in wait of I knew not what. The scented candles had burnt themselves out, and the darkness was broken only by the dimness of the moonlight upon the window.

Then I suppose I dozed again, for I awoke to the sound of the door opening, and a candle casting its rays around the little chamber of delights. It was Leonie who had come to me. She came into the chamber and knelt by the bed, stroking my hair gently as though trying to rouse me from my slumbers. The nightdress she wore was of white lace, which clung to her womanly curves most appealingly.

She spoke in her own language and made signs and gestures to let me know that Fernando would not spend more of that night with me, and that I was to return to the smaller cabin which I now thought of as my own. My feelings of desolation at this news must have been evident in my face, for then she embraced me in her soft, warm arms, kissed me, and made much of me. Then, using the same means of communication, she led me to know that Fernando had thought much of me, that he was delighted to have found me. Leonie even told me, in jest, that she was jealous that she would be replaced in her master's affections by me, and that we should become enemies if affairs continued in the same way.

She signalled to me to stay where I was, going out of the cabin hurriedly and returning in a few moments with a large earthenware bowl, a pitcher of warm water, towels and sponges, and then, as before, a silver tray, marvellously worked, of unguents, soaps and perfumes. Pouring the water in the bowl, she dropped crystals of I knew not what substance into it, causing perfumed foam to rise in a fascinating manner that I had never experienced before.

Then, quite without either shame or lasciviousness, Leonie threw off her own garment. She walked to me as bare as the day she had been born, raising her hands above her head in order to adjust the plaited coil upon her head that trained her hair tight over her scalp. Despite the satiation of my senses, my heart beat faster when I saw for the first time the nakedness of her whole form, admiring the grace and strength of her body, the firm weight and richness of her bosoms, the gloss and shine of her chestnut skin, the two black circles that ornamented her upper body, and the dark mystery that lay hidden in the black triangle where her thighs met her belly.

She took my hand, pulled the sheets from my body, pulled, telling me that I was to get up, then led me to the washing utensils, and began to wet me, soap me, rub my skin, and anoint it with new perfumed and cleansing oils. The delicacy, softness and sensitivity of her touch was thrilling to me, yet the relaxation which my whole physical person now felt meant that I enjoyed, but I did not take fire. When I began to reciprocate her touch and service, my fingers, her skin – the feel of her softness and feminine shape, quite different from the texture of Sophie's body – all brought a new kind of happiness to me. We were together without pretence, without fear or guilt, and the future seemed to hold much delight, delight for which I only had to wait.

Fifteen

As I returned to my cabin, perfumed, the hunger of my senses slaked, in the darkness I saw the sea sparkling with a phosphorescence that echoed in its watery element the stars that lay scattered in profusion. The softness of the sheets on my bed welcomed me, and the gentle rocking and swaying brought me only pleasure. As my mind slipped away into the darkness of sleep my loins became pleasurably and lightly aroused by the pictures that drifted through my mind – Fernando gently touching my feminine parts, Leonie answering his touch with her gentler fingers, Sophie's clumsy yet eager caresses, and fleetingly, the violence of John Barebones between my legs.

I was awoken in the light of morning by a commotion upon the decks. There was the crying of a man's voice which sounded as if it came from high up in the rigging. There was the thud of footsteps running by my cabin towards the prow of the ship, and from all sides I heard voices, raised in excitement, calling out in pleasure. But, alas! I understood almost nothing of their words.

'You must understand, my dearest Balthazar,' said Miss Chaunce demurely, 'that in my time on board ship – both ships, the English one and the Portuguese vessel – I had not been true to my own nature. I was living a lie. I was pretending to be what I was not. I know', she said, holding up her hand to me as though I were to object to her words, 'that you will say that as a Puritan girl in London I was not true to myself, either. That may be so. But during the time I spent in the Denver household I had managed events so that I was

121

able to find the experiences that I wanted. I was always ready with the right word, the bold action that would achieve the results I sought. But you will observe that so far, while I had been on the Portuguese vessel, I had been an almost completely passive agent, allowing fate to act upon me. Now I resolved that I should be bold again.'

I bowed to Miss Chaunce, and riposted.

'Madame, it is your boldness that draws me to you. With your boldness I am like a little child. Be bold, madame, and I shall be putty in your arms!'

Miss Chaunce stared into my eyes in mock severity, shook her finger at me, and warned me of the consequences for my intrepid words.

'Mr De Fado, Mr De Fado, disrespect will be punished!'

I felt joy in my heart as she continued her narration.

Curious as to the cause of the commotion on the deck above me I accordingly rose from my bed, took a bottle of perfumed waters that remained in my cabin from the previous day, and liberally spread its contents over my skin, rubbing it into the space between my breasts, the pit under my arms, the upper part of my thighs where the slightest movement of my legs would set off a tantalising exhalation, replete with female passion. Then, putting on my naked body the fine dress that I had worn to visit my lover the night before, I set about the task of arranging my hair in an alluring style. I was ready to step out into the world of my new and greatest of all lovers.

As I took to the deck two sailors were hurrying by, excitedly chattering between themselves. I believe they smelt my perfume before they set eyes upon me. They turned and looked at me with astonishment in their eyes and fell silent. Then they backed away from me, slowly and with respect. From this behaviour I understood that my figure was as I wished it to be, stately, a fitting companion, perhaps, to the Count.

I had been afraid because I did not know in what condition I had been when the sailors had discovered me floating with John Barebones upon the raft. I did not even know whether I had been naked or clothed, whether I had been raving or calm; indeed, whether I had been handled lewdly by any of the men who must have been my rescuers. But now I resolved to put such speculations out of my mind.

I walked slowly up the steep steps that led to the upper deck, where the Count's cabin was situated. It was at the stern of the ship, and the front part of it jutted out above the rest of the vessel and commanded a view of the whole. By a balustrade at this front part stood a company of men clustered around the figure of the Count, and when I saw him amongst other, everyday people, his commanding air, the poise of his body, the fineness of his limbs caught and held my attention above all the others. Beside him stood a short man, bald, powerfully built, clad in voluminous brown pantaloons and a loose cotton shirt, that revealed his copious body hair. I guessed that he must have been the captain, for he held a tubular device to his eye. I learned later that the function of this instrument is to bring distant objects closer. It is named a telescope, something then quite new to me. Another, possibly the second mate, bare-torsoed, and wearing a red felt cap, manipulated another device made of brass that I later was told is used to calculate, by means of the sun, the position of the ship upon the great globe itself.

From time to time the Captain kept taking his eye from the telescopic device in order to shout commands to the sailors who were busy on the decks below. From the constant noise of voices, feet and general activity I could only guess at what was going on, for the seamen were still invisible below the level of the balustrade.

Then I looked in the direction of everyone's eyes, and joy suffused my whole being. Upon the far horizon rose out of the deep blue ocean a peak, green with forests, steep and rugged, and on either side of this lay a jumble of smaller elevations, while beyond for many leagues stretched a flat coastline, irregular with clumps of great trees, and edged with glaring white sand. Then I smelt the scent of this land – heavy with the odour of hot plants, sweet with the smells of perfumed flowers, with another smell lurking in the background, heavier, more musky, more rancid. My nostrils quivered, and my body became suffused with a delight that had never been in me before, as though the air itself could pleasure me. And the memory of the boundless delirium of the night before came back and stayed with me. Sometimes it seemed that beneath the strong perfumes I was wearing I could still smell the odour of my body as I lay satiated in bed, alone after Fernando had left.

Then I called out to my lover – for as such I was now thinking of him. 'My dearest Count, now that we have nearly arrived at our destination I trust that you will give thanks to the gods!'

As one man the group around the Count turned, becoming aware of my presence on the deck with them for the first time. Their jaws dropped. My figure was stared at with curiosity, with shameless desire in the eyes of the men. Eyes were on my upstanding breasts, and especially, so it seemed to me, on the space between them, which was so cunningly brought attention to by the cut of my dress. Eyes were on my waist, on my loins, as if I had been naked in front of them. My female parts were yearning again for Fernando's touch, and a wetness was spreading on to my thighs as I walked. My thighs, being now heavier than previously, caressed each other lightly, the feel of the soft silken skin further arousing my senses. I was an object of admiration and lust to all who saw me, and the signs of their desires further enflamed mine.

The Count, my lover, stood erect, in response to the proud walk that I now assumed, and watched me, not with lust, not with vulgar curiosity, but rather with the eyes of a critic, skilled in judgement. Then he stepped forward, reached out his arm with a gallant gesture and bowed. I knew I had behaved in a manner of a woman fit to be his mistress.

'Madame, you honour our vessel with your presence.

124

But why do you say 'gods'? Is it not for us to honour the True God, of whom there is but one, and none other like unto Him?'

Then I noticed for the first time in the knot of sailors a man with staring eyes, a priest, thin, stooping, pale and wizened. He stared at me with an unashamed expression of lust.

'My dear Count,' I responded, laughing, 'when Venus rises from the waves, bringing the protection that her delightful self can give, is it not only right that you give thanks to the gods for conveying her to you?'

At this the whole company laughed; even the priest made a wry gesture of amusement with the corner of his mouth. Then I stood with the men in the place of privilege, on the right of the Count, watching the functioning of the ship, listening to the orders, and wondering at the almost miraculous effect of the telescope when I admired the view of Brazil by means of the cunning instrument.

Thus the hours passed by in the most delightful manner, amongst a group of men who deferred to Fernando, the Count of Braganza, my lover, and I took a joy in being amongst their masculinity and close to my lover. The occasional touch of his body on mine, the perfumed airs that assailed my nostrils, the scent that rose from my own body, the reminder that the odour carried on it (of the passions of the night before), the anticipation of a repetition of that previous night's joys: all these emotions blended together to create a sensation in which I was ready and, indeed, aching for love, open to it, permanently ready for it.

Finally, as the late morning brought the oppressive heat of the tropical sun, Fernando laughingly made us to believe that he was tired and needed to rest. The other men took their leave, looking at me with a mixture of envy and amusement, and I was proud that my body was now the focus of so many attentions. When Fernando came through the door of his cabin, his first action was to remove his upper garments completely so that the musk of the pomander that he wore around his neck on a chain aroused my senses even before he touched me. I loosened the fabric around my bust so that its untrammelled beauty would be open to him, but he merely stood looking at me, moving around my body, like a giant cat hunting its prey. Then when he stood behind me he touched my neck with his lips, but so lightly that I was unsure whether it was a butterfly or his hungry lips.

He turned me around and smelt the perfume between my breasts and touched the swelling organs themselves with lips and tongue, coming teasingly close to my pink buds where all sensations came together. He complimented me on the beauties of my womanhood, the lightness of my skin, the delicacy of my breasts, and I could see that the perfumes that I wore were intoxicating his senses. Then he knelt down, opening my dress below my navel, where the little hairs on my feminine organs met the soft curves of my belly. He buried his face in me, while his hands felt under my dress, and tossed my skirts, as I fell back on to the bed.

I let the clothes, useless and unwanted, fall to the floor at my feet while his nakedness was pressed between my thighs, and his tongue tasted the perfumes that rose from them. The natural ones, of my skin, the tantalisingly sharp perfumes that I had applied, the muskier scents that were oozing from my female parts, all drew him to me and inflamed him. In a few moments his tongue was inside my private lips, teasing the soft pink flesh, opening up my channel until it was aching to be filled, pressing and sucking the inner lips, inside the very folds where my senses were more powerful than in any other part of my body. Each time his tongue pressed me there, I cried out in joy, and my senses set my whole being alight. Then his whole body was above mine, kneeling, and he held my buttocks, one in each hand. My legs wrapped themselves around his waist, his shaft was in my hand, the swollen tip hard between my ready fingers, and both our bodies were wet with the liquids that poured out of them, the waters of passion, the heat of desires. His burning brand took me, my body

126

was wracked with the agonies of shared joys, and for longer than I could ever have imagined it possible the pain of delirious pleasure continued until I no longer remembered who I was or where we were.

We lay together quietly for some time, in peace, lulled by the sound of the waves and the soft cradle-like rocking of the boat. As I drifted in and out of sleep it was as though my whole life had become a dream.

Then the coast was upon us and rowing boats were all around. Before us lay San Cristován, not a great city like London, but a small settlement of mostly simple wooden houses, jumbled together near the great peak that formed such a landmark from the seaward side.

This settlement, and the wild lands that surrounded it, were to be my home for many years, and, indeed, I believe that I would be there still if it had not been for a dire stroke of fate that befell my lover and myself. But more of that when the time is right. I shall content myself for the present time with describing my first impressions, which are those that *any* traveller would enjoy on arriving in the Brazils for the first time.

The ship was met by small boats of wood that were rowed through the heavy surf by four men – black-skinned, finely muscled, their flesh shining in the brilliant light, clad only in white cotton breeches, barefoot. I sat in the front of the little vessel with the Count of Braganza standing beside me, wondering at the animation of the scene on the shore. Here were people of every description. There were black skins, red skins, yellow skins, all intermingling with the fair complexions of people of European origin. And for a woman coming from a Puritan family in cold England, I was surprised to see naked flesh everywhere I looked. Many of the lower classes wore only a single garment, as had the rowing men in the boat, and in the case of the women the cotton skirt – sometimes simple, at other times highly ornamented, dyed in colours and decorated with lace – was sufficient only to cover their legs to a little below their knees. For the rest, the belly, breasts, shoulders and arms were quite uncovered, and I remember well the delight and curiosity I felt on that first day when I moved through the lively throngs on the foreshore, admiring the unashamed beauties of so many of those who were near to me.

But in the midst of this joyful throng stood a group of men: Portuguese like Fernando, dressed not in the popular style of this country, but rather in the aristocratic garb of their homeland, as was Fernando. The fineness of the brocades, plumed hats, embroidered waistcoats and ornate collars was a strange sight indeed, and in the heat of the morning the group appeared uncomfortable.

Then, when they saw my lover, they came forward to greet him with the greatest deference, bowing low and uttering what seemed to be formal compliments and expressions of friendship. My lover returned each declaration with impressive formal gravity, so much so that for some moments the eye of my imagination conjured a vision of him acting in just the same way in a royal palace in front of a king.

Then the sight of two women drew my attention. With skin that shone polished black in the sun, they walked past, chewing on pieces of sugar cane, each with full, naked rounded breasts, pointed and heavily nippled, that swayed in the most alluring manner.

Such were some of the impressions that I felt on my arrival in Brazil. However, there is little to be gained by describing in detail every event of the following days. Suffice it to say that I began to understand some of the customs and to comprehend some of the language of my exotic new companions.

For the first weeks my home was in the Governor's palace, the residence of my lover when he carried out his official duties. It was the finest building in San Cristován, with terracotta floors, blue and white tiles on many walls, windows whose shutters stood open much of the day, allowing the caress of the sea breezes to delight and freshen our bodies, and verandas strung with hammocks that were a pleasure to lie in. The ceilings and many of the pillars were made of the massive dark timbers of the country, smelling lightly of resin.

In this palace, so pleasant that it seemed almost designed to maintain the senses in a continual readiness for pleasure, I was given private rooms, well-furnished and appointed, with a supply of clothes – fine ones for public use, light simple wear for when not appearing in public, and also styles more fantastical and indecorous, worn when my lover's fancy took him – in order to stimulate his desires when in my company.

And with me lived Leonie, and her task was to minister to my every need and desire as well as managing the other menials who waited upon me. But Leonie was more than a servant for she became close to me, a friend with whom there were no secrets, no barriers, no pretences.

Sixteen

'I am sure', said Miss Chaunce to me with a smile, 'that you have guessed by now, my dear friend Balthazar, why my relations with Leonie were not purely those usual between mistress and servant. From the days when she tended me while I was recovering from my ordeal upon the high seas, I had known that there was a possibility that we should find solace together in the long hot afternoons so typical of those climes, when life passes slowly and lazily and little work of any sort is attempted.'

I bowed to Miss Chaunce wordlessly, and begged her to continue her story.

Our physical relations were not entered into suddenly, in an excess of passion, as had happened in the case of Sophie. I did not strive to make a conquest of her in order to satisfy my instincts, and to bring myself pleasure. Indeed, I cannot say *when* we first became full-blown lovers. In that climate, nakedness was normal at times between ladies in circumstances unthinkable in our country. Indeed, in the land of Brazil, behaviour that would be scandalous in England is regarded as quite normal. As a result, our physical instincts were allowed a free rein. In that city in those days the pleasures and pains of the tender passions in all their variations were freely indulged, enjoyed, even talked about openly. At the same time, however, women from Europe such as myself who passed as aristocratic were in a small minority, and were jealously guarded by their husbands and masters. During this time, therefore, I was not at liberty to go about, to visit whoever I wished.

Men I only met in the company of my lover, Fernando, Count of Braganza. Other than when he visited me, which was very often, my company was entirely that of other women, and while there were many male servants in the house, I did not know at first which were in the confidence of my master as informers.

It was the normal custom for personal handmaids such as Leonie to be with their mistresses while they performed their ablutions, and it was considered to be disrespectful for a servant to wear any more clothes than their mistresses did, so from the very first days of my life with Leonie I was in intimate contact with her. It was one of the pleasures of my life to lie in a big earthenware bath upon the veranda, screened from importunate glances from the garden by cotton sheets laid over screens, while Leonie bent over me, her breasts loose and bare, massaging my shoulders, rubbing foam into the space between my breasts, ordering me to stand up so that her hands, slippery with soap, could run up and down my legs. The memory of my previous night of passion with Fernando was often still with me, and the contrast between the hardness of his body and the urgency of his desire, and Leonie's curves and softness, would cause my senses to smoulder and I would sometimes lapse into a waking dream, letting my hands respond to her caress. Soon I would find that I was touching her upon her shoulders, or that my fingers were upon her back, exploring the silky skin where her spine met the softer curves of her buttocks, where she was built more voluptuously than I was.

Then she would laugh with pleasure, and almost by accident, or so it seemed, her dark hands would gently nip the pink ends of my breasts, rigid and erect with sensuous excitement. I would involuntarily sigh, low and long, and perhaps without being aware of what I was doing my hand would press more firmly upon her, or when she kneeled, move forward to the place where her belly and her thighs, firm yet full and heavy, came together at a woollen black triangle. Then my fingers would run through her hard secret hairs. Her hand in turn might return to my nipple, and hold the sensitive tiny organ between two fingers, pinching enough to arouse the fires and bring a delighted yearning to my body, but not so urgently as to make the passions break, thus launching us both on a stormy ocean of pleasure.

I cannot, as I say, remember when it was that I first lay with Leonie upon one of the great oaken Portuguese beds, of which there were two in our chambers. But I remember that I felt as though I were afloat upon an ocean of warm joy as sweet as honey while Leonie played upon my feminine organs, freshly washed yet smelling of the secretions that lust spreads upon our organs as a bait. I remember that I lay and watched her fingers, dark and slender, silken yet firm, running through my golden hairs, lightly pressing the nails into the pink skin that bordered my secret lips. I remember, too, that I responded to her touch by bringing my warm nakedness close to hers, so that the silk of her body, fuller, stronger, darker, accepted the pressure of mine, as though in protection. The empty hours stretched ahead of us on those afternoons, and the slow rise and fall of my ecstasy filled them, as gradually my female channel opened itself to Leonie's caresses. I let her fingers tease the sensitive places that revealed themselves, and the juices ran out. Her mouth was upon my breast, upon my neck, upon my belly. My secret parts would wait like a flower, offering honey to my companion, and I would hold her head between my hands as she set upon the bloom, like a bee, or a butterfly, sucking the honeyed saps that blossomed under her tongue.

These shared passions were not like those that I enjoyed with Fernando, my true lover. He would often come to me in the middle of the day, and we would enjoy our midday meal, drinking wine, eating many courses of food extracted from the local forests, such as roasted meats, fruits and herbs, accompanied by cultivated foods – rice and beans cooked with many piquant flavourings. The heavy yet appetising fare relaxed my senses, and the wines would stimulate them, making me more direct in my suggestions, more lewd in my conversation. During these private midday refections I would dress in the lightest clothes, sometimes no more than the dress of the women in the street, merely a light cotton skirt around my legs, barely covering the knees. Fernando's caprice was for me to wear my hair hanging straight over my shoulders in a very simple style, scarcely combed, so that I appeared to be a woman of the lowest class. He would watch me eating, breasts bare.

'Your flesh is so pale, my dearest, and the pink of your breasts is so vulnerable, that it almost appears as though you are too delicate for this bright world of ours, here in the Brazils. Eat more, eat more.' Here he would hand me a piece of strong wild meat on the bone, and he would watch, his face swollen with lust, as I held it in my hands and chewed into the dark flesh, letting the juices run down over my chin. Then he would be behind my chair, like me, naked to the waist, and he would grease the tips of my breasts with the fatty liquid, lubricating, running his fingers over them, maybe taking a glass of red wine and pouring a little on to them. Then he would lick the mixture, tasting it, and I would feel his manhood thrusting out in response to the provocation that the perverse usage of my body afforded him.

As he stood thus with me he would sometimes ring a bell that stood upon the dinner table, bringing in one of the women who waited at table, in order to ask for a fresh jug of wine, and would let her stand close by us in order for her to refill his glass when he was ready. The women were dressed in the same manner as I, and he enjoyed a piquant sensual pleasure in watching the contrast between the dark skins, black hair and full figures of the serving maids and my own fine pale body, with my blonde hair and blue eyes.

As dinner ended he would command me to raise my skirts above my knees and sit with thighs well parted. He would force me to eat fruits that produced sweet juices in abundance as I bit into their flesh, and he wanted to experience those sweet juices upon my flesh, sometimes seizing a slice of watermelon or jackfruit and pressing it upon my legs, then taking the sweetness into his mouth. He became passionate when he saw me eating sweets with the brown molasses that country produced in abundance, often mixed with cream and various perfumes to give it a delicious savour. He invariably wished to spread some upon my female breasts, covering up the delicate pink of the tips with its dark stickiness, and he would push his hands far under the skirts, and smear the sweet substance all around the areas which naturally were becoming wetted with the natural secretions of my passions.

Then he would lift me in his strong arms, and would carry me to the place he chose for our mingling – I would already be in a delirium of yearning for the pleasures only he could bring. It could be on the bed, or it might be in a hammock. Sometimes we chose to couple upon the bare floor, or standing upon a veranda behind white sheets that flapped in the hot winds of the prime hour of day.

But I remember the hammock as an instrument of love above all others! The hammock is a device peculiar to the natives of that region, only recently appearing in the Old World, cunningly constructed of twisted cotton and affording a most comfortable alternative to the bed. I would lie in one of these, the last vestiges of clothing long cast aside, legs and arms splayed out wide, and he would lick the whole of my body with his tongue and lips, removing all the sweetness and oils from my skin, while my rising tide of passions, further stimulated by the heated air, led me spontaneously to replace the sweet foods with my own perspiration. Often he would ask me to lie crosswise over the hammock, so that my legs and head were arched downwards towards the floor, allowing him to take me with legs around his waist and his masculine staff filling me, thrusting in and out, again and again and again.

Then again I might take him in my arms, and with my body over his, he would take my pink flower in his mouth while his staff would plunge between my lips. And at other times his fancy would tempt him to make me lie on my front over the hammock, with the white cheeks of my rear opened to his explorations. Often I would play the man, and, thrusting his body down upon the hammock, sit above him, forcing him to lie still and passive, while I stirred his manhood to greater and greater passions, grasping the swelling head of the staff between my fingers and bringing it again and again to a point when it would have exploded into my hands. Each time I would restrain it by grasping it tight at its base, holding the precious fluids in, stirring it around inside the entrance to my honey-pot, mixing my emissions with his. Again and again I would call out in ecstasy before bending over him and taking the end of his member in my mouth, moving my lips around the wide head, rubbing the most sensitive spots with my tongue, sucking gently, restraining with firm pressure the moment when it would explode in my mouth, urged on by the cries of joy that Fernando uttered whenever I let him approach satisfaction.

Then I would allow his member to delve into my fringed purse again and he would lower it gently into me, letting it stretch, fill, slide and excite, until he was calling out in rapture in time to my own cries. My body and his intermingled, our nerves thrilled together, and we grasped, kissed and caressed until the moment when I felt his manhood overflowing inside me, and our voices moaned gently together, our frenzied movements became gentler, our bodies became satisfied and luxurious and we lay silently in a dreamless sleep of reason.

The life I led at this time made a new person of me. I quickly learned the language of Brazil and even became a member of the Roman Catholic Church in order to adapt myself to the customs and society of the country.

Early morning mass was the time when well-bred women (those who had been born in Portugal, or whose parents had both come from the same mother country) went out in the streets, appearing in public to the general populace. I would wake in the pre-dawn cool to the sound of the cathedral bells, with the light of the forthcoming dawn gently shining through the shutters. If my lover had chosen to

136

spend the night with me I would embrace him fleetingly in the drowsy half-light. The warmth and firm smoothness of his body would put me into a dreamy state of delight mixed with happiness at the prospect of living a new day.

Then Fernando would leap from the bed, and, pulling a robe around himself, hurriedly leave me in order to commence his heavy duties as Governor. Hearing his footsteps fading away into the distance, Leonie would enter my sleeping chamber carrying water for a perfunctory wash, and clothes suitable for entering a place of worship.

Soon we would be in the town square, on one side of which lay the Governor's residence, arcaded and white-washed, my home, while the cathedral was on the far side. It was delicious to walk over this space with the pink of dawn ahead of us. We wore shawls over our dresses as was the custom, and in my hands I would carry a rosary, finely made of gold, crystal and rubies. Here and there other couples, a mistress and her servant, turned out in similar style. Ahead the cathedral loomed, the finest building in the whole of San Cristován, with its carved stone portico. From its ornate tower the pealing of the bell summoned the faithful to prayer and worship. I had become one of the Old Faith because I had to conform to the customs of the land of Brazil; I certainly felt little spiritual compulsion.

But what other sorts of fascination it held! The ornamentation of the interior was profuse, and was covered in ornate and gilded plasterwork. There were a great many painted figures, some of which carried a very marked character; the female saints, for example, being apparently in a state of physical rapture, as though in congress with an invisible lover. It appeared that many of the congregation were influenced not only by motives of piety but, also, for the younger and more attractive members it was an opportunity to see and be seen. The well-known libertines would stare around at the most attractive females with a shameless curiosity, and, whilst some women worshippers repulsed their bold stares with contempt, there were others who clearly were not above encouraging them. Many were the assignations arranged by a gesture of the hand or a proud toss of the head!

Commonplace, too, was the surreptitiously passed note, or the message hidden in a space between two stones. Whilst I stood amongst the worshippers in the portion of the cathedral used by the upper classes and their servants, I saw all around me the dark passionate eyes of the women, all the more alluring for belonging to faces that were often partially covered by their shawls, thus adding to the mystery of their wearers. And often a lady, high-born and proud, would momentarily let drop her shawl as if by accident. Then would be revealed a face of beauty and luxury, framed by rich black tresses and augmented by a fine figure, and an alluring bust only partially covered by her clothing. The laces might be loosened, as if by accident, attracting the eye to the space between the breasts, a clear invitation to some sensuous rogue ornately dressed, with black moustache and bulging eyes!

Now, in my early days in San Cristován, I had as yet gained no position, and outside my rooms Fernando had never acknowledged me. As a result, my glances were prey to any man who cared to try his luck with me. But I was unable and unwilling to taste the joys of illicit assignations, tempting though they would have been. For in those first months, even years, I wished to build up my position so that I would be more than his mistress, if less than his wife, and I was unwilling to jeopardise my position in his regard by engaging in any adventure which, if found out, could lead to my ruin.

Through my intimacy with Leonie I learned much about the society of San Cristován, and one of the things that I was told by her was that the frequency of relations between high-born ladies and their personal servants was no less commonplace than between the same ladies and others of their class, and that such behaviour was not generally frowned upon by husbands. Thus it was that the more virtuous ladies, who would never stoop to taking male lovers, were often not averse to the pleasures that another woman of her class could provide.

At this point Miss Chaunce moved her chair nearer to mine, and, leaning towards me, put on one of her most enchanting expressions, knowing that I was powerless to resist her attractions.

'You must bear in mind that I was a most striking figure in the society of San Cristován, for I was tall, very pale skinned, with luxuriant blonde locks and clear blue eyes.' *She stared at me with them wide open, and touched me upon the knee lightly as she spoke, knowing what effect her actions would have.*

The general mass of the ordinary people were dark complexioned, and dark-eyed. Only the upper classes were truly white, but they almost all had black or dark-brown hair, and brown eyes, while even those with lighter hair did not possess my clear complexion and light eyes. Now, for myself, I have enjoyed relations of the most passionate kind with people of all complexions and hues, yet I have observed that, in the matter of the tender physical relations, there are two contradictory sources of attraction. Some, nay, most people have a predilection for a certain type of lover. Some men love full-breasted women, others those with small breasts. Some men like copious body hair on a woman, while others prefer fine, smooth bodies. And so with the colour of skin and hair. But at the same time there is another impulse, do not you think, my dearest friend? The man who has been satiated with blonde women will suddenly conceive a passion for the dark! One who has lived all his life amongst the dark regards the blonde as a rare pleasure! And, of course, a woman whose embraces have been confined to those of her husband will conceive of a passion for another woman!

Teresa Chaunce stroked her blonde locks as she spoke, and seemed to be taunting me with her provocative words. 'Do you doubt my words?' *she said.*

139

'I do not doubt their truth,' I replied, 'but I am curious as to the application of the principle.'

'Well fie, sir,' she rejoined, 'We shall see about that?' At this she rang the bell with a distinctive rhythm of sounds, as though it were a message in code.

One of Miss Chaunce's assistant Ladies of Pleasure answered this message in cypher, no doubt having been forewarned what to expect before my arrival. To my astonishment, it was as though one of the ladies from Miss Chaunce's tale had entered the room! She must have been no more than twenty years of age, and her complexion was of the type that Miss Chaunce had suggested to me in her story – a fine brown shade, with black eyes, glowing with animal spirits and youthful desires. Her hair, black also, was thick, strongly growing, and long, hanging heavy about her shoulders. Her body was of the voluptuous type, and the fabric of her simple white cotton dress was thrust up and out by her heavy, but pointed breasts.

She looked me up and down with open lust in her eyes, and stood behind her mistress's chair, her arms about her neck, touching her mistress's white skin, stroking her soft golden hair, rearranging the fabric of her dress as it covered her breasts.

'You see, my dear friend Balthazar, how I have arranged every detail for your delight. You know but little as yet of what I have to offer in my establishment. I wish to introduce Maria to you.' Maria curtseyed to me, laughed, and looked my body over as though trying to let me know what was in her mind. 'Delights of all description are to be found here if you know how to ask! As for today, I wish you to understand the truth that a variety of female types stimulates the appetite.'

At this Teresa Chaunce led her young companion to the bed, and allowed herself to be partially disrobed, insisting at the same time that her companion do the same. Now they were both in brief undershifts that scarcely covered their shoulders and breasts. The skirts of Maria's garment bared much of her thigh above her knees. She knelt by her mistress,

140

who was now stretched out on the bed, and turning to me, indicated by a gesture that she wished me to sit close to them. I was already in that physical state where a touch or an embrace would be sufficient to make my passions rage so violently that no further check on them would be possible.

For her part, Maria was delightful to observe, with her sturdy frame and heavy but firm breasts moving free of stays under her shift, which served to stimulate the appeal of her nakedness rather than cover it modestly. Now the two women were lying in each other's arms, and Teresa was passive under her young friend's caresses. Gradually the mature beauties of Teresa's pale body emerged from her light clothing, and at their invitation I loosened Maria's shift and drew it down over her polished brown skin, exposing the dark full points of her breasts, full thighs and black triangle of joy. My senses were roused to an extraordinary degree as I watched Teresa Chaunce's melting passion of golden hair and white soft skin yielding under the caresses of her companion.

Miss Chaunce was sighing softly with joy as Maria's tongue lingered upon the pink tips of her breasts, yet she spoke. 'Balthazar my friend – divest yourself of your dreary clothing. Enjoy what has come to us, as I enjoy it!' In a trice I was as bare of everyday clothing as they were! My staff was engorged, and my senses maddened by the touch of my two companions. Their eyes feasted upon the size and rigidity of my member, and they both came to it at once, the soft white hand of Teresa, the firmer, darker touch of Maria, the fullness of Maria's lips upon its tip at the same moment as the firm but delicate touch of Teresa's hand at its base: all these and many more combinations of the two contrasting and different women thrilled me and brought me to a state where I thought only to penetrate. So, whilst Teresa's lips were upon my member, Maria had turned herself so that the plenitude of her backside was offered to me. The two globes guided my gaze inward, where the black mystery of her secret hairs stood guardian to a pair of lips that opened their pink and perfumed interior to my shaft.

141

In the frenzied passions that followed, the sight of Teresa's womanly parts promised further joys even while I was enjoying the buttery depths of Maria, and when I was in Teresa, Maria's nakedness waited like an invitation for my return! Thus we spent many hours in fine sport.

When I dressed to go, Miss Chaunce and Maria shook hands with me.

'So, my dear Balthazar, do you now understand that variety is one of the principles governing the stimulation of passion?' asked Miss Chaunce with all the severity of a schoolteacher who has just completed a demonstration for the benefit of a slow pupil.

Seventeen

The following day Miss Chaunce was in her usual seat by the fire. She greeted me demurely, as though the unexpected pleasures of the previous day had not taken place.

Let me return to the first weeks after I disembarked in San Cristován. I was unsure of what my position in society consisted. Being assigned Leonie as my personal servant, and occupying rooms in my lover's mansion was nothing unusual in this society. Many retainers and hangers-on also lived in this great building, which was, indeed, so large that it was impossible to be acquainted with all who lived there. As the first days went by it became clear, to my disappointment, that my position was a humble one, despite the respect with which Fernando had treated me on board the ship and the passion that I aroused in his breast when in private.

When, in the morning Fernando, as Governor, held open house for the general populace, in order to accept petitions, to adjudicate disputes, to meet those who wished to transact business with him, he sat at a great carved table, surrounded by his retinue. At the close of the morning it was the custom, when he was so disposed, to lunch with these same men, and sometimes in the company of their women. But as many lacked wives, it was accepted that mistresses of long standing and high status could attend in their stead. Excluded from these gatherings were the more casual females, and mistresses of inferior social position. All this information and more I discovered from Leonie as my command of the language improved.

Imagine my mortification, then, when I was never invited to dine with this company, and to realise that when he came to me for dinner, he was invariably alone. In company with others of his class, at social occasions in the evenings, or when riding out of the town on days of holiday, I was never asked to accompany him.

Determined as I was, then, to make myself more than simply his plaything, I decided that the only way to improve my position would be at a dance. This was a form of dissipation that was held every month in the dry season in one of the dealing halls in the port, cleared of encumbrances for the occasion. People of the lower classes were free to attend only if they possessed the light but formal clothes that were worn by the dancers. Beyond this, it was customary for most people who were members of society to appear at the revelry, although some jealous husbands did not allow their wives to attend. If one takes into consideration the fact that there were few legitimate wives in the upper levels of society, one can appreciate why many of the females at these events were, like me, adventurers!

The first time that I attended I was in a state of great excitement for I imagined that I was going to enter into true society and make a great deal of new acquaintances. In the candlelit interior the music was provided by a group of musicians with lutes, hautboys, small kettledrums, and various other percussion instruments that I had never seen before. The music itself was a rhythmical mixture of folk tunes from Europe, and the insinuating rhythms of African origin which the slave trade had brought to these shores. The engaging and sensual nature of the music encouraged the dancers, especially the females, to move their bodies in the most suggestive way conceivable, and, as many of the dances required male and females to dance together with their bodies touching closely, the atmosphere of the event was lustful and lewd in the extreme.

The married women congregated in one corner of the floor, and kept themselves somewhat remote from the main body of the revellers, while the society men with Fernando

144

at their centre formed their own group. While Fernando did not move around nor introduce himself to the others, many others walked the floor, eyeing the many women who stood in wait, glowing with excitement and eager to enter into conversation with anyone who chose to speak to them.

When I first entered I was overwhelmed with surprise at seeing the many single women. How finely dressed they were, all alone or with simple maids in attendance, all waiting for the world to come to them. They were like parrots, brilliantly turned out in clear greens, blues and reds, and the bodies and features of many of them were of the finest. There were colours and complexions of all sorts, from the palest ivory to the rich dark hues of Africa; there were figures of every type, tall and slender, short and petite, voluptuous and heavily developed. Most of the women dressed so as to draw the eye to their individual charms. Low-cut bodices flattered the attraction of a buxom woman, skirts tight-fitting around the thigh drew attention to the slender bodied, while a tuck around the backside teased those who lusted after more ample charms. Bare arms and backs promised further nakedness; dresses that lifted to reveal silken stockings and fine ankles and calves promised secret charms still more deeply concealed.

As I walked through this throng, my nostrils inhaling the many perfumes of musk, rose, incense and attar that they carried on themselves, I felt at first despair at ever standing out from so many other women of beauty. I intimated as much to Leonie, who was in attendance. She laughed softly, and whispered, 'Do not despair! Your beauty is noteworthy amongst so many. Look more carefully around you. Look at the wives!'

And, as I glanced across at the group at the far end of the dancing floor, I understood what Leonie wanted me to notice. They were all staring at me with astonishment and concern, and I realised that gossip travelled quickly in such a closed society, and that they were alarmed to see me. They themselves were quite different from the rest of the company. Some of the women had chestnut hair, or in one or two cases, dark blonde, and the majority of the complexions were excessively pale, as of a woman who, having a naturally delicate skin, rarely ventures into the sunlight. But none of these women were like me; light blonde, clear complexioned, tall, finely formed. And the whole company had their eyes upon me.

I did a tour of the hall, and, passing the knot of men who clustered around my lover, Count of Braganza, I curtseyed to Fernando in a formal manner, hoping secretly that he would distance himself from his companions and come to me, acknowledging publicly our friendship. But he contented himself with returning my bow in the same manner, not showing in any way that we were acquainted.

I was angry at this behaviour until Leonie explained to me that it was the custom in San Cristován for men of position not to show openly which women were their mistresses at any time, unless they reached a position of trust and influence, in which case the permanent nature of the relationship became recognised publicly.

I spent the rest of that evening watching with delight the gyrations and convolutions of the dancers, taking pleasure in the music, which was quite new to me, and refusing with haughty disdain all approaches from the many men who passed by me. When I returned to my rooms that night I was filled with despair at raising my position in this land about which I knew so little. But when Fernando came to me I did not let him know my feelings, not even referring to our cold meeting that same evening, and contented myself with enjoying the pleasures that only he could bring me, and bringing his raptures to the greatest heights possible.

During the following months I concentrated upon perfecting my grasp of the Portuguese language, and receiving instruction in the Catholic Church. And when my lover, as Governor, held public court I attended, but always kept a distance from him, so as not to cause him embarrassment or to lead him to suspect that I was eager to improve my position in relation to him. But all that time I was engaged in watching how the ladies of society behaved, what they said when they were introduced to him, and how they spoke to each other in general conversation.

Then, one day, the time was right for me, and amongst others, some of whom belonged to the very highest society, I went up to Fernando, dressed in my finest clothes, enjoying the admiring glances that came my way. I held myself erect and haughty and acted out the part of being his social equal. I curtseyed to him in the manner that was normal for a woman of the upper classes, put out my hand to him, and spoke in a proud voice, using the accent that I had observed to be normal amongst women of that class, and referred to some item of gossip that Leonie had reported to me that day. 'Really, Count, I do wish that you would keep me informed of these pieces of news, rather than allowing our servants to pass messages on!'

He looked truly discomfited at my complaint, bowed to me respectfully and murmured some words of apology. But in doing so he had acknowledged me to the rest of the court. From then on it was easy to move forward in my public position, using a combination of play-acting, jealous wiles and the magnetic power of the attraction that I held for him.

I well remember the day when I first accompanied Fernando on a social occasion, one of the most informal types of reunion in which society took part. An outdoor repast was arranged on the estate that he owned outside the town. We commenced our journey just before dawn, and the many helpers carried the hampers of food, the bottles, the awnings and the cloths that were to be set out for our comfort and pleasure. I was taken there, as was fitting, along the narrow paths that ran between the stands of great forest trees intermingled with bush and sugar-cane fields, in a hammock held by two bearers, one on each end of a long pole. Leonie walked alongside, and Fernando accompanied us on horseback, much in company with the other invited guests. We had left, as I said, before dawn, and the darkness of the vegetation, decorated with millions of fireflies that twinkled in a faerie manner, affected my imagination powerfully. The sky lightened as we drew near the estate and its wooden residence came into view upon a slight elevation. It was much simpler than the one we inhabited in the town, made largely out of unpainted hardwood logs roofed with terracotta tiles. As we approached, the paths became busier, with other parties converging upon the house, using similar modes of conveyance, and there was much friendly banter between us.

As the sun rose the servants laid out the cloths, cushions and hampers, and erected the awnings so as to prepare a protection against the heat of the day. I settled myself down upon a little knoll in a commanding position with the house a little way behind, and the sight of the delightful vista of trees, brightly coloured flowers and green, naturally grown lawns, was accompanied by the sounds of monkeys and parrots, and other large colourful birds that particularly haunted those parts. Soon other ladies in a similar position to me, whose relationship with their lovers had acquired a permanent and recognised quality, congregated around me. As I looked from one to the other I reflected on the fate that had thrown these women together, and on the variety of charms that they possessed.

To my right sat Purificação, the mistress of one of my lover's colleagues. Somewhat younger than I, her complexion was golden, her figure extremely full yet stately, her shoulders broad, her neck long and regular, and her breasts well-formed with an appearance of extreme firmness, to which her light casual dress only served to draw attention. On my other side reclined Zenilda, younger than any of us, with a slender figure, long legs, a long narrow body and a bust that consisted of small, widely separate breasts high upon her body. Dressed as we all were in white, loose, simple country cottons we were an appealing party, and my senses were soon on fire when I saw how many of the others seated in other groups were continually casting their glances in our direction, especially when I realised that the figure that enjoyed the longest inspection was my own.

I could see plainly that I was recognised as the leader of the women, and I was delighted when some of the married ladies came up to where I was sitting and greeted me with respect and deference.

As the morning's pleasures unfolded I began to feel a great sense of well-being sweeping over me. I looked around at the scene and admired the fineness and handsome qualities of those men who had joined our group. Dressed like the women in simple garments, as befitted a country outing, they wore loose shirts, white cotton pantaloons, and light stockings and shoes. At first we partook of a copious refection, in which dishes of all types, including meats, game, vegetables, rice and sweet potatoes were promiscuously presented upon the tablecloths, washed down with copious draughts of light wines and cane spirits mixed with fruit juices. These latter cordials had the effect of raising our spirits, and the games, when they commenced, were boisterous, I should point out that it was the custom on occasions of this sort for games to be played which, back in the more formal and restricted society of England, would be considered quite unseemly.

A great favourite was blind man's buff, in which one person is blindfolded, and others taunt him, encouraging him to run after them, and, so it seemed to me on these occasions, inviting capture if the embraces of the person involved seemed appealing. Men, women, masters and servants all participated in the game, and as a consequence the opportunities for illicit touches were great, especially when a particular variant was practised in which more than one player was chosen at the same time. Upon this occasion, during such hours of recreation, my lover Fernando was able to leave behind him the burdens of his office, forget temporarily the formality of his position, and become as carefree as anyone else.

At one point in the game I was running away from an ugly fellow whose embraces I did not desire, when I accidentally blundered into the path of another of the blind players, and was captured by her. It was Purificação, and we both fell together on to a mound of short grass. For some moments our bodies were touching, and I closed my eyes, luxuriating in the comfort I felt at sinking into her ample yet shapely charms, with her softness and sweet perfume. Then, just before I pulled away from her, to the sound of laughter and good-natured banter from the party, Purificação squeezed my waist in a significant way, a squeeze that was full of hints and hidden meanings. When I stood again, and let her place the blindfold over my eyes, my heart was racing at the promise of illicit sensuality.

Then, in my blindness, I became aware of the sounds that my companions uttered as I blundered my way over the grass. Soon I became able to distinguish one person from another simply from their laughter. I heard Fernando's laugh, then close by the voice of Leonie, and others around me. I continued to feel my way here and there, hoping to distinguish again the sound of Fernando's voice, but he had fallen silent.

Then I heard what I took to be him. There was only one brief sound, and I ran in its direction. In a moment my arms were around a man's waist, and I felt his torso, exploringly, sensually. We tripped and fell together. One of his hands tried to loosen my blindfold, and his other was on my breast. My heightened passions were rising, looking foward with pleasure to the joys that I hoped we should share in the course of the hottest hours of the afternoon, when the custom was to retire to bed. Then the fabric was off my eyes, and I saw that the touches that had moved my appetites had come not from Fernando but from another – a young man of my own age, whose lascivious expression left no doubt as to the strength of his feelings. Then I looked further, and saw that Leonie was captured by the Count, with many screams of delight on her part. She struggled against his embraces, whilst he, in fun, continued to entwine her in his arms, letting them slip just enough for her to run a little further, then clasping her to him once again. She looked straight at me, and a question passed through my mind, to be put out of consideration almost immediately.

As the day progressed, the sun crept up the sky until it was nearly overhead, and the heat became so intense that the party was disinclined to exert itself unnecessarily. I lay under the awning with my companions in a lazy drowsy state. We talked of our lovers, our passions, of the tender emotions, for members of this society spoke with great openness about their private feelings and habits.

'My lover', said Purificação sleepily, 'is sometimes insatiable, coming to me time after time, all night. Yet at others he is quite uninterested in entering me. But not, I think, when he has been unfaithful, for then his passion increases!'

'But how can you tell that he has been unfaithful?' I asked, in alarm, for it was a possibility that I had never seriously considered, Fernando's passion for me appearing to have continued unabated.

'When he comes to you in a different way, you will know. Or perhaps, if he has been with someone different, the perfume of the other woman can still remain upon him,' replied Purificação indifferently.

Zenilda opened her eyes, for she had appeared to be asleep. 'My lover does not attempt to conceal his affairs from me,' she laughed sleepily, lying closer to me, and putting her arm around my neck in the most affectionate manner, as though there were no barriers between us. 'Indeed, he has often taken my closest friends. It only makes him the more passionate when he returns to me. And the thought that my friend has been intimate with him makes me more passionate, too.'

Just then, I noticed that Leonie was no longer in our party, and that likewise Fernando was nowhere to be seen. A moment of suspicion passed through me. I stood up and gestured to my companions. 'Please feel free·to speak to the servants if you wish to retire to the house. They will find rooms for you. They are at your disposal! I think my master calls!' I said, with a suggestive wink to the company, walking towards the house.

The interior of Fernando's country house was, as I have already indicated, much simpler than that of the Governor's palace in the centre of town, and up to the day whose events I now recount, I had rarely been there, for he usually used it for entertaining friends. I walked through the cool, white, roughly plastered rooms, passing by groups of guests who were now retreating into the cool of the indoors, reclining upon sofas and couches, asleep in some cases, in chairs and on the bare terracotta floor.

Then I came to that part of the house forbidden to guests. It contained Fernando's private apartments, where he enjoyed the opportunity to relax in complete privacy. The servants who guarded this inner sanctum looked surprised to see me there but, acknowledging who I was, bowed awkwardly and let me pass.

As I approached one of the bedchambers, I heard a soft moaning sound. The heavy mahogany door of the room stood slightly ajar. I crept up to it, moving soundlessly, and peered through the gap between the door and its frame. I saw on the bed exactly the sight that had been passing through my mind since hearing the chatter of the women in the garden outside.

Fernando and Leonie were entwined upon the bed, the same bed that I had myself used with Fernando for hours of passion. They were both totally naked, and the dark gloss of her body, as faultless as any polished carving in wood, made a contrast with Fernando's pale skin that stirred up my senses to an extraordinary degree almost as soon as I saw them. They were engaged in a violently passionate love-play, but had as yet not consummated their desires with the most intimate act of union between a man and a woman.

All was revealed to me as a spectator. Fernando's staff of passion rose thick and heavy from the dense mass of hairs that covered his lower belly, and the hands of my serving woman, whose delicacy and sensitivity had brought sweet joys to me on many occasions, were now upon it, squeezing, rubbing, bringing the head of the organ up to her mouth so as to excite it the more. I noticed that she held it at the base in such a way that when he came close to an involuntary emission of his seed she was able to hold him back, thus prolonging and increasing their shared joy. Soon his fingers were deep within the little purse of joy that was hidden deep beneath her own thick hard bush. Its lips were wide open as I had seen them so often when her senses were in a state of passion, and I saw the slippery pink flesh that lay hidden inside.

Now she was upon her back, legs wide apart, his tongue within her crack, and she cried out again and again in joy as he found out the parts where her senses were at their most acute. Then in a moment he tore himself away from his pleasant task, and his body was upon hers. She was melting with passion and the heat of the day caused her whole body to perspire heavily, but he treated her with gentle care now, as his member hit slowly against the first lips of her femininity, withdrew a little way, then pressed in further, stopping, letting her channel loosen, waiting for her rapture to rise to new heights. I could see right inside the hot perfumed slit as Fernando's member drew back, stretching it wide open. Then, while she held his organ in such a way that it still did not discharge itself into her body, she encouraged him to enter fully, and both abandoned themselves to their lustful passion with cries of joy, shouts of pain, and writhings and gestures of the most violent sort.

As for me my emotions were overwhelming, so powerful that I lost all sense of time and place. At first I felt jealousy, then anger at being wholly dependent upon this man who had even saved my life. My anger intensified into rage, and I was ready to rush out, search for any appropriate weapon and kill both lovers *in flagrante delicto*. Then, to my astonishment in the midst of the emotions that were shutting up the gates of my reason, the familiar sensation of lust began to appear. I saw Leonie's body being pounded by the thick engorged staff that Fernando was thrusting into her again and again, up to its hilt. As I watched the movement of her breasts heaving rhythmically in time with Fernando's thrusts, I was seized with desire to touch them, to further stimulate her pleasure by squeezing her nipples, hard and erect as they were. And as I saw her feminine parts strained open, with the masculine organ of my lover swollen to its mightiest and moving in and out, I began to experience a new form of jealousy, in which I wanted to share their desire and pleasure, but suffered no resentment at their snatching illicit minutes of rapture.

My own rosy slit ached with longing as I beheld the scene in front of me and my little bud of pleasure felt tense and rigid. Honey began to seep from between my secret lips and I pressed my thighs together, thrusting my buttocks forward. I slipped my hand under my skirts and began softly to stroke the blonde hairs on my Mound of Venus.

Fernando was lingering over taking his pleasure fully and just as Leonie's cries began to reach a crescendo he would slow himself down. Then she would moan in resignation and move backwards and forwards on his rigid staff desperate to reach the pinnacles of ecstasy, but he pushed her back on to the bed and gently withdrew from her, his organ shiny and dripping with her delectable juices. Then, as her excitement waned a little, he would enter her again, thrusting slowly and gently at first, kissing her belly and sucking at her dark erect nipples until her cries grew louder. This process was repeated again and again.

My own excitement mounted as I watched their coupling. My fingers pressed and rubbed at my stiff little pleasure bud. I thrust my fingers up inside my honey-pot as far as I could reach and I could barely conceal my own cries of joy as I considered how pleasurable it would be to feel Leonie's tongue flicking my bud whilst Fernando filled me from behind with his great staff. I had great difficulty preventing myself from springing into the room, throwing myself on to the bed and entering into the fray. But I resisted and contented myself with pleasuring my parts whilst gazing upon them. Leonie was now lying upon her stomach, her legs over the side of the bed, her glossy buttocks pointing upwards. Fernando was standing behind her, and I could see the moisture glistening upon his erect organ. Then he spread her thighs and entered her with a great cry, and began moving towards his final ecstasy. So my fingers became busier, I pressed my thighs together harder and rubbed, flicking again and again that special place hidden inside. As they reached their final pleasure I did so, too, and my involuntary scream of delight was drowned by theirs.

I crept away silently, and rejoined the ladies with whom I had spoken only a few minutes ago. During a pause in our idle chatter I whispered in the ear of Purificação and made an assignation with her after the cathedral the following morning, a suggestion to which she assented eagerly.

So ended the day of my life when I had gained a position much to be envied and lost my lover as my exclusive property. But, in recognising that I could share him, with my friend and servant, I was opening the gates to more and fresher pleasures. The next period of my life was a happy one, too, and in it I enjoyed many advantages. But, like so many good things, it was destined to be cut short in the most unexpected manner.

Eighteen

Now that I was one of the leaders of society, I appeared everywhere with my lover as his official consort. When he held court in the forenoon, taking petitions, meeting with the society of San Cristován, I would be at his side, dressed in the finest fabrics imported from Spain, Venice or France. When I passed through the square in the pre-dawn light with my faithful servant and intimate friend Leonie on the way to the cathedral, it would be as one of the leading devotees, so that if by chance I were behind time I would see all faces turned to me as I entered the dimly lit interior, the priests waiting for me to settle to my place before the began the ceremonial of the mass.

When the dance was held I was the undisputed leader of the women, and now I was accepted by the married women, even if unwillingly, as one in authority. Fernando and I would open the proceedings by taking a few stately steps, after which other representatives of high society would follow our lead. While we were together thus at the head of the revelries I would see other women out of the corner of my eye who were like I had been in the early days, and felt a certain pride in what I had done for myself. Alas, having so much I forgot that everything changes, and that all we believe to be durable, upon which we place our trust, will inevitably come to an end! Perhaps it was my pride which fate chose to punish by taking from me everything which I believed was unalienably mine. I cannot say. But punished I was.

Perhaps the beginning of my fall goes back to that day when I saw Fernando taking his pleasure with Leonie. My senses took fire, for I saw the possibility of more unrestricted and unbridled practices, in which I could taste pleasures that had been closed to me until that time.

When I was alone with Leonie at the end of that day, we were enjoying the routine that we so often shared – I was unclothed, and my friend and confidante was equally naked. I enjoyed the sight of her high-set breasts, so heavily tipped, so velvety to the touch, and I luxuriated in the feel of her hands upon my nakedness as she rubbed perfumed oils into my skin, so that if Fernando came to me that night I should attract him as strongly as a flower draws bees. I put my hand on her waist and stroked the light-brown softness of belly and thigh, then ran the tips of my fingers through the hard dense bush that covered her mound of love in a delightfully hard and resistent thicket.

'So my master has entered your well of honey again! I saw how abandoned you were when he thrust himself inside you today. As your master he has the right to use you in such a way, of course. But I am a little sad that you did not see fit to let me know that I was to share my lover with you, my dear!'

My words, spoken even while her hands were moving sensuously upon my skin, ignited in her the ardent fires of passion that now formed a background to all of our lives together. For me, too, the prospect of the joys that we might be about to share together awakened a yearning in my private places, and I felt my wetness spreading, mixing with the perfumes that she had spread even in this secret place. The fact that this secret was out teased her desire, and she looked at me in adoration, wanting to enjoy more unrestrained mutual caresses. But that was not my intention at this moment. Instead I dismissed Leonie sharply, and she left, downcast; and I took to my bed, waiting expectantly for Fernando to come to me.

When we lay naked together, I used all my skills, all my gifts, to raise his expectations ot the highest degree. I held his staff softly in my hand, exciting it with my mouth, my tongue, or with a butterfly's touch of my nipples, until his whole body was aroused, perspiring with the heats of passion, hard with desire yet submissive to my arts. Then I kissed him upon the lips with my mouth and spoke to him softly.

'So even though the passions that we share are so fine, so strong, so insatiable yet so deeply satisfying, you desire my servant, and take your pleasure with her in secret, unaware that I watch your every move, your every caprice.'

Fernando looked at me with alarm, and I felt his manhood slacken in my hand even as I spoke. Then I went on. 'But there are no secrets between us, my Lord and master. I only wish to please. If my beauty, my passion, my arts of love, so craftily applied to your pleasure are not enough to stop you from taking my serving maid on occasion, I am sure that it is through no fault of my own, for I am sure that I have never failed in ministering to your passions.'

Here I paused for a moment, and kissed his body in ways that would rekindle his desires. 'But', I continued, 'I believe that it is quite natural in a man', here I laughed in the most friendly way possible, 'to find other ways to re-kindle the passions that might otherwise become stale. By finding other objects for our sensual impulses, for example. And what better than with my maid servant, whose beauties and charms are so different from my own. She is so eager to please and to give pleasure, and has no secrets from me?'

At this I pulled the sheet over our bodies in order to cover our nakedness, reached out to a stand that lay beside our bed, and rang the small brass bell that I used when I wished to summon Leonie to my presence. He did not speak, but I knew that he understood then what my intention was, for when I put the bell down, and passed my hand over his manhood, it had sprung back to life again, and was so hard and distended that I was afraid to grasp it too strongly, in case he discharged his fluids there and then, spoiling the joys that I had planned for him.

Then Leonie was in the doorway, and at a gesture she came forward to the bed, standing by me, as her mistress, awaiting orders. I kept my hand upon Fernando's staff, and I knew by its rigidity that his passions were stirred by the presence of his clandestine lover.

'Leonie, how can you stay fully clothed beside your mistress when she is naked? You remember the custom. You must divest yourself.' At that she looked abashed, but, carrying out my command, loosened the laces that held her dress above her ample breasts and shoulders. With a shake of her body the thin cotton fell to the floor, and she stood, still somewhat uncertain and shy, awaiting my orders, clad only in a short lace underskirt, that shut out from our gaze her full buttocks, her upper thighs and her delicious private parts. And I knew that they waited only for a touch from one of us, her master or her mistress, for the floodgates to be loosed.

'But my dearest Leonie, you are still clothed,' I said. My own private parts were now yearning to be caressed and aroused by first one of my companions, and then another, and I moved slightly so that the bedclothes fell away from my body, revealing my own pink tips to my two companions. 'Come on to the bed between us, and allow your master to remove the garment that hides your delightful charms from both him and me!'

Soon she was beside me on the bed, kneeling between my lover and me, and the sharp but sweet perfume of her body aroused my senses, as did the sight of her ample breasts and bare thighs. Fernando's hands were on her body, touching her breasts, pulling the thick nipples, feeling the weight of them, and then her thighs were opened by his eager hands and the final little garment had been pulled off her body. Fernando commanded her to turn to me, and her lips were on mine, her hands stroked my breasts, my thighs, the flesh of my belly, while Fernando watched the rising passion that we shared with the light of desire in his eyes.

Then I lay passive, allowing my female lover to treat me as a man might treat a woman: roughly thrusting her private parts against mine, rubbing her body against mine, biting and slapping, until I called out again and again in passion. But the rapture continued, her head was between my two hands, and her mouth upon the tender flesh of my belly, upon the soft skin between my thighs, and her tongue gently excited the wet flesh that, pink and aching with sensation, guarded the entrance to the very pit of my womanhood, all wide open to her gaze, to Fernando's eyes and awaiting whatever my two lovers wished to do with it. For now my sensations were raised to a pitch I had never shared before, knowing how two people are gaining their pleasure from my pleasure and aware that at last we had no restrictions, no secrets. Then I felt a change in the movement of Leonie's tongue inside my womanly parts, and I opened my eyes to see that Fernando had come at her from behind, for she knelt to her task, and her nether parts were high in the air, inviting Fernando to use them at his pleasure.

So now all three of us were crying out in ecstasy. Not only was our own pleasure immense, but the sight of two others enjoying similar pleasures, each in his or her individual way, raised our delights to peaks unknown hitherto, certainly to me, and no doubt to Leonie and Fernando also.

Then we lay quiet together, limbs entwined in a shameless mingling of bodies. But it was not to be so for long, as Fernando's passions were soon stimulated once more, and he demanded that I do to my servant what she had done to me. Ah, Balthazar, my dear friend, can you understand the perverse joy that I felt in playing a part which had until now been reserved for her! As my lips sucked at the womanly perfume that dripped from her fringed purse, so recently enjoyed and used by my own lover, she tasted both sweet and bitter as I discovered each intimate fold of flesh, so much bigger than my organs. As I uncovered each point of pressure, each little piece of suction in the pink, perfumed and sticky honeyed interior, my own organs were being touched, pressed, licked and gnawed by Fernando. Then I felt his organ stretching my secret lips open, pressing in and thrusting, as the passions that welled up in me teased me on to thrusting my tongue ever deeper inside her, pressing far into her orifice, deeper into the very source of her honeyed essence.

'And so began, my dearest friend Balthazar, that period of my life where I was devoted to procuring willing subjects for my lover, Fernando, where every day I searched anew for new sources of novelty. A pleasant task, you might say!'

I bowed to Miss Chaunce, respectful, acting like a true friend, which I hope she believed me to be. *'Madame, your gifts, at least so far as they are known to the world at large, suppose you to be a true master at such activities!'*

At this Miss Chaunce smiled, wistfully it seemed to me.

'My dear friend. It was a pleasant task, yet it was also a sad one. I had found true freedom from the guilt that had bedevilled my early life, yet I was not free. I knew that at any time I could lose my high position in my adopted society if I were to fail to pander to Fernando's tastes, and in truth his tastes became over the months and years more arbitrary, more varied and more capricious.'

At first I procured discreet liaisons from amongst the women of the lower classes I saw in the cathedral. I would, as before, attend with Leonie as my companion. And whenever a maid of one of the society ladies appealed to my tastes, I would whisper a word in her mistress's ear upon leaving.

'My dear, you have a most charming maid! I believe that there are some *services* that she might be inclined to carry out for me! If you should wish, I can lend you my maid as a replacement for the duration!' A nod and a wink, and it was done.

As I became more practised in the art of finding lovers for Fernando, I attempted to procure other types. Purificação was one of my more ambitious conquests. An established mistress, she was not exactly a member of high society, but she had a certain status.

She was younger than I, and her statuesque person reminded me of Sophie, with whom I had enjoyed my early passion. Her body was like Sophie's, with large globular breasts, full thighs, buttocks well-developed and rounded, yet compared to Sophie her allure was more powerful, her charms bigger, her presence stronger. I could see from her lustrous black eyes smouldering even in church that her sensuous impulses would ignite with a mere touch.

So when she accepted my invitation to my quarters in Fernando's residence I made much of her, talking of this and that, mentioning love for a moment, then passing on to other things, observing her blushes, sensing her rising curiosity. Then I would speak more frankly about my own pleasures with the opposite sex, as we had on that day in the country. Finally there came a moment when I sensed that her curiosity had been fully aroused, and I spoke freely.

'My dear,' and here I put my arm around her neck, stroking her hair, looking admiringly at her body, especially where her fine full breasts came together, 'you are of just that age when, I remember well, the fires of love burn most hotly. I am happy, for myself, that I followed my instincts at that time, and enjoyed many rapturous experiences with my girl friends, free of any shame or regrets!' Then I stroked her flesh around the neck, shoulders, breasts, wondering at her yielding softness, letting my lips brush her body, as lightly as a butterfly touching a rose petal.

When my lips touched hers without any dissemblement, I knew that Purificação would be mine, for hers responded with all the fire that I had seen in her eyes when I looked at her in church.

From that opening, it was only a short step to us sharing the bed throughout the whole of a warm and humid morning, and to her losing all sense of shame in the delights that we enjoyed together. I luxuriated in the touch of her full breasts, the softness and responsiveness of her parts, that were so easily awakened, so liquid and sweetly perfumed, like a lotus blossom, and so quickly raised to a peak where

163

she lost all restraint in the excess that I was able to bring her.

Once that task was accomplished, and we took daily pleasure in each other's bodies, it was my role to introduce Purificação to Fernando. For each of his new conquests it would be different. In the case of Purificação he decided that he should take her in the morning when she and I were sharing the illicit joys of the bed, and that I should pretend that the intrusion of my lover was quite unexpected and shocking.

This I accordingly did, watching with vicarious pleasure the sight of Fernando taking Purificação from me, with her secret lips damp and open, having already enjoyed moments of ecstasy under my touch. When she saw Fernando disrobed but for a cotton cloth about his loins and felt him take her body and commence kissing and touching, she knew not how to respond. She was so passionate by nature, but she also felt shame. She screamed and cried with shock and surprise, yet was eager and curious for the experience of a man whose sexual powers I had recounted to her in much detail. In no time at all, her protestations had turned to cries and sighs of rapture. And all this time I had to make as though I was shocked at the intrusion, utterly ashamed and dismayed.

But the dangers Fernando and I encountered in our secret meetings with Purificação were as nothing to the situation in which we found ourselves soon after. A scandal occurred when I had persuaded two ladies of high society to enter into clandestine relations with me simultaneously. This was a new experience for me, to make love to a pair of ladies, each so different from the other. The one, whose name I no longer recollect, was tall and slender, graceful, with narrow thighs and abundant hair upon her organs, which were perfumed like honey, small, tightly closed against my exploring caresses, cool to the touch. Her friend, in contrast, was more heavily built, with full buttocks, thighs and breasts, and a hot silky body that perspired freely when her passions were raging. Her pit of joy was hot and its flesh yielding, covered in soft sparse down, wet and open, strongly perfumed with a sharp womanly odour that aroused my senses beyond all measure. Once I had initiated the two in the joys that we could share together, we all three lay for hours in each other's company, shameless, exploring our secret delights, stimulating each other repeatedly. I found pleasure in the smallness and bushiness of the one and the size and softness of the other. Then I lay passive almost in paradise itself while one after the other raised my senses to peaks of desire. First a light cool, sweet-smelling body was upon me, then a heavy soft, bitter one!

I was lying thus upon the bed, when a noise from the doorway caused me to look over to the entrance of the chamber. There he was, my virile lover, the man who accepted the pleasures that I procured for him. He was naked, and the state of excitation his manhood was in told me that he had been observing us clandestinely for some time. He raised his finger to his lips, enjoining me to silence, for he could see that my two companions were lying with their faces away from him. He would be able, therefore, to approach without disturbing us at our diversions.

As so often happened, the perverse joy of being observed at pleasures that many people would dismiss as disgraceful served only to heighten the passions that were carrying me along with them. I lay now arm in arm with my soft, heavily built companion, mouth to mouth, while my private parts were the possession of my slender friend, whose cool, firm narrow lips sucked my perfumed honey with joyful abandon.

Now Fernando was behind the slimmer woman, his gaze on her nether parts, thrust upwards towards the ceiling, displaying shamelessly their aroused and inviting charms. After a few moments of admiration his arms were around her thighs, and, oblivious to her struggles and protestations, he opened her legs to their widest, and lowered her body on to his erect manhood, burying his member in her secret crevasse. Passion had her by the throat, and even as she called out in shock and protestation, her senses reached the heights, causing her angry cries to turn to those of joy and satisfaction. My other companion called out in fury to both of us.

'Depraved people, my Lord Governor. And you, Teresa, how dare you use respectable people so, as if they were nothing but whores to be procured and used according to your whim?'

If the situation had not been so fraught with danger I should have laughed at her speech. To think that a woman should believe that her pleasures with two other women were 'respectable', while the entry of a man on to the scene was enough for her to be considered a 'whore'! Yet that was the custom of the women of San Cristován!

To cut a long story short, the two women left our presence in high dudgeon. Their husbands came to know what had occurred and soon Fernando, Count of Braganza was known all over San Cristován as a man who conspired with Teresa Chaunce to procure and corrupt respectable married women. Every man in the society of San Cristován became afraid that his wife might be the next to be taken by the Governor and his scandalous companion. Suddenly the open court that the Governor of San Cristován held for his subjects every morning became deserted of supplicants. When I went to mass in the cathedral, the crowds of worshippers would draw away from me, for, of course, everyone was afraid to be seen in our company, for fear of being branded with the same badge of shame that we now wore.

Fernando decided that it would be most opportune for us both to retire for some time to one of his estates in the interior of the country, farther inland than the one where I had first discovered his passion for Leonie.

In Brazil there is so much land that estates extend for uncounted leagues over forested hill and valley, stretching on into the remotest parts of the interior, where no civilised man has trodden. And amongst these empty fastnesses, where the most fertile soils have been found, are cleared

166

lands upon which sugar cane is cultivated. By these fields lie the mill and factory that turn the cane into raw sugar, the slave quarters, and the mansion house of the owner.

Those with vast estates of this sort could retreat into their midst with scarcely a chance of being molested by outsiders from the city, for each estate was a world unto itself, with the owner behaving as though he were the emperor of his private realm, where no other person would dare ever to interfere, provided that taxes were duly paid to the Portuguese Emperor. It was to these dominions that Fernando proposed to retire, waiting until the scandal died down. He would carry out the essential business of the Governorship through communications that agents would deliver to him whenever necessary.

And so it was that, only a few days after the disastrous episode with the two married ladies, Fernando and I were riding on horseback along the narrow tracks that took the place of roads. We were traversing a tract of forest land that had been scarcely affected by the hand of man, where the magnificence of the forest trees as they reared huge out of the soil is scarcely to be appreciated by one who has never seen them. The thickness of the undergrowth that lined the fringes of the road was so great that it seemed almost impossible to leave the area of the track and take off into the jungle.

Our entourage was small, much shrunken compared with that day when we set out with the leaders of society in San Cristován. Now there were only a few servants, carrying our most important possessions, some basic supplies, and our faithful companion, Leonie.

To keep our spirits up I was telling Fernando and Leonie of the joys that awaited us in Fernando's manor house, and how I should, as Mistress of Ceremonies, design and carry out for my lover and master great revels that should provide him with pleasures of the flesh of every conceivable description and type. All, of course, within the limitations of his country estate – a sort of rustic pleasure dome.

'And so', I was going on, addressing Leonie as well as

Fernando, 'you must allow me to take the lead in finding for you those who can carry out your wishes in the most delightful manner. I know, as you do', I continued, drawing my horse closer to his, and placing my hand upon his arm, affectionately, 'that there is very little joy to be had from using the services of women who have been pressed into this work. Even though your estate possesses many slaves, amongst whom countless charming females are to be found, each of which is obliged to carry out your every whim ... Despite this power that you have over so many, my dear Fernando, I beg you to take my advice and to proceed differently!'

At this he bowed slightly to me, and the ghost of a smile played over his lips, as though in rueful agreement. I was glad that I now had the power to dispel his cares.

'My dear Teresa,' he said, 'I know that you have skills that are not given to other women. You have always been able to guess my most secret caprices. I give you free rein on my estates.'

'You have spoken, so I must obey,' I responded with a laugh. 'I shall devise pleasures for you that no other person in Brazil has enjoyed! I shall bring lovers to you who will join our household purely because they will find it a joy. I shall attract them to you like moths to a lamp. I shall set their senses on fire, and shall cause them to behave with such abandon that your passions will be alight constantly. Just think,' I went on, 'now that you are free of your duties, we shall be able to refine our lusts and the means to satisfy them. We shall be in the seventh heaven.'

Fernando had coloured at my words, and I believe that my speech caused his desires to stir there on the road through the forest. I went on, trying again to take his mind off the cares that still oppressed him.

'Imagine what we could achieve together. The finest women from the estate, large women, with heavy breasts and thighs, whose fringed purses are so engorged and swollen with lust that they beg you to satisfy them in that way only you know. Or small slender purses, tight, closed, re-

168

quiring all your force, gentleness and skill to open them and find the hidden gold. Imagine the scenes we could view together, of women taking women, men possessing women – men possessing men, even! You have only to say what you desire, and I can make it come true!'

In a split second, there appeared from amongst the undergrowth bordering the road a group of figures that astonished us to the extent that we halted speechless in front of them.

Nineteen

Three Indians stood staring blankly at our party, showing no emotion, and giving no indication as to why they were there and what they wanted of us.

There were two men and one woman, each as naked as the day that they had come out of their mother's womb. The bareness of their bodies was made all the more astonishing to me when I saw that they had removed all the hair from about their person. Their skins were golden, and shone in the sunlight as if polished. Their physiques were fine, firm, both men and woman being muscled and well-proportioned. At first I could not keep my eyes off the two men, for they had such an air of energy and strength that I longed to be able to reach out and touch them, and find out how they would go with a woman like me once their passions had been set on fire. I could not remove my eyes from their masculine organs of generation, for in each case they hung down heavy, wide and long, firmly shaped, standing firmly free of bodies from which all private hair had been removed, so that their skin seemed as naked and fine as a woman's. I longed to take each one in my hand, gauge its weight, press and handle it, feel it respond to my touch, rub, kiss and take it into my mouth, bring it to the point when its passion was uncontrolled, and enjoy its power as it discharged its liquids over me!

Then my eyes were on the woman, and I was delighted by the tiny pointed breasts, high under the armpits and topped by swollen nipples. I feasted my eyes upon the place between her slender thighs, as hairless as the cheeks on her face. The little slot was swollen and rounded, but tight

171

shut, inviting my tongue to excite it and encourage it to open. I wondered how she would behave when she became swept away upon the tidal waves of the passions that we all share. I wondered how her skin would feel upon mine, and how the touch of her fingers upon my own organs would be.

Then I remembered the other women whose passions I had shared, and thought how their womanly organs, hidden beneath layers of clothing, carried upon them a sense of secret shame. I thought of the thick and tangled private hairs, which in many cases were so dense as to hide from my eyes the slit that was the source of ultimate delights. It seemed to me, looking at this Indian woman's organ, shamelessly displayed for all of us to look upon in the bright sun and open air, that I saw an uninhibited state of nature that I longed to share.

Their bodies were covered in labyrinths of patterns – at that time I did not know whether painted or tattooed – in dark blue, black and red. The way that the shapes caressed the body, wandering over thigh and breast, arm and private part, back and belly, excited me and stirred me in such a way that I longed more strongly now to touch and explore. But as my thoughts were following such directions, those of my lover had taken quite a different turn. He shouted out and waved, seemingly in fury, standing up in the stirrups, seemingly ready to attack them in anger, even though they had shown us no harm.

'Filthy creatures, away, keep away from us here! Leave us in peace! Go back to the jungle, and stay there!'

The three Indians stared back at us blankly, apparently not understanding what Fernando was saying. Then one of the men raised an arm in which was held a small bow, and took an arrow from the cotton string about his waist. At this gesture Fernando called out the louder, took from his waistband an ornately patterned pistol, raised it to his shoulder and fired at the man. He fell, and blood poured out of a wound in his side. The other two Indians remained silent, but took him up, carrying him between them, and ran off back into the forest.

'Fernando, how can you use those simple creatures so? They meant you no harm!' I called out in grief at the thought of such a fine man being harmed for no purpose.

'Meant no harm? They are dangerous creatures, Teresa. Be warned. Thirty years ago, this country was infested with them, much to the detriment of the people who lived here. They are cannibals, my dear; more like wild animals than human beings. Until recently they were a great danger to us, and we are lucky that most have been exterminated from these parts. Our life would not be secure if they were still here amongst us.'

It was a subdued party that several hours later arrived at Fernando's manor house, built between the cane fields and the forest on a grassy knoll set about with flowering bushes. It was a delightful spot, and in the distance the sugar mill, the slave quarters, the houses of the overseers and of the free workmen mingled prettily with the serried rows of sugar cane.

After resting in the heat of the afternoon and washing ourselves, we took a tour by the light of the setting sun around the plantations. I must tell you, my dear friend Balthazar, that when I was in Brazil I found the practice of slavery most distasteful, for the whole of my life has been spent in a quest for freedom, freedom in which my passions can mingle with those of others. So many creatures deprived of the most elementary dignity, unable to deviate in any way from the paths set out for them by their masters and mistresses, at the caprice of their overseer at any moment, was to my way of thinking an insult to the human spirit.

Nevertheless, the sight of so many rustic people, clad only in the customary garb of the country – a pair of breeches for the man and a light cotton petticoat barely covering the thighs above the knees for the women – stirred my sensibilities and hinted at what might lie in store for us, if I were able to find those with the necessary spirit for the finest voluptuousness. Indeed, that same day, just before we were due to return to the manor house,

I conceived of a plan to introduce Fernando to a type of pleasure that departed considerably from what we had undertaken before.

There was a woman engaged in a light carrying duty, with a pannier upon her head, who had the height and build equal to that of many men. She was powerfully muscled, and broad shouldered, and her skin was of a glossy dark brown, the colour of chocolate. Her breasts caught my attention, for they were of a fullness quite out of the ordinary; heavy, mobile, yet firm and pointed also. Her thighs, hidden by the little petticoat, so inadequate at concealing such an exceptional body, promised delightful pleasures still hidden.

I sent a message by way of Leonie for the woman to come to the manor house after dark, and to use my name with the servants in the house in order to gain entrance. After the sun had gone down, Fernando sat upon the veranda for some time, and drank quantities of wine, in order, no doubt, to deaden the worry that was afflicting his mind. After eating a copious supper, he ordered me to accompany him to his sleeping chamber. I complied with his request, but he was in such an advanced state of intoxication that his caresses were sufficient upon my womanly organs to excite them and bring them to a pitch at which they ached for satisfaction. But he was not able to perform the penetration I required in order for my lusts to be extinguished.

Then he was asleep, and I stole out of bed in search of the woman whom I had invited to come to the house. She was, as I had ordered, waiting upon the veranda, kneeling upon the wooden floor, back straight and perfectly poised with her straight spinal column and broad and heavily muscled shoulders. Indeed, in all the simplicity of her station in life and rusticity of her manners, she seemed in stance to be a queen, born to rule.

She started when she saw me, and seemed afraid. I knelt in front of her, strongly aware of my own nakedness under the thin cotton shift that I wore.

174

'What is your name?' I asked.

'Elizabeth,' she answered, and stared at me. I admired her eyes, far apart and big, and her prominent cheekbones.

I commenced asking her about her life, her work, and her friends and family. I gave her a glass of wine to drink, and questioned her about her lovers. By now she confided in me, and confessed, after I had given her a second glass, that she had three lovers, and that she had succeeded in keeping from two of them the existence of the others, while the third was willing to share her with the others. I urged her on to reveal more of her secrets by telling her a little of the adventures I had experienced in the past and how I had succeeded in gaining my high position despite being a foreigner and starting from nothing at all.

'I like to have more than one lover, mistress,' she said, 'because the differences between them allows me to enjoy each one the more. Remembering the others when I am with one makes the pleasure the greater.'

'Tell me how they differ,' I said.

'Ercole is the youngest,' she said, shyly, her eyes lowered. 'He is smaller than I am, and very slim, with the skin of a woman. Yet his male organ, his manhood, is longer and thicker than any of my other lovers, and this excites me. But the way he touches me is gentle and soft, unlike James, who is a true giant, strong and hard of body. Although his masculinity is not so large as Ercole's, the power of his body makes me feel like a leaf upon the wind when he takes me, and he can come into me again and again, all night long, until I am exhausted.'

She paused, and I filled her wine cup once more, and offered her food to eat. She consumed with relish all that she was given, and I questioned her further.

'And your other lover? How does he thrill you?'

'By having no secrets. By speaking to me honestly about his desires. By talking to me of my beauty. Sometimes he restores our passions by bringing another woman to be with us, and taking her first in my presence, never sparing me even the most private intimacies. She is always of a

175

different type to me. Sometimes she is a very small, slender woman. Another time she will be an older woman, or a very corpulent woman. But, on each occasion, once he has satisfied her passions, he will come out of her still hot and hard, and, all sweetened with the honey from the other woman's most secret recesses, fall upon me hungrily, and devour me with his kisses before pressing his manhood into my yielding crevice.'

These words kindled my own passions in turn, and I raised my hand to touch her upon the soft skin around her neck and shoulders.

'If you are attached to the arts of love, as I am myself, you may find a new way of life opening up to you.' At this she stared at me, wide-eyed, steadily, in a manner that had only one meaning.

I allowed myself to draw nearer to her, and as I did so it became inescapably evident that, while the natural perfume of her body was fine and sweet, her labour during the day in the hot sun, and her lack of perfumes and unguents meant that her body was exuding an odour that was both attractive and repellent at the same time. I rang the bell for the house servant, and water and toiletries were brought into an adjoining chamber.

Once by the great bowl of perfumed water, we stood together, and as an example to her I pulled off my thin cotton nightcoat. Then I loosened the thin cotton skirt that still covered her nakedness, slipping it over her full but hard buttocks and loins, until we were together with our bodies pressing, both, to my joy, unashamed. My eyes feasted upon her full and powerful charms as she sat in the warm steaming water, sinuously flexing her torso as my hands massaged the soap and perfumes into her skin. Her body was lithe as a panther's, her waist slender and long, and as my hands kneaded the firmness of her breasts, feeling the swelling of the thick hard nipples, she responded by pulling me into the bath with her. She ran her firm strong hands over my soft flesh, hungrily holding my nipples between her hard fingers until I began to sigh with the coming ecstasy – noises that she reciprocated in time to the squeezings of my hands upon her globes.

I was intoxicated with the joy of discovering this new body, and my mouth sought out the flesh – so firm and heavily muscled – covered by such fine skin, as dark and soft as velvet, that formed her lower belly, her upper legs and the insides of her thighs. I poured oil distilled from scented palms into the black bush that protected her private feminine lips from my gaze, and the perfume mingled with a rank odour that drew me in to find the well of her sensuality, and to press and slide, lick and kiss, suck and penetrate. Then, almost without knowing how it was, we were upon a couch near the bath, and we towelled each other's nakedness, without shyness or reservation, and each kiss brought a burst of ecstasy, each pressure stimulated a sigh. When her body was above mine, her strength and power had the weight of a man upon me, but the sensitivity of each touch was a woman's.

'You are so pale, so soft,' she said into my ear, as her hand caressed the golden down upon my lower belly, and teased open the pink-lined lips that lay in their midst. 'Your honey is so clear and sweet,' she continued, licking the juices that had once again covered her probing finger, 'that I feel I could eat you whole, like one little honey-cake!'

I ran my fingers inside her womanly slit, wondering at its smoothness, its stickiness, its size, its perfumes, and each pressure upon the swellings and roughnesses that were the points of her greatest sensitivity to physical pleasure caused her to cry out in pleasure and flex her body towards mine.

Then we were in the chamber of my lover, Fernando. He was still asleep, deeply drugged with alcohol, and we were still unclothed as I encouraged her to lie in the bed on one side of him, with me on the other. My desire grew as I saw her monumental body beside his sleeping form, naked and loose. I took his soft masculinity in my hand, gently, softly, so as not to wake him, and I was thrilled when I felt the

177

slight firming of his organ, naturally heavy and full, but weightier now when beginning to distend with the blood and passion that he carried within him.

I took Elizabeth's hand and drew it to the same organ, and showed her where to hold it so as to touch the spot where his sensitivity was the greatest. It thrilled me to see her hand beside mine upon the private part of my lover, and when my lips brushed the tip of his organ Elizabeth reciprocated by taking the lower parts of his shaft into her mouth, so that it sprung into its fully engorged girth, and the first oozings were filling my mouth with their sticky discharges. Now my lips were against those of Elizabeth, and they were lubricated by his male juices. I watched as her lips closed around the thick and swelling head, my hands upon her own tumescent nipples. Then she pulled away to let me take my turn at this delightful task, and her hands excited my body.

When, at an invitation from me, she knelt over him to take his staff into her, I saw that her thighs were stronger than Fernando's, and that the magnificent size and development of her thickly haired crevice was such as to take all the vigour of his manhood within it with the greatest of ease. In this she was quite different from many others I had introduced him to in the past, who had been slender and tight in their loins, and where he had to fight and struggle to stretch the little slit wide enough to take in his full girth.

As she moved up and down in rhythm, the perspiration started to stand off her skin, and her breasts swayed in time to her body. I wished to be part of her in her coming ecstasy, and I knelt behind, my body pressing against hers. I swayed in time to her sinuosity, and, while one hand touched the wet shaft of his organ, slippery with the honeyed essence of Elizabeth's slit, the other ran through the strong dense hairs that thatched her secret places in a dense undergrowth.

Fernando seemed still to be asleep, for his eyes were still closed, and Elizabeth's breathing was becoming deeper, more raucous as her pleasure intensified so as to be almost like pain. The heat from our bodies bathed us both in sweat. Then a sudden flurry of voices outside made us start. The light of flames against the sky illuminated the room, together with our struggle and fright. There were people hammering against doors, breaking down wooden walls and running about in the corridors downstairs. Fernando awoke.

An arrow shot through the window, and another, and then a third. All were alight, burning with a wad of cotton soaked in tree sap attached to them. Fernando leapt off the bed, with his manly organ still standing straight up in front of him, and tore the burning shafts out of the wooden walls, where they were ready to gain a hold. But the smell of smoke drifting up from downstairs told us that this was not an isolated outbreak of fire. Then a sound of roaring, like that of great waters, came up to us from what we knew must be a larger conflagration.

I grabbed at a brief lace petticoat and a bodice in thin embroidered cotton as I rushed to the door, full of that instinctive fear of fire in an enclosed space. I ran naked down the stairs, behind Fernando and Elizabeth, who were both, like myself, utterly without clothes.

In the darkness outside there was a crowd of Indians, armed with bows and arrows – not the small weapons we had seen that morning, but big ones, which I was later to learn were exclusively used for war. The warriors stood by the doorway, waiting for us to come out of the house, and as soon as we were on the veranda they fell upon Fernando, hitting him in the face, dragging him away by the hair. Even in my terror I had the presence of mind to put on my sole articles of clothing; then I, too, was hit in the face and dragged away, and I fainted and knew no more.

Twenty

I returned to consciousness in darkness in a clearing in the forest. My hands and feet were tied by rough cotton thongs, and I lay outside a circle of Indian men squatting around a fire. My head ached and my dress was torn and soiled. I raised my head, and saw on the other side of the circle the prone figure of Fernando, apparently still unconscious. The men were talking in low voices in their own language. I called out to them, and indicated, when they turned round to look at me, that I was thirsty and wished to drink. But they merely laughed, imitated my gestures in fun, and went back to their conversation.

Then I lay back and watched the stars as they moved slowly through the sky, thinking back upon the past years of my life, and the strange twists and turns of fate that had carried me hither and thither, from success to loss, from comfort to imprisonment, from Boston in Lincolnshire to this clearing in the Brazilian jungle. I remembered being captured by sailors who thought that I was a man, and how I had awoken from captivity in the dark hold of a ship.

Then I thought once more of my dear parents taken from me so unhappily by the plague, and suddenly I felt like the most miserable woman in the world. I thought of all the happiness that my sensual pleasures had brought to me, and how much others had enjoyed my presence, and then I felt desolate once again, for I had lost that source of joy, and now was an outcast, going I knew not where, to I knew not what end.

But in the end, despite my misery, I fell asleep. I awoke

to a raging thirst and an aching head, and I saw that the men around me were preparing to continue their journey. Now Fernando was awake, and we greeted each other with many expressions of sorrow as we were forced to stand whilst the thongs upon our legs were taken off. Then, with our arms still bound, we were each led like a dog or captive goat, barefoot, along paths through the trees. My feet soon became swollen and scratched, and it was almost impossible for me to walk without constantly stumbling from pain. But the men who had captured us were strong and powerful, and continued down the forest path without ever letting up their gait. I was carried over the broad back of one of them as though I were a sack rather than a woman who had only a few days before been the star of society.

At this point Miss Chaunce had reached the end of yet another day's narrative.

'*You will find,*' *she said,* '*it hard to imagine that I, who appear to you in such sophisticated guise, seeming so much of the fashionable world, could have lived through such strange and outlandish adventures. Yet, my dear friend, it is true, and as a result of these adventures, I have little patience with the prudery that infests all levels of society in this land of ours.*'

I bowed to Miss Chaunce. '*Miss Chaunce,*' *said I,* '*few would ever accuse you of prudery!*'

She laughed at this, and went on. '*Yet in this realm of England few people, men or woman, ever care to remove all their clothes, even in the most intimate of circumstances. You will have observed this prudery, no doubt,*' *she said, smiling her sweetest smile.*

I felt unaccountably embarrassed at this, and I must have blushed somewhat at her words.

'*My dear Balthazar, we must cure you of this prudery. I shall only continue my narrative on the morrow provided that you follow my example and remove all your clothes this evening. For you will find that few of the characters in tomorrow's narrative used clothing!*'

182

Miss Chaunce stood where the ruddy flames from the fire played upon her fine and exquisite features, and she commenced loosening her overdress, a red velvet garment, and pulling down the many petticoats she wore under her dress. Then, pulling off the basque that she had over her shift, she stood clad merely in loose thin cotton, and lifted up one fine slender leg, so that I could see a length of white and shapely thigh, inviting explorations further up, where sensations become more acute. Then she pulled off one stocking, and threw it to me with the accompanying garter. My passions soared as I took these precious pieces of clothing into my hands.

'Now you must follow me,' she said, as she approached and pulled at my clothing, quickly unbuttoning my jerkin. She forced me to remain upon the chair, pulled at my boots, unbuttoned my shirt, and unlaced the fastenings upon my breeches. I was aroused beyond endurance as my clothes fell away from my body under her practised hands, and I watched the full-breasted nakedness of her body moving, lithe but mature and womanly under her shift.

In a trice Teresa Chaunce let all her garments fall to the ground and slid off the final stocking so that she was quite naked before me. I observed the white and gold magnificence of her body: the soft golden hair upon her Venus Mound, the pink flesh that crumpled together formed the closed lips of her honeyed slit, and the white of her thighs. She walked to the bed, raised her arms above her hair in order to take out the pins that held her coiffure in place, then let it tumble golden and free around her breasts and shoulders. She gestured to me to stand, revealing my own shameless uncovered stiffness, and to walk over to her, while she lay upon the cushions, legs open in invitation. Our mutual nakedness aroused my senses to an extraordinary degree, and when I lay upon the bed beside her my male organ, erect as it was, was in such a state of excitement that the slightest touch would have caused it to reach a climactic state and prematurely spill my seed upon her soft and yielding skin, making us both lose the pleasures that we wished so ardently to share.

But Teresa Chaunce was alive to the risk. She instructed me to lie still upon my back, and, turning her nether parts towards my head, she took hold of the base of my male organ in such a way as to inhibit it discharging its fluids before the right time. Then she put the end of my staff in her mouth and commenced caressing and licking, so that my sensitivity to these touches reached a point where I was nearly frantic with desire. These sensations were much increased by the sight of her own female organ above me, with the lips pink and already drawn far back by the stimulation that her enjoyable task had wrought upon her. She indicated, by lowering her soft buttocks, that she wished me to stimulate her rosy bud with my strong tongue. I accordingly set about the task, plunging it into the delightfully scented crevice, where the plentiful lubrication copiously welled up from deep within her feminine parts at each touch from me.

Then, as the shaking and sinuosity of her body told me that she was nearing the peak of her own pleasure, she released her hold upon the base of my shaft, and let me discharge the full volume of my male emissions into her mouth. Then we lay still for much time, me admiring the uncovered loveliness of her womanly parts, with such a fine combination of golden down and pink flesh. But all too soon the hour came for my departure, and I reentered the world, clad and covered once more.

Upon the following day I met once again with Miss Chaunce, who began her narrative where she had interrupted it so pleasantly the previous day.

And so our journey through the forest continued, with me being thrown back and forth upon the shoulders of my captors, and Fernando forced to walk naked, barefoot and bound, much bewailing his fate and begging his captor to let him free, or even kill him, rather than submit him to such great indignities. Yet the warriors that were our captors remained stoical, tireless and silent.

As the day drew towards its close we arrived in the Indian settlement. It was in a clearing in the forest, a mere circle of huts, built in the most cunning manner out of entwined leaves and jungle creepers, the whole raised off the ground by fine hardwood tree-trunks. There were seven of these constructions, and as we approached out of the forest more men, as naked as the ones we were already acquainted with, cried out in surprise and pleasure, laughing and pointing at Fernando and me. Then the women, both young and old, came running out of the huts, staring at us, clustering around in excitement, sometimes reaching out to touch our bodies or to hold a limb, seemingly making fun of us.

Fernando and I were made to sit down together in the centre of the clearing, while the women formed rows of dancers on either side, singing, moving in time, clapping their hands, seeming to celebrate our arrival with joy. The warriors were greeted by a small number of elders, but men were greatly outnumbered, and soon they all went off together into one of the huts, leaving the dancing women. I could see them through the open entrance drinking quantities of a liquid that seemed to make them intoxicated.

At this point my fatigue and fear had reached such a pitch that I was hardly aware of where I was. They took me to a small hut, a little way from the rest, where I was tied by one arm to a central pole. There an old woman gave me a gourd full of water to drink, and a few pieces of manioc cake, a bread-like food made of the grated roots of a native plant, that is much eaten by both Indians and settlers. This frugal repast revived me to some extent, and curiosity about my condition and future returned somewhat. After some time the warriors who had captured us came in a dense throng and entered the hut, all painted and wearing feathers around their necks and upper arms.

In the midst of them was Fernando, bound by the hands and, like them, painted and wearing feathers. He was tied three yards or so from me at the foot of another pillar. Hardly had we exchanged more than a few words when a warrior came into the hut holding a great club. He was painted and feathered with the same labyrinthine designs, and he ran at Fernando again and again, seeming each time ready to club him upon the skull, but always pulling away at the last moment, while the rest of the warriors stood around the hut cheering him on. All this time Fernando bewailed his fate, crying out with fear, begging for his life to be put to an end, saying that there was no reason left for him to live and that he was the most miserable of men.

Then all but one of the men went away. He came towards me, leaving Fernando weeping on the other side of the hut. He spoke to me in bad Portuguese, saying that he was an Indian like the rest of them, but that he had been captured by settlers, and had spent several years as a young child with them. He had managed eventually to escape from what felt to him like imprisonment. He talked to me for some time, telling me that his people were saddened by the loss of one of their tribe – by this he meant the man that Fernando had killed on the road the previous day. It was the custom for vengeance to be exacted upon outsiders who had killed any members of the group, and that consequently they had captured Fernando and me in order to carry out their duty to the warrior who had lost his life. Execution was planned, when the time was right!

'Why', I asked, 'do you wish to kill me? I did not kill your countryman. It was he,' said I, pointing at Fernando, who by now appeared to have lost his reason, the violence of his uncontrollable weeping seeming to have taken him over.

'Indeed,' he replied. 'But you are his woman, and you must stay with him.'

'But I am not to be executed?' I asked.

'This we cannot say. It is not for me to decide.'

Then he began to speak more about himself and his people, explaining how they only wished for peace, and that they had retreated far into the forest away from the settlers in order to be left alone and to live their lives according to their own ways.

As he spoke I began to picture myself amongst these

people, living among them as one of them, and wondered whether it would be possible for me to change my life so greatly. Aweiri (for that was the name of the warrior who spoke to me) was squatting upon the floor, close to me, and even in these strange and frightening circumstances, my curiosity about the more tender passions – the physical bonds that bring man and woman closer to each other – exercised my mind.

Aweiri was of medium height and well-made, with powerful shoulders and arm muscles. His hair upon his head was black and glossy, as straight as the hair in a horse's tail. Elsewhere his skin was as smooth and fine as any woman's. Over his torso he had smeared rough squares of red paste, oily and with a slight odour of musk and pepper, and an oval of the same substance covered the area around his mouth. Then my gaze fell upon his male member, and once I began to stare at it, I could not bring myself to tear my eyes away, for it was so thick and heavy, so well-shaped, so naked with its surrounding growth of hair removed. His powerful thighs were smeared with lines of the same red oily paste. I wished to hold, to take the oil on to my hands and rub it into his member.

I asked Aweiri about his experiences in the land of the settlers. 'And did you ever take a woman from amongst the settlers? Did you ever go with a woman who was not from your tribe?'

He looked at me, long and hard, unsmiling, and held out his hand to my face, stroking it gently, touching my golden hair, dirty and uncombed as it was. I looked down at myself: my limbs were all scratched and bitten by insects. The light cotton undergarment that still covered my body was torn in so many places that my nakedness was clearly visible in places through it – my thighs were open to Aweiri's sight, and a tear in the cotton below my breasts showed the soft flesh about my navel. One cord that held the loose bodice upon my shoulder had broken, and I had tied it in a simple knot to stop this piece of clothing from falling off me. His face was closer to mine now, and I understood that

187

the natural womanly perfume of my body must have been extremely powerful, for I had spent two days without bathing. It seemed that our lust took light at the same moment: when his fingers pulled at the knot of the cord, letting one side of the bodice fall from my swelling white breast, revealing its proud pink end and its firm but heavy feminine magnificence, my hand strayed to his torso, and its hard oily strength was pleasing to me.

With my one free hand covered in the red paste, I let it touch lightly against his still slack member. At the first momentary contact, Aweiri's whole body flexed in passion and his member leapt like a struggling fish and filled my hand, thick and strong like a living thing, rigid and ready in a moment to possess me. In a trice my skirts and bodice were tumbled above my waist, and his hand, strong and hard, ran over my breasts, holding their tips between his finger and thumb, before grasping my thighs between each hand and forcing my legs apart. My hand upon his staff was wettened by his first emissions. Then Aweiri's hand was inside my womanly parts and the hardness of his thrusting fingers awakened them so that my body glowed with passions that now craved satisfaction.

But his strength and vigour were such that in just a moment his body was against mine, weighty, oily, hard, and the huge girth of his member pressed imperiously against the wet and melting lips of my womanhood. The excitement that I felt grew like a whirlwind, rising up in a moment instantly so strong as to be uncontrollable. I cried out again and again, and the narrowness of my opening was thrust apart, wider and wider as he bore into me, crying out too in his powerful ecstasy. For a few moments of supreme pleasure I was fuller than I had ever imagined I could be, then my inner chamber filled with pulse after pulse of his male juices. He throbbed rhythmically within me, then it became fainter, until we both lay quiet. But it was not, apparently, the custom for men like Aweiri to spend much time in love-games, for he then stood up and was away.

Fernando's redoubled rage made me turn my face in his direction, and he was furiously pulling at his cotton bonds, bellowing out insults in my direction, and threatening Aweiri and all the other inhabitants of the village with destruction by him and his friends from San Cristován. But, while some might have felt guilt at having betrayed a lover in his very presence, I knew that, in such a situation, we could only be concerned with preserving our own individual lives. Furthermore, I had already performed many services for Fernando, Count of Braganza, services which many a woman in my position might never have consented to give, which included watching him taking his pleasure with women whom I might have regarded as rivals.

I therefore contented myself with speaking back to him in a low and calm voice. 'Fernando, my dear friend, remember who you are. You are the Count of Braganza, Governor of the city of San Cristován, and, although your present position is far from what we should like, you must maintain your dignity. And, my dear Count, you must not malign me so, for I am only taking my pleasures where I find them to be most advantageous for me, as I have assisted *you* to do in the past!'

I lay back on the bare earth of the hut, and looked up at the leaf roof, dim in the evening light. I heard voices, the clucking of chickens, the sound of wooden utensils being beaten. The same old woman came into the hut carrying a pot of water and two gourds, and a pile of manioc cakes. I thanked her when she gave me them to eat and drink, but in his fury Fernando threw his portion back at her.

Twenty-One

Evening came, then night, and the people of the village gradually retreated into their own huts and fell asleep. Silence reigned, but in the jungle it was loud with the sounds of insects and night-haunting animals. Gradually I, too, lost consciousness and sank into the deeper darkness of sleep. Then I was awoken, still in the darkness of the night. The obscurity was almost impenetrable, but the red glow of a distant fire illuminated some shapes enough for me to distinguish what was around me, if with a little difficulty. Fernando was squatting beside me.

'Come, I have broken my bonds. To think that such a people thought to hold me back!'

I started, afraid of him. 'What will you do? Where will you go? Do not be foolish, you cannot escape from here!'

He pulled me roughly by the wrist. 'Come with me. Rather freedom in the jungle than captivity here.' Then he raved about how we should both flee and collect a force of settlers who would return and wreak vengeance upon the tribe.

I looked at his naked white body, and wondered how he should survive alone in the forest in such conditions. I ordered him to leave me, reminding him that we were in this terrible situation not only as a result of the scandalous behaviour that he had forced me to take part in (forgetting in my distress the pleasure I had shared through executing his commands), but also because of his brutal killing of one of these people's band. Ignoring my advice, he took my arm and began to pull at my cords, saying that he would carry me off bodily. I raised my voice in protest, threatening to scream and wake the whole village, thus making it impossible for him to escape and perhaps bringing down upon his head further punishments in addition to the ones in store for him.

In silence he ran out of the hut, with not a stitch of clothing, nor weapon, nor implement with which to ensure his survival. That, I believed at the time, was the last that I should hear or see of my ex-lover, the Count of Braganza, the man who in his time awakened in me more passions and joys than any man before him. But everything passes, everything is transitory. I lay in the darkness and looked forward to the new day with as few regrets as I could manage.

When it was discovered the following day that Fernando had escaped his bonds, there was fury on every side. But it was plain from that time onwards that no one now knew what they should do with me. At one moment I felt in danger of my life, so threatening was their behaviour, while at other times it seemed that I was being treated as one of the tribe, for several of the women approached me with kindness and spoke to me in their own language almost as a friend.

From that day on I was still tied by cords, but they gave me one or two yards' free movement, so that I could spend the day sitting outside in the fresh air, and at night could sleep under the roof of the hut. I was thus able to observe life around me. The food was varied and wholesome. I was fed on fruits, manioc cakes, water, and sometimes a little game meat or fish.

From the first it was the beauty of the people around me that attracted me and led me to stare at them with great attention. The women's smooth and slender bodies were of great interest, especially the younger ones with their small, tight, high breasts. They seemed to be quite unashamed of the nakedness of their secret parts, all of which appeared totally hairless, so that the lips of the little slit itself were there for all to look at.

Their appeal was made all the stronger by the decorations that they used – a little cotton thread around their loins, forest blooms in their hair, or necklaces of woven cotton and shell around their necks. And the paint they wore gave them a strange attraction in my eyes. The pigment glistened upon their bodies, applied in a multitude of different modes – criss-cross patterns over thigh and belly, labyrinthine designs that emphasised the form of the women's breasts and arms. Sometimes thick oily paste covered the whole body with a single colour – white, black or red.

As the days went by – I was tethered in the same place, with only short breaks for carrying out the necessary offices – my desires for these naked people grew, and I wondered what it might be like to be one of them, naked and unashamed. Little did I know what lay in store for me!

At night I hoped again and again that Aweiri would return to me, and that perhaps our relations should in future combine the intensity of passion that we had both felt with the lasting joys that I had delighted in so much in my previous lascivious adventures. But Aweiri never showed himself at all at night, merely contenting himself with acting as an occasional translator during the day. I later learned that he had been afraid to be seen going with me, on account of the uncertainty of my future fate.

The days passed in idleness and captivity. Now that the only thing to occupy my mind was the sight of so many bodies, I became obsessed with the physical pleasures, and at night I found that as soon as I closed my eyes and sleep came to me, my dreams would be filled with my past pleasures. Sophie's heavy full breasts were caressed by Fernando's soft hands, and his male member, rigid and straining, plunged in and out of her secret parts, while my first lover, the sailor who had forced me to touch my private places by guiding my fingers into the slit, took Leonie. She knelt above him, like a man above a woman, and her hands caressed his thighs, held his masculine staff in her hands, and caused it to grow and grow as his excitement rose to its peak, then it stretched her lips and opened her passage with a vigour that led her almost beyond endurance. She cried out again and again while lowering her body on to his.

'I cannot stand it, my love! How big you are and how narrow I am!' I awoke, and my hand was buried deep between my legs, the fingers were touching the little folds and swellings, finding the bud of passion, and as my desire rose, the sweet juices flooded my parts and I called out quietly in pleasure.

The following day two of the women who had previously showed me some friendship came to me. They indicated by means of words, signs and gestures that they were called Timba and Itui. They sat beside me on the dusty ground, and indicated that I was in a very dirty state, inviting me to accompany them to the river, where I understood correctly that it was the custom for women to wash.

Timba and Itui untied me from my bonds, and encouraged me to stand and exercise my limbs for a few minutes, while they collected necessaries from their sleeping huts. Then they took me by the hand, one on either side of me, each with a basket on the other arm, and led me away from the village circle. Down a path we went through low-lying bush, until we cleared a low rise and ahead a river stretched out, wide and dark. The prospect of bathing my body in the balmy stream made my heart leap with joy. Where the path ended at the river-bank there stood a small hut, which I later learned was exclusively for the use of the women.

Unlike the village buildings, this one had walls all round and a low opening, so that it was impossible for outsiders to see what was going on inside. As we walked towards it, my new-found friends talked to me in their own language, laughing and pulling at the remnants of my clothes with distaste. I understood them to be saying that I was to become one of them, and adopt their ways, that I should learn to act in their manner, and such like. Yet I still felt uneasy in the women's company, in their shameless nakedness. The hairlessness of their bodies was more overwhelming when I was in close proximity, for it made them seem still more unclothed, with the little slit of their private parts perfectly visible to me, and I wondered at its neatness and smallness with the Mount of Venus as soft and smooth as a baby's flesh. I tried to imitate the way in which they spoke, using their words, while gesturing agreement. My incorrect speech caused them much amusement, but my intention seemed to be well taken.

Inside the hut the heat was reduced and spaces within the thatched roof let in a cooling breeze and a soft light. The two women told to me that I was now to abandon my ragged clothes. I must have looked a sorry sight, for my torn garment was terribly deteriorated, and my full breasts were bared every time I moved my body, with my belly open to any cooling winds that blew into the hut.

Nevertheless, at first I was reluctant to abandon these garments, which were my last links with civilisation, but Timba and Itui both sat me down on a pallet of wild cotton weave, and resumed talking, this time pulling at my clothes. I guessed they were still trying to show me how it would be better for me to be like them, for they stroked their own bodies, and took my hand, inviting me to feel and admire the smoothness and firmness of their naked flesh. As they invited me to touch, my womanly passions rose up more powerfully than ever and I began to wonder whether it might be possible even here to enjoy those mature and abandoned pleasures which had previously brought me such delight.

I looked at my two companions questioningly, asking myself whether these women might desire me. The feel of their flesh beneath my hand would have stirred the senses of anyone, I am sure. Timba was plump, not tall, while Itui was slimmer and of greater height, but both had skins of such silky softness as I had never enjoyed before. Now they were exploring my body in return, stroking my cheeks, my shoulders and thighs, and pulling the shift down off my body, admiring my breasts, comparing the rosy pinkness of my nipples with their own, and encouraging me to pull the petticoats down over my thighs, until I was soon as naked as they were.

As the dirty rags fell away and the whiteness of my body emerged to their gaze, I began to experience a thrill of liberation, an excitement which sent my pulse racing. Indeed, when I looked down at myself, I saw that I was now beginning to be covered in a rosy blush, starting at my face and travelling downwards over my breasts, my belly and inner thighs. My two new friends looked in wonderment at this phenomenon, and showed me by gestures that they found my nakedness beautiful. They encouraged me to lie down beside them so that they could satisfy their curiosity further. It was the little golden hairs that most excited their attention, for, as I have already told you, the bodies of men and women alike were totally lacking in any hair apart from that which grew on their heads. They looked at the golden fuzz that protected the little pink slit that still, my dear friend Balthazar, gives and receives much pleasure! Itui lay beside me, her legs pointing the way of my head, and in pure wonderment, with no apparent lustful intent, reached out to my secret place and began to stroke it. Then Timba, who was kneeling beside me at the other side, leaned over and investigated me in the same way.

My passions were now being aroused, but I did not yet know if my two companions wanted me to return it, so I contented myself with reaching out to Itui's private parts, and stroking her little mound again, as if admiring it. She showed no embarrassment at this and, indeed, seemed flattered that I should take so much interest in her body.

Now I should tell you that both of my companions were covered in the remains of much red and black paint. They indicated the pigments on their bodies and the dust that covered parts of their feet and ankles, and pointed to me. This, to my imperfect understanding, meant that they wished to go down to the river to bathe. They took from one of their baskets a mess of puréed herbs and roots, and, with their arms around my waist, they led me in the direction of the river. In response to their intimacy I had placed

196

one arm around the torso of each of my new friends, and was able to run my hand up and down their bodies, and feel the swell of their hard little conical breasts, noticing how those of Timba were a little fuller and more womanly than her friend's. Sometimes one or other of them would turn her face to me and smile brilliantly with perfect white teeth. I enjoyed the sensation of the sun and the warm gentle breeze caressing my naked body, and the thrill, already beginning to make my female parts melt in hopeful anticipation, of knowing that every part of my body was open to the gaze of a stranger – her gaze, her admiration and (who knows?) her secret desire.

Suddenly we were by a clear pool, cut off from the main stream by a semicircle of rocks, and I followed my companions into the warm water, delighting in the sensation of being with them in such an idyllic situation. They anointed my body with a mixture of herbs and roots, which sloughed away the engrained dirt from my skin, restoring its tone and freshness, and imbued it with a natural perfume. Here I abandoned myself to the pleasure of sharing their innocent nakedness, the feel of their small firm hands in my most secret places, and gradually I responded to them, lathering Itui's hair, rubbing the herbs into their skins and delighting in their unconscious sensuality.

Then we were back in the hut, the three of us close together on the cotton. They showed me how they maintained their bodies' smooth hairlessness, for they had tweezers cunningly constructed of slivers of wood bound together. Itui lay with her legs wide apart, whilst her friend explored her womanly parts fold by fold, pulling out every tiny new hair so as to maintain the smooth perfection.

I waited, my most secret places all excited now and only waiting for the touch of their hands in order for me to experience joys unfathomable. My feminine parts were producing honeyed essences in profusion, but I kept my legs well together, so as not to embarrass my companions, for I did not yet know the limits of their sensibility. Then they turned to me, and I lay, waiting to see what they wanted to do with me. Would they wish to open my legs wide and pluck out my golden hairs? I doubted whether I would be able to let them do this to me without the force of my desires overwhelming all restraint and modesty, even in their presence.

But we went no further in our play, and I was merely told to follow them, as they made to return to the village.

Twenty-Two

*'My dear friend Balthazar, I must tell you that my presence
was to have a most profound effect upon the life and customs
of this tribe. Rather than narrating this tale to you chrono-
logically, I propose to move forward a little. I was soon to
discover that the members of this tiny nation were not given
to excessive pleasures of the flesh. My experience with
Aweiri was the case that taught me this point, for despite the
beauty of so many bodies, and the constant display of everyone's sensual charms, the coupling of man with woman was
quick, furtive and carried out with none of the refinements,
variety and finesse that I have learned to seek.'*

'Madame, you speak truth. Such finesse! Such refinement!'
I said, bowing, and speaking from my very heart.

*'As people lived in communal huts, there was little oppor-
tunity for private meetings, and in most cases the sexual act
between man and woman was carried out in the most perfunctory manner, often after dark, in the bushes and forest
adjoining the village. But with my gifts and influence, Balthazar, much was to change!'*

When we returned to the huts I was walking beside the
women, as naked as them. Whereas I had been treated with
scant respect as a captive, I now was surrounded by a
crowd of curious people, who stood awed and amazed by
my bare skin, so white, and by my golden hair, which some
reached out to touch and feel. Also my body attracted
them, for my full-breasted narrow-waisted, long-legged figure was a complete contrast to those of the women of the
tribe.

199

Timba and Itui led me through the crowd, brushing away those who disturbed them by coming too close and leading me into one of the big open huts. Inside, in the semi-darkness, I was shown to a woven hammock with a reed mat below it, and was given to understand that these were to belong to me. As I looked around the building, I saw similar structures all around, hanging between the tree-trunk poles upon which the roof rested.

I followed their instructions, and lay in the net, and the two women shooed the other villagers away. Timba made much of me, kneeling beside me in the semi-darkness, touching my hair, and stroking me upon the breasts and belly, upon my legs and arms, tracing imaginary lines with the tip of her finger. Each time her touch strayed over a nipple, or upon the sensitive flesh at the top of my thighs, my nerves thrilled inwardly, and I felt my secret parts take fire and my juices flow.

Itui came back shortly with one gourd full of dark-blue paste in her right hand, and another of a red oily substance in her left. Then she untied from her cotton thread a handful of little stick-like objects. They crouched beside me, one on either side, and I was strongly conscious of the perfume that they carried upon their bodies: sharp and sweet, with a hint of wood smoke, and some other smells that I could not yet identify. Then I saw that the sticks were brushes, with animal bristles attached to the ends with a sort of gum. Two sets of hands pulled me out of the net, and I lay upon the ground while they commenced drawing labyrinthine blue patterns that meandered over my body. The little bristles under their touch teased my senses, the line spiralling over my breasts and circumambulating the rosy tips that waited rigid and excited, longing for the pressure of Itui's fingers, for the suction of her mouth, and for me to writhe and cry out in the pleasure of it.

Slowly the line travelled over my belly, on to my naked thighs. My body was turned by their gentle arms until I lay upon my front, and my buttocks, my lower spine, the backs of my legs, were open to the touch of my two friends as they readied me to be one of their band.

Then I was turned round once more. My legs were opened wide, revealing my golden bush in its entirety to them, and they looked at it with renewed fascination, staring and talking much between themselves. I lifted my head and looked at myself. My womanly organ was aroused and ready for passionate congress. The delicate flesh that was usually hidden from sight by the lips was now erect and reddened with lust, so that it stood upright like the crest of a rooster, pressing through the delicate fuzz of my pubes. Passion had caused my honeyed juices to ooze out, so that much of the flesh around my golden hairs was sticky with odoriferous nectar.

The surprise and unashamed delight of Timba and Itui at what they saw made my senses sharper still, so that I waited throbbing with desire and lust, for the slightest pressure upon those parts would have been enough for me to reach instant joy. But it was not to be. Laughing and joking at my condition, they completed their task of fitting me to enter the group decked out in the way that pleased them. Taking the second gourd in her hands, Itui poured the red oil on to her hands, and rubbed some of it on to my pubes, emphasising their colour, in this way drawing everyone's eyes to my most private parts and their state of excitation.

There was another small hut in the circle, apart from the one that had been my home for the previous days. Now Timba and Itui led me to it. Inside it was dark again, and cool, although now that I wore no clothes the heat of the day was less troublesome than it had been before. The whole of the building was plaited together with such care and ingenuity that it seemed as though I was inside a giant basket, cunningly woven. The light came in through the roof, and, as a result, once we were in the hut we felt utterly cut off from the world outside.

Lying in a net was a man of commanding presence. I learned his name was Ruweiri, and from the two women's gestures and explanations I understood he was the chief man of the village, and that they were his wives. He was the tallest man I had seen so far in the tribe, and his body was strong. Now he was reclining, his body relaxed, but there was a lithe power in his bodily form that told me of his strength. Like so many of his companions here, his body was covered with rough designs in coloured oils, and the sweet musky perfume of the oils permeated the hut.

He gestured to me to sit near him, upon a carved piece of wood that served as a seat, raising me only a very short way above the ground. Itui sat near. She seemed to be telling Ruweiri about me and her experience with me that day. Then Timba returned carrying food laid out upon a big leaf. There was roast whole fish, fruits and manioc cakes, and gourds of a fermented white drink that was sharp and intoxicating to the taste. The four of us sat in a circle upon the floor, eating busily in silence.

The slight intoxication that the drink caused me was pleasant, but it only served to rekindle the desire that I felt in my belly, loins and thighs, while the points of my painted breasts swelled and hardened from the excitement that came from within me.

I saw that, as we drank, Ruweiri's gaze was often upon my body, and he seemed to be admiring my painted and adorned naked white flesh. I could not prevent myself from reciprocating, with long stares at his fine well-muscled body, the power of his loins, and the weight and girth of the male staff that lay between his thighs, fully exposed to my curious stares and ready, as I hoped, to grow and stiffen. As he drank he placed his arms around each of his two official wives, and he stroked their fine skins with sensual pleasure, touching their buttocks and breasts, appearing to be talking about me and comparing our respective good and bad points. Then, at a word, the two women stood up and left.

We were alone, and he touched the ground near him, indicating where I should sit. The musky perfume that the oil upon his body produced was in my nostrils as he took up a bowl of the drink, and, sipping a little, offered it to me, watching my lips as I sucked at the liquid. I luxuriated in the sight of the lubricated smooth power of his body, so close now, and I took his hand and guided it to the tips of my breasts, indicating to him to take my body and explore, excite and give pleasure.

My insides were on fire and my breathing was heavy. My heart raced, my skin perspired. Two bodies touched, and the coloured oils and paints made them slide together. The hardness of his staff was in my hand, and its lubricious upstanding shamelessness tempted me to let Ruweiri have his way and enter me, quickly, finally. But I wanted to teach him how to extend and deepen his pleasure. I held his member tight at the base, so that I could hold back his peak of pleasure for later, and raised him to higher and higher crests of joy by pressing and rubbing the swollen tip, by licking and sucking it, by holding it against my own body. I took his fingers in my hand and guided them to my own womanly organs, now once again swollen, wide open, crested with desire, and showed him the lumps and buds where touch most aroused my senses. The honey that I was oozing so copiously mixed with the oils which were upon his hand, and the paint that had been smeared so liberally over my pubes. Now I felt myself reaching my highest state of satisfaction. I lay back, opened myself to him, and felt his staff open me, wider and wider as it pressed in, slow and steady, filling me with passion as I cried out again and again. More and more abandoned became my joy, and groan followed groan from Ruweiri as we together approached the final heights of passion. Then within me his staff swelled for the final time, and burst after burst of his male liquids brought on the final spasms of pleasure, and we lay together quietly.

We were still together upon the mats when Itui returned to the hut. She seemed pleased to see us entwined together, and laid herself down in a hammock, looking at us, and talking quite unselfconsciously with Ruweiri. I had no doubt that they were talking about me, discussing my charms and delights. But now the evening was darkening, and the village was settling down to sleep. Ruweiri climbed into Itui's hammock, then Timba entered the hut soon after and took another, leaving me alone in a third.

During the course of that night Timba came to me. Her body lay on mine and it was warm and smooth. Later, when I spoke their language better, I came to understand that Aweiri had told Ruweiri that he had had relations with me, and that the manner in which I had responded to him had been unlike that of any woman from the village. He had been excited by my movements, the way in which I had touched him, by the natural perfume of my body, by the golden hair that had ornamented my pubes, and the hair that grew under my arms. Ruweiri had forbidden Aweiri to approach me again, and had ordered his wives to dress me as one of them, and let him alone discover what powers I had. And I had pleased him beyond anything he could possibly have imagined! Timba lay upon me, and the heat of her skin was upon mine, and her hot breath was upon my ear. She spoke many words whose meaning I did not know, although I guessed correctly.

'You have pleased Ruweiri more than I can please him. You have stolen his heart. Teach me how to please him in the same way, and you will have a friend who will remember you for your entire life!'

That night I initiated Timba into the delights of sophisticated relations of the most tender kind.

Her body was not oiled or painted, and its dry silky perfection surprised and delighted me, my desire returning even after having been slaked so thoroughly by Ruweiri. My hands were on her breasts, so high, just under the fold between her arms and her torso, and I delighted at the feel of her nipples, raised and naturally swollen. As I held them, as erect as tiny masculine engines, Timba moved her body in a sinuous manner, and sighed slightly. My lips were upon the soft flesh under her chin and between her breasts, and my hands were upon her lower belly, upon the little mound that displayed the lips of her pubes so shamelessly. Her body became warmer, her breathing deeper and harsher, and with a sudden flood my hand was covered in the sticky pungent emissions that flowed from the depths of her little purse. With one hand I sought out within the firm slippery lips the source of her essence. With the other I guided her hands to the source of my delights, and the tips of her slender fingers ran through the still oiled mat of hair that guarded it. She understood that she was to imitate what I was doing to her, and she obeyed the imperative of my own thrusts and feelings within her.

My body was on fire, my passions were released as Timba's hands found out my zones of delight, and Timba was following in the wake of my pleasure. I was just on the brink of joy and of giving vent to my feelings with cries of unstoppable pleasure, when I looked up in the dim dawn light and saw the outline of Ruweiri's body, by the hammock, watching us! Sensing my movement, Timba turned her head and saw him, and at the same moment both our delicate womanly organs reached their peak of pleasure, and we called out again and again in joy. We had commenced a new era!

Twenty-Three

Thus began a period of my life that lasted many years, but I know not how many. Living in such an unchanging tropical climate, where the weather every day was like the one before or after, there was no way of measuring time accurately. But during this era I lived as the female chief, co-ruler with Ruweiri.

My gifts in the tender emotions and the lustful passions were my saving graces once again. I became for the villagers a veritable Goddess of Love. I was the white-skinned stranger who had brought the arts of passion to these people who had always felt the stirrings of desire strongly, but who had, until I came into their lives, always restricted the expression of these urges to a few very quick and simple actions.

After that first day the whole village was in a ferment, for word spread rapidly, and all wanted to share in the new practices. There was no privacy. The following morning set the pattern for some time. Ruweiri, Itui, Timba and I were together in the perfumed dimness of the chief's hut, replete after a night of unrestrained love. I lay in the hammock, and Ruweiri reclined on the ground beside me, eating a repast that had been prepared by the two other women. I had been briefly to the river with my female companions, and was freshly perfumed and cleaned.

Once Ruweiri had finished eating, the two women came and sat close to me. I was on the opposite side of the hammock to Ruweiri, who reached out and commenced rocking it to and fro, holding on to my shoulder, while Itui on the other side pressed against me in order to return my swinging body in the other direction. Above the background sounds of children's voices, chickens and the occasional shout of the men, or the higher-pitched voices of the women, there was a faint creak as the hammock moved to and fro on its mounting. Then, while Itui held me by one hand, my thighs and hips were subjected once again to Ruweiri's passionate touch.

Behind him, Timba caressed his torso, causing his staff to stiffen and grow, so that I could not tear my eyes from it, imagining the delights that lay in store for me. Then Itui and Ruweiri turned my body until my legs pointed in the direction of the chief's hungry eyes. Her hands were upon my full breasts, and Ruweiri watched with delight as her fingers took my rosy nipples between them, as I had done to hers the night before. My body thrilled as the points hardened and grew under her touch. In the mean time Ruweiri's hands were upon my knees. He pushed them apart as far as they would go, and gazed hungrily at the golden hairs that decorated my womanly parts. He stared at the pink lips that were, even as he watched, beginning to stir and swell under a tide of passion. I felt the juices flow inside me, I felt the tender hidden flesh swell, I felt my body loosen and invite his entrance.

Timba had poured red oily paste upon his staff, the better to lubricate it, and she held it in her hand much as I had held Ruweiri's the night before (so quickly do men and women learn). I was tempted to lean over and take the domed end in my mouth, sucking the juices, tasting his masculine perfume mixed with the musk of the paste. But I knew that they all wished me to remain passively awaiting their pleasure, so I lay still and luxuriated in each gesture and touch upon my skin.

Now he pulled my body further forward, so that my nether parts were pointing straight out, away from the fabric of the hammock. Itui took my ankles in her hands, and lifted them, pulling them back, revealing the whole of my private parts, while Ruweiri caressed them, first with the flat of his hand, then with the ends of his fingers, causing the lips to draw back. Then, plunging deep within, he explored with his index finger the slippery, sensitive interior, and I felt the honeyed essence of my womanhood pouring out of me, covering his hand, his fingers and my own soft flesh with its stickiness. Timba had raised his manhood's sensibility to its greatest extent, and I contented myself with stroking its odoriferous lubricity a few times before I lay back and let Itui gently rock the hammock forwards so that, as Ruweiri knelt and Timba aimed the staff at me, his manhood filled me to the deepest chink, without either him or me moving a muscle. But before my passion boiled over in time with his, a casual glance in the direction of the door showed me that many people were peering into the hut. The surprise caused me to lose my excitement, but Ruweiri's passion continued unabated, and his staff plunged in and out of me, to and fro, in and out, as Itui rocked the hammock, both women sharing in the pleasure of watching their own husband's sexual pleasure.

This is how I became the village's Goddess of Love, for through my guidance this tribe became adepts in the art of passion. There, far from the reach of the settlers, a civilisation dedicated to the joys of the flesh grew up, and I was its chief votary, its principal leader. Itui and Timba told their friends and family what they had learned from me. Many people had seen through the door of the hut what the four of us had done together. Now everyone wanted to become like us, and I was the woman who could lead them.

They built me a hut, situated on its own near the village. It was of a different design from the others, for it was made to my requirements. Beautifully woven, in the villagers' traditional manner, the construction was round, with a reed floor and a raised circular couch in the centre. Everyone in the village, like all Indians in Brazil, were in the habit of sleeping in hammocks. But I judged that it was not a fit structure for the arts of love, and that I would have to use a couch in order to draw out the greatest pleasures from my future encounters.

The couch was covered in piles of cut grass bound tight

to create a firm but comfortable surface upon which I could lie with my consorts, and over it all a mat was thrown, constructed of a variety of dyed reeds, thus creating a beautiful and rustic effect. The entrance, unlike that of the others in the village, was capable of being shut from prying eyes by a loosely woven screen that let air and light filter in, creating during the day a dim, soft light that was perfect for the practice of the arts of love.

It became the custom for those young men who wished to learn the passionate arts from a true mistress to come to me. Sometimes they would come in pairs. They would stand together, awkwardly waiting for me to take the lead, their bodies golden in the dim light, slender, soft-skinned, well-muscled. They were, like young men anywhere, hungry for adventures with women, but they were sometimes shy, too. I remember one time in particular, when two stood humbly in front of me. I could see clearly that one was naturally more modest than the other. Even in this situation, the shy one stood with his hands clasped in front of his masculine organ, unwilling to let my gaze settle upon it, whilst the other was quite unabashed at my survey of his body, and even stood with his legs splayed apart, as though to make his member thrust out a little at my gaze.

I patted the couch and they came to sit beside me, one on each side. The bold one put his hand upon my leg, so that his fingers brushed the inside of my thigh, and I felt the stirrings of desire within me, desire for both of them.

'Do you like the way I look?' I asked the bold one. 'And my skin, does it please you?'

He nodded at me. His hands were now upon my shoulder and back, feeling me hungrily.

'Why do you not touch me upon my breasts?' I said. 'A woman always likes to have her breasts touched. But at first gently, just brush the tips of your fingers over the pink,' I continued, taking his hand and guiding it. By now my desire had grown, and I stroked his soft flesh – as soft as a woman's body, it seemed to me. As my hand wandered over his narrow slender torso, I saw his male member stir and thicken, rising somewhat from where it lay upon his thighs. I turned to his companion.

'See how his manhood has come to life!' I said, pointing, then I held the shy one's wrist in my hand, moving it away from where it covered up his own member. In repose it seemed bigger than that of his companion, and I brushed it with the back of my hand, while his bold friend was still exploring my womanly globes with his hands, following my instruction and treating them gently. The shy boy's member reacted with great rapidity, jumping up to a state of semi-excitation in a single movement, and I could not resist the temptation to hold it between my fingers, rejoicing in the sensation of its stiffness and width. Following my every whim, my other hand sought out that of his companion, and the sensation of holding one in each hand brought me great pleasure.

'Now you can both kiss me upon the lips, then upon the skin under my chin, my throat, and upon the cherry tips of my breasts too, if you should wish.'

I lay back upon the hay-smelling bed. On either side of me the sinuous movements of the boys' bodies, lips, fingers, stirred my passions and excited my senses, and I felt myself nearing that stage when all restraint is thrown off and instincts alone lead our behaviour. The two boys' approach to me was dissimilar, for the bold one took me with vigour, pulling and pushing, pinching and even hurting, whilst the other, shy one was much more gentle, his touch coming closer to what my own instincts demanded from a lover.

I ordered the bold boy to bring to the bed a small pot that stood nearby. It was filled with clear perfumed oil that I often used whilst in a passionate embrace. As he walked to where the pot stood, he seemed to take pride in his erect manhood, which stood up straight and swollen, bouncing as he walked, ready at the right moment to enter me with passion.

Now, following my commands, I lay upon the circular couch in the balmy half-light, the shy boy kneeling behind

211

my head, whilst the bold one was in front of me, between my knees, staring with passion at the pink lips and golden hairs of my fringed purse. Following my commands, the two boys commenced massaging the oil into my skin. Their hands were all over me – upon my breasts, over my belly, and, especially, within the compass of my two thighs. The golden halo around my pubes was soaked in the musky liquid, as the bold boy's fingers worked the oil into the lips of my womanly parts. Encouraged and guided by me, he entered into the very interior of my most private crevice, so that the flesh stood out, crested. At my urging, he came to me, and with his mouth performed those offices upon me that his masculine organ would normally have performed. He followed my commands.

'Now run your tongue very gently above the entrance, in the deepest part of the valley. But when you feel a hard lump you must stop. Do not press it hard; lick it gently and very slowly ...' He obeyed and my body flexed with the first uncontrollable impulse. Then I held his erect organ in my hand, and pulled it towards me, holding it tight at the base so that it should not discharge its duty prematurely, and I called out repeatedly with ecstasy.

When it was the turn of the shy boy, we were more tender. He laid his body upon mine and entered me again and again until I was exhausted, but still he came at me, with a gentle strength that always succeeded in stirring me up.

212

Twenty-Four

The years I spent amongst the villagers were very happy despite the monotony into which my life fell. Here, although I was a queen and had all that I could possibly desire, I lacked variety. Soon after I was accepted as one of the tribe, I proposed that I should go escorted by a group of villagers back to San Cristován, there leaving them, and returning to my old life. But I was told in no uncertain terms that I was free to do whatever I wished, provided that I did not leave the village.

Nevertheless, it was a great pleasure to see how the whole of their little society had become, like me, addicted to the arts of love. People began to cover themselves suggestively, for now it was understood that total nakedness practised each and every day was less enticing than raiment that both revealed and hid from sight. It was also appreciated, following my example, that the surprise of finding unexpectedly bushy hairs upon the pubes, or a small tuft, or total bareness, was superior to uniformity of custom.

A sort of fabric was manufactured out of beaten bark, and it was used to construct a variety of short kilts which some of the women wore, finding that it increased their allure. For myself, I too took pleasure in attiring myself in a garment of this sort, and hiding my most private charms from the curious gaze of others. In addition to the short kilt, I strung coloured stones, shells and feathers on twine in order to fashion a necklace to adorn the upper part of my body and draw attention to my magnificent, full, upstanding breasts. My skin was now exposed to the sunlight, in a way that it never had been previously, and it became smoother, fed as it was by frequent applications of the many oils and vegetable pastes which were in frequent use in the village. Soon it turned a golden colour that set off my blue eyes and blonde hair to perfection.

I encouraged the construction of a type of hut that would allow some privacy, for the barrack-like living spaces that the tribe were used to were no incentive to the exploration of the passions.

However, pleasant though my sojourn in the jungles of Brazil was, as with all the other episodes of my life, it was not fated to last. I shall now recount to you, my dear friend Balthazar, how it was that my village of love became for ever lost to me and how I returned to this bustling London of ours.

I well remember the day before the great disaster hit us. It was a feast day, held to celebrate the harvest of the palm fruit. The men had been in the forest for many days fishing and hunting to ensure that there was plenty of meat for everyone. In addition, an intoxicating manioc cordial had been fermented; as much as anyone could drink.

The fire in the centre of the village burnt high, I sat in the place of honour, upon a low seat carved out of a single piece of wood. On one side of me sat Ruweiri, while on the other were Itui and Timba. In front of us were leaves laid upon the ground as plates or tablecloths, and upon them stood the manioc drink in great gourd bowls. As I drank, the feeling of intoxication tingled in my body and I was ready to enjoy all sorts of physical pleasure. People of the village kept bringing us pieces of food to eat – the flesh of wild animals, whole fish grilled in the coals of the fire, crabs and fresh-water lobsters roasted dry in their shells. There were palm fruits in abundance, and roots and berries from the jungle. We ate and drank, and all around me in the semi-darkness I could see the bodies of the villagers, enjoying similar pleasures. As time went on, the music and dancing became more general. Men and women danced together, and their bodies touched insinuatingly, stirring up each other's passions. As desire grew, modesty was thrown aside. Women danced with women, and men with men. Ruweiri had drawn my body close to his. His two consorts were at my side, each holding on to me, caressing, arousing my sensibilities. Wishing to reciprocate their attentions, I placed my hand upon Ruweiri's organ, and its firm state of excitation told me that he was ready to take me. Together we walked out of the area that was illuminated by the glow from the fire, and sought a private corner near the huts.

I knelt down in front of Ruweiri, and took his stiffening member in my hands, and with light touches from my mouth raised it to a keener state of readiness. Itui was beside me, and she lent her fingers to my pleasant task, supplying a further source of passion. Between us we prepared him to enjoy the very peaks of pleasure with all three of us. He wanted to take me first, and his two wives held me in the way that I had been taken on the hammock all those years ago. They lifted me from the ground and with one wife on either side, holding my legs out wide, they swung me towards his body. He stood ready and waiting, his manly staff stretched out, plunging into me in time with the movements that the wives imparted to my frame.

I cried out in joy as our pleasure overflowed, then I knew it was the turn of the other two women, and Timba and I lifted Itui up in order to perform the same action with her. But it was not to be. There was a flurry of excitement from the area around the fire, and people ran to see what was happening. A stranger had entered our village circle. His features were much like those of the Indians who lived within our group, but he was dressed like one of the settlers, with a pair of ragged, tight-fitting breeches and a loose cotton shirt, badly soiled and torn, as though he had spent a long time in the bush, far from civilisation.

He did not speak the language that we used in the village, but conversed in Portuguese to me. He was the guide and tracker for a Catholic priest, a very devout man, once a gentleman who had in the past been rich, worldly and powerful. But he had several years previously repented of his ways, and had resolved to devote the rest of his life to poverty and missionary work, visiting Indian villages and converting as many people as possible to the True Faith.

He had spent many months travelling about the forests and jungles in the interior of Brazil, and he had used João (for that was the name of his Indian servant) as a guide, in order to help him to find villages and prepare the inhabitants for his visit, before commencing to preach and convert them to the Faith. This news filled me with contradictory and confused feelings. On the one hand, I was overjoyed at the chance of meeting someone from my own people after such a long time in the jungle. I looked around the dim edges of the campfire circle, at the trees and bushes, and the rough leafy huts, and imagined myself in a civilised place, wearing fine clothes and mixing with my own kind. I thought of my underdress – still wrapped up and kept safe from ants hanging from a beam in my hut, unworn for many years, but ragged and torn nevertheless – the last object I possessed that linked me with civilisation. But on the other hand I was full of apprehension, afraid for what this visit would bring, for I knew that meetings between settlers and Indians rarely made for happy outcomes.

The following morning João left, saying that he was to go back to his master, but that he would return to the village, bringing the priest to us as soon as he could lead him here from where he was presently camped. One day passed, then another. I was lying that afternoon with Itui near the river-bank, having bathed with her, rubbing oils into her skin while she did the same for me. I was caressing her breasts, touching the baby-smooth flesh of the bare mound of her pubes, which she insisted on maintaining in the old-fashioned bare style. I was luxuriating in the sensations that the touch of her fingers upon my own womanly parts was arousing in me. Then I noticed that she was shivering, and the touch of her skin was hot with fever. She could scarcely walk back to the village, and I had to support her with my arm.

When I returned, I found Ruweiri and Timba, like Itui,

sick and shivering. Indeed, almost everyone in the village was similarly affected.

The Indians had lived lives that had been so isolated from the common run of humanity, with its myriad sicknesses and fevers, that many had no strength to resist even relatively minor ailments brought from the settlers. It seemed to me that João must have carried with him some illness from the civilised world. He had not seemed affected himself but perhaps, over a period of time living with the settlers, he had acquired the strength to resist the distemper and had simply carried it to the village, like a burr, upon his person.

As the day wore on, the village became quiet. I seemed to be the only one who was not ill. Suddenly I heard a strange sound coming from the forest path that led into the village. It was a plainsong chant, such as might be sung by the monks in the great cathedral at San Cristován. I ran into my hut, and took down my old undergarment, putting it over my naked body. Before the priest appeared out of the undergrowth, the great cross that he carried loomed up above the bush like a beacon. Then he was standing in the centre of the circle of village huts. Beside him stood João. Tall and imposing, with a naturally commanding and imperious expression upon his face, the priest had brought illness before him, and now he was singing a devotional song of his faith, concerning Divine love!

'It may occur only once or twice in a lifetime,' said Miss Chaunce to me philosophically, 'that a meeting occurs which is overwhelming in its strangeness. I believe you will agree with me,' she went on, 'that this meeting was of this type!'

I bowed to Miss Chaunce, and begged her to continue, taking the opportunity of sharpening my quill pen.

With a moment's shock I saw who it was I was looking at. Fernando, Count of Braganza – he had become a priest, and was now standing before me, singing a devotional song! Older, his beard grown, his hair long and matted,

217

thinner and with his aspect changed – no doubt as a result of his austere life – it was him.

When he saw me he ceased his singing.

'So, Teresa Chaunce,' he cried out, 'God has led me to you after years of searching. When I was alone in the forest, naked and afraid, I came to see that my sins had brought me to this pass. I vowed that if ever I should survive the wilderness, I would devote my life to the Faith, as a priest, and in addition, I should travel through Indian villages, preaching and converting, until I found you again. I cannot say how long I wandered through the forests, naked and starving, but eventually I was found by itinerant gold prospectors, who fed and clothed me and returned me to my people.'

At this he fell upon his knees, and gave thanks to God for his good fortune. But the following days were terrible times, for the illness that he had brought with him took many lives, and left the few survivors weakened and broken. It was with sadness that I left my companions, but there was little more I could do for them, and Fernando and João were the only people who could return me to civilisation.

'Of the journey back to San Cristován, my dear friend Balthazar, and the events that led to my being placed upon a boat bound for Lisbon, with enough money to purchase a London-bound passage and more, I shall say little. Suffice it to say that my benefactor had felt such guilt for the way in which he had used me in the past, and was so eager to expunge the weight that the burden had placed upon his soul, that he used the influence of his powerful family in order to perform this service for me. For myself, I felt no regrets for the time I spent with him, but was happy to receive the fruits of my ex-lover's spiritual discomfort.

'But before we finish today's tales, Balthazar, I wish to recount the one time, before my departure, that Fernando succumbed to temptation and allowed the passions that had so dominated his earlier self to come to the fore once more.'

* * *

The journey back to San Cristován took us much longer than the Indians had taken from Fernando's residence, for we were unfamiliar with the routes, and several days were spent on the road. It was the evening before our return to San Cristován when we were staying the night in a settlers' village. The wooden house that we stayed in consisted of two rooms. I was in one, Fernando in the other, while João our guide and servant stayed upon the veranda.

I lay upon a simple wood and string bed, my eyelids drooping in slumber, when there came from the room next to mine the sound of wailing, punctuated by noises as of a whip or strap being wielded. There were moments of silence, then the wailing started up again, full of plaint. I recognised Fernando's voice, much changed though it was, and stood up to go to his door and knock. Then I stopped by the wall that divided his room from mine, my attention having been arrested by a knot of wood that had fallen out of the partition, allowing me to look through to the adjoining bedchamber.

There was a single candle burning in his room, and he was kneeling in the middle of the floor, staring up at a small reliquary that he had hung upon the wall. His habit was stripped off his shoulders and torso, so that his skin shone white in the dim light. Between his hands he held a heavy thick leather thong, which he switched repeatedly in the direction of his right shoulder with a single swift motion; each time the heavy leather fell upon his back with a loud slap. Then his body would shudder convulsively, and the sweat stand out upon his skin, as though he were suffering from extreme pain. Then he cried out, 'Oh Lord, forgive me my sins! Lead me away from the temptations of the flesh.'

At that moment I knew that my former lover had not totally forgotten the feelings he had shared with me in our previous life together. He was now forced to castigate himself in the hope that his hidden lusts would disappear.

I turned away from the knot-hole, ready to return to my bed, but I tripped in turning, and fell noisily against the wall. There was a moment's silence from Fernando's room, then his voice called out to me. 'Teresa? I am in agonies of remorse. I have wronged you. And though I repent, I need your forgiveness. Come to me and absolve me.' His voice was low and anxious.

'Of course, Fernando,' I called back, using his first name, as a woman would to a man who is close to her.

Inside the room it smelt of his sweat, and his face was drawn and pallid with the pain of what he had done to himself. His body was like the one I had known so intimately before, if thinner and harder. I imagined him taking me there and then, and I found to my surprise that my passionate feelings for him had not abated. I could feel the juices of my secret places flowing at the sight of his familiar torso.

He threw the whip across the room to me. 'Take this and beat the sin out of me, Teresa. Beat me until I am purified of the thoughts that I have about you.'

I could not resist asking him, 'But what thoughts could you possibly have about me, my dear Fernando?' He replied without leaving anything to my imagination.

'I think always of your skin, the silky feel of your skin against my body, I think of your breasts, of your womanly parts, the passion that I felt when my manly staff penetrated them!' He gestured at the leather thong lying before me. 'Take it!' he said.

He reached up to the low ceiling, and clung on to a beam, so as to stretch his body, still clad only from the waist down, and the muscles and sinews stood out hard, the veins swollen. I commenced using the lash upon him, and at each blow he called aloud – whether in pain or pleasure, it was hard to tell – commanding me to beat him harder. As he winced at each blow, the habit fell down his body until it dropped away completely, revealing his nakedness and his male member already partially engorged with passion, and he called on me to lash him harder. This I did, and now my own passions were excited by the sight of his condition, which became more pronounced the more I struck his back, his buttocks or his loins.

My womanly parts were on fire, and after his staff had reached a state of full and lubricious excitement, I could not resist the temptation to throw modesty aside and grasp it, use it with abandon, pull Fernando to the ground, and, giving my skirts a toss, lower myself upon his rigid and tumescent body.

So commenced a night of passion as lascivious as any I had passed with him before. But this time his sensuality was suffused with guilt and shame, and after each passionate struggle, when his engorged staff discharged copiously and repeatedly, he demanded more castigation, more punishment. Yet each lashing was followed by more torrents of lust, and, still clad in my ancient, torn and soiled undergarments, my body was hard-used by the night's delirium.

Twenty-Five

I do not propose to tell you the tale of my return voyage across the Atlantic Ocean, nor of my brief sojourn in the city of Lisbon, awaiting a passage to my homeland. Suffice it to say that eventually I found myself upon the quayside in London, near the Ratcliffe Highway, alone in the world, possessing only my physical charms, my memories and experiences, and a purse containing a few gold pieces, a hoard which I wished to see grow rather than diminish.

As I walked through the streets of London I was struck, as all visitors are, by the wealth of the city: the many people apparelled in fine fabrics, with much gold braid, rings, fine stones, and such like; and the many imposing new stone buildings that rose up on either side of me, replacing the antiquated wooden constructions of yesteryear. But that day I also saw conformity all around me. There were still many of the Puritan persuasion to be seen in their dark and sober robes, although the style was not as prevalent as before. But even those who had adopted the gayer garb of our times were not truly joyful, it seemed to me. There was none of the natural grace that was always to be observed amongst the people in whose lands I had spent so many years. The sky was grey, and the cold east wind that blew up the Thames made me shiver and wonder at the sadness of life in such a country. I asked myself how I was to find a way of living that would allow me to enjoy each day with the style and enjoyment I had become used to, even in the midst of the trackless forests.

I commenced my day by going to a shop that sold women's dresses, and outfitted myself with as much finery as it seemed reasonable to use. I was now in velvet and silk, with finely embroidered linen, and I believed that I would make a fine impression no matter where I went.

It was not long after this that I found myself sitting in a tavern and, in order to increase my strength, I was partaking of a repast of roast fowl and claret wine laced with spices and sugar. Whilst I ate and drank I passed the time by observing the society around me in the hope of finding some route to my future. As I was watching the antics of a group of young blades, dressed in much finery and continually blaspheming against all that is worthy, I was approached by two men dressed in much the same way, but apparently more respectable in their demeanour.

'We have not observed you before frequenting this establishment,' one of them said to me, opening the conversation in a dull manner.

'No, nor likely to have done,' I replied, 'for I have been on a voyage to the Americas, and have but recently disembarked.'

I saw them exchange a glance, as though they had read a secret meaning in my words. How simple I was, to have risked falling into their company. But when we embark upon a new adventure, the chances that we take are very great, and it is only by our errors that we learn how to protect our interests. Soon, after more cordials, gallantry and proposing of toasts, it was suggested that we should pass some hours in chambers of theirs that lay nearby. This was soon accomplished, and we proceeded through a gateway into a courtyard, and thence up some steep and dark stairs into a small and somewhat close chamber, chiefly furnished with a large four-poster bed, richly hung with velvet, but also with some stools and a side table. Bells were rung, and a serving wench entered, built up a fine log fire, then brought more wine and sugar with which to further increase the cheer between us.

They made much of me, complimenting me upon the fineness of my complexion, which, it was true, was better than that of most of the inhabitants of London, for the fine climate of Brazil, its warm airs and delightful breezes, had improved my flesh, and the light that had fallen upon my body had made it at that time a most attractive light golden colour, which many men found most appealing.

The young gallants were of similar ages, but William was dark-haired, brown-eyed and strongly built, while his friend James was quite the opposite – slender, fair-skinned and golden haired. William was bold.

'You will find, Miss Chaunce, that I take the lead in all things in my friendship with James. I am sure that the sight of your beauties, once bared, will excite his passions beyond all measure. You will not be ashamed, I believe, to display to us the hidden charms of your thighs, which, if at all equal to the grandeur of your bust and shoulders, will be a fine sight.'

I laughed at this gallantry, and found it excited my own senses to lift my dress, petticoat and undershift high up, so that the two young men could feast their eyes upon me, for I wore silk stockings and red silk garters fastened above my knees. Then I loosened the stays and laces about my bust so that my breasts became freed from constraints, and stood out freely, proud to be naked in front of such an appreciative audience. Then I spoke to them.

'But, my young gallants, why do you hold back? Why do not you divest yourselves of what encumbers you, so that I, too, can take my pleasure in your company?'

At this William laughed, and consented to remove his breeches, while his companion was less forward, taking off only his doublet and shoes. Then William was kneeling between my legs, my arms were round his body as he pressed his face between my breasts, and his hands sought the soft skin inside my thighs.

'Miss Chaunce, your beauty kills me! Let me take you before my friend can have either of us!'

I lifted the shirt off his body, and my hands felt his well-muscled front, where his staff was standing rigid, throbbing slightly, ready to enter me and stir up my passions. Then I saw that James had opened his breeches, and stood behind his friend, his member hard and upright, if smaller than that of William. Then we all three, in a state of growing rapture, moved to the bed where I lay, still largely clothed. William's tongue was inside my secret place, opening the lips, exciting and teasing the soft flesh while his friend held William's nether regions in his hands, stroking his friend's powerful thighs, touching him inside his crack, thrusting his hand under William's body in order to squeeze his friend's bulging organ and the twin stones at its base.

Then, in a frenzy of passion, William was upon me, thrusting his baton into me, rubbing and pushing with tireless abandon. He soon discharged his male liquids, hot and sticky, deep inside me, then we lay, his softening organ still within. After some minutes it began to stiffen, for James' hands were rekindling his friend's passions. He suddenly slid his member into William's nether hole, causing the member inside me to resume its full girth and return to the exquisite game of love.

Then it was the turn of James to enter me, then of William again. We spent the whole night long in our games, until all three of us fell asleep exhausted.

It was only after I left their chambers the following morning with the gold piece that they gave me in exchange for the night of shared love, that I came to count my bag of money, and found that, for the coin that the two young men had given me, they had taken five more.

I felt sad and lonely in the extreme as I walked through the streets of the City of London, looking in the shops of Cheapside, admiring the fine buildings, such as the new St Paul's Cathedral and the Mansion House. But I was not alone for long. Soon a finely dressed lady of about the middle years of her life accosted me. She was well-spoken, with an air of almost aristocratic distinction. She had observed me staring at the goods upon a mercer's stall in Cheapside, and embarked upon a casual discourse, enquiring my opinion of the goods on display.

She skilfully moved the conversation to more general

topics, such as the doings of fashionable society, the court gossip of the day and suchlike. She observed by my answers that I was not accustomed to the society of London, and I admitted to her that I was, indeed, a stranger in this great city, knowing scarcely anyone.

At that she began to make more of me, inviting me to partake of luncheon in her private chambers on the newly constructed outskirts of town. I was impressed by the size and modernity of the house to which she accompanied me, talking all the while about the influential people that she knew – who was up, who was down, and suchlike – not neglecting, of course, to inform me of her name: Phoebe Grey.

Her chambers were magnificently apparelled, with many rich hangings, much fine upholstered walnut furniture, a dining table big enough for eighteen, and heavy and ornate silver in abundance. She was greeted by two maids, young girls, well-dressed considering their station, with full lusty figures and dresses cut in such a way as to reveal much of the charms of their ample busts to the gaze of any interested party. They looked me over with bold curiosity that took me aback somewhat, and ushered me into a close small chamber, well-heated with a fire, containing a number of comfortable armchairs and tables. At a word from Phoebe the two maids retired, returning in a short while carrying much alcoholic refreshment, with which we enjoyed good cheer.

She asked me abut my life in Brazil, expressing astonishment at my tales concerning my life amongst the Indians, and was pressing with her questions concerning my relations with Fernando, with Ruweiri, and with any other men who I happened to mention.

Then the truth that I was beginning to suspect became apparent.

'Here', said Phoebe with passion, 'in this establishment, we entertain only gentlemen of the highest echelons of society, Teresa. I am sure you understand my meaning. I feel that we are friends already, do you not agree?' At this

227

she put an arm around me, and winked in the most suggestive manner. As for me, I thought for a few moments, considered how vulnerable it was to be a woman, alone and friendless in a strange city, and decided to accept her offer, for that is what I was beginning to understand it to be.

After I had spoken, she embraced me warmly, and expressed her pleasure and joy, talking of her 'other good woman friends', offering to introduce me to one of the best of these, a woman called Sophie Denver. As soon as I heard that name my mind went back to the act of betrayal that had started me upon my voyage of adventure. Almost without my knowing it I was in a state of anger and resentment, when all at once Phoebe rang a small bell, gave orders to the servant girl, and my old friend Sophie walked into her parlour!

But it was no longer the same Sophie, for the years had passed and she was not the innocent young girl that I had known. Yet her plumpness still retained some of its former attraction, and her face radiated a type of smouldering sensuality that I could understand would be appealing to many men in search of pleasure. But all I felt was fury and resentment. As soon as her eyes lit upon my face she remembered who I was, and expressed in her coarsened features both guilt and regret. Her repentance was so great that she threw herself upon my feet, begging my forgiveness, narrating her tale to me. She herself had very soon after my departure been unable to maintain her secret affairs without being discovered, and as a result had, like me, been expelled from her parents' house. She had been forced to find the means to survive as best she could, until she was invited to enter the establishment of Phoebe Grey, from which time she was content.

I am a naturally soft-hearted person, despite the many adventures and tribulations that I have been subjected to in my eventful life, and I was unable after such a peroration to refuse her plea for forgiveness. So we embraced, and swore never to betray each other again. I then narrated as much of my life's experiences as seemed fitting to tell that night.

But we were not to be left alone for long. Soon Phoebe was at our side, inviting us to accompany her to the dining chamber, for there was a company of blades asking for us. Once in the room, a most merry scene presented itself. There was a party of four men, all richly dressed, with the arrogant manners of those who enjoyed money and position. They were aged between thirty years and forty, I judged, and their behaviour indicated that they had been enjoying many potions of strong drink before coming to Miss Grey's establishment.

The two maids who had served me when I arrived at the house earlier in the day were with the party, not wholly as servants now, for both of them had allowed the party to remove her overdress. Their short-skirted petticoats afforded us an enticing view of their well-made legs, covered only in short stockings that were tied below the knee by garters. What is more, each when I entered the room was allowing the stays and laces around her ample bust to be loosened, revealing to the party's eager stares the heavy and full-tipped nakedness of her breasts. Once Sophie had entered, she, knowing what was expected of her, joined the others in this amorous horseplay, removing her overgarments, inviting the party to loosen her clothing in any way that they so desired.

I could not tear away my eyes from Sophie's naked breasts, for we had learned much about the arts of love from each other in our youth. Her bust was now ample, and, while full rounded and pendulous, had still retained much of the firmness that had been so delightful in her youth. But now that they had increased so much in girth and volume, the dark-red nipples had expanded to a striking size, bigger than two crown pieces each one, and were tipped with points as thick as my little finger.

The sight of her parts occasioned much laughter and ribald comment, and one of the gallants held her in one arm, while he held a seeming maid in the other. His lips explored first one breast and then another, all the while calling out to the rest of the party with comments and comparisons. I was not happy to enter into this abandoned scene, so I contented myself with sitting quietly in the dark of an alcove near the doorway through which I had first entered.

Soon the game became more abandoned still. One of the serving maids was kneeling upon the table, with her breasts bare and hanging free. Then one of the rakes took a glass of claret wine, and gently poured it upon the upper part of her chest, so that the drink ran over her breasts, dripping off each red-tipped nipple like a waterfall. At this, another of the group lay upon the table, under her bust, and, raising his mouth, drank the elixir as it dribbled off the woman's form.

Not to be outdone, the other maid lay upon the table, surrounded by the many glasses and laughing faces, and, raising her garments high above her pubes, let her stomach lie flat, the navel forming a little hollow. She invited one of the party to pour a quantity of wine into the plain of her belly so that she had only to raise her body slightly in relation to her lower parts for the drink to pour in a waterfall over her private parts. One of the gallants lay with his face between her thighs, drinking with gusto the liquids before they could spill on to the table.

At that, another of the party led her to a couch by the fire, and without throwing off any of his own clothes, but contenting himself with loosening the ties to his breeches, he handed her to one of his friends, who held her body in his arms and thrust it back and forth, impaling her on the first gallant's own staff, much to the delight of the rest of the company.

But there was one gallant who took little part in these revels, and upon reflection, I noticed that his stance and manners were more commanding than those of the others. I accordingly went to sit with him, and commenced conversation, while the rest of the company enjoyed further revels of the type that I have just described.

Twenty-Six

My new companion introduced himself to me as Nathan Roundhorn. I informed him of my name, and when he had heard it he laughed. It was a knowing and world-weary sound, a cynical one.

Teresa Chaunce,' he riposted, 'Teresa Chaunce, and what chance has brought this saint to me? By what ministrations of Heaven have I been sent such a companion?'

He spoke lightly, apparently in jest, yet appeared scornful of the conventions, as though he were continuing with normal social intercourse merely because it was expected of him, although his melancholia and lassitude no longer allowed him any true pleasure in life. He was a man of medium height, of dignified comportment, a quick eye and a fine manner of dressing, which created an impression of great distinction.

He commenced interrogating me about myself, asking again what fate had brought me to him, upon such an evening when he felt that, although he was still far from being an elderly man, his existence no longer brought him the joys that it once had. In reply I informed him that I had only the day before returned from many years upon the American continent, and that my life had passed through so many twists and turns that I was quite unable to imagine being a prey to the black humours that had taken a hold of his soul.

I asked him what manner of man he was, and how he had come to suffer from such depression of spirits.

'I was born in a most fortunate condition of life,' replied he, 'being blessed with a father who was both successful in

231

overseas trade and respected in his dealing which his fellows here in London. When I was rendered an orphan by the death of both of my parents I found that I had become the heir to a very considerable fortune, with little inclination to emulate my father's industrious bent. As many young men in my position have done before me, I thus devoted myself to a round of dissipation and pleasure. Luckily, my wealth is so great that the bills that I have run up in the course of my entertainments have made little or no impression upon the amounts of my capital. I could, if I so wished, continue to commit follies and extravagances for the rest of my life.'

'But', I interjected, 'you now feel a revulsion for the pleasures of the flesh, and have resolved to live a more continent life hereafter. You are planning, perhaps, to take upon yourself duties of public office in order to make recompense for your worldly good fortune, not to mention for your wasted years?' I spoke with some cynicism.

At this he laughed knowingly. 'My dear Teresa – you do not object to my taking the liberty of addressing you by your Christian name? – you underestimate me. I do not envisage taking such a course of action in the near future. No, my problem is of quite another sort. In a few short years I have experienced all the pleasures that money can buy in this great London of ours, not to mention the polite dissipations that country society offers to eligible bachelors such as myself. I refer, of course, to such lures as the hands of the ugly daughters of rich men, or the beautiful ones of poor men.'

I laughed at his worldly-wise philosophy. 'And where, Nathan Roundhorn, do you place me in your system? For I have no fortune, nor do I belong to society in this, my native land, although I have done so in other places, at other times.'

'I cannot say,' he replied, eyeing me keenly. 'But I shall perhaps be able to form an opinion as we become more intimate.'

There was a pause in our conversation, and we sat silent

232

for some minutes while watching the antics of the others in the party as they pawed and teased the serving maids. I noticed that the strong drink that Sophie had already consumed had caused a flush to suffuse her features, and that her ample charms were less appealing than those of the maid servants.

'But to have experienced many pleasures is not of itself a cause for melancholia. Many would envy you your good fortune,' I continued.

'You misunderstand me,' he replied. 'I am eager for further pleasures of the sensual variety, but I find that little excites my sensibilities as they once did. I have run through the gamut of delights that our London ladies – and, I must confess, gentlemen too – have to offer, and have found some to be agreeable, but I now demand something new. Until I find it, I shall remain continent.'

At this moment one of the gallants pulled Sophie towards him, and, having loosened the drawstrings of his breeches so that his staff stood out firm and swollen, he was encouraging her, with her full bust uncovered, to press his staff into the space between the breasts. She complied, and by dint of much rubbing and squeezing, he was experiencing the pleasures that normally are reserved for the channel of joy between a woman's thighs.

I returned my attention to my companion. I understood his predicament. 'As I told you, I have spent much time in exotic places and climes, and have learned things that I could not have acquired had I restricted my experience to London! The pleasures that you are familiar with in no way represent the limits of sensual refinements. I assure you that I have much experience in this field, which could bring rapture to your dissipation again.'

After I said this, he stared at me for some minutes, apparently intrigued. Then he stood up, without saying a word, and left the room.

The following morning I awoke in one of the sleeping chambers in Phoebe Grey's establishment. The evening's indulgences had been pursued until the coming of dawn.

Soon after, while I was still lying under the blankets, Phoebe herself entered the room and sat upon the bed, coming straight to the purpose of her visit.

'You passed some minutes in the company of Nathan Roundhorn at our revels last night,' she said seriously.

'I meant no harm,' I rejoined.

She leaned forward to me, and patted my hand. 'Of course, nothing to be ashamed of. Mr Roundhorn is a fine gentleman, if a little too worldly wise for a man of his years.' She patted my arm again. 'He has been much trouble to me in recent weeks, for he is dissatisfied with what I can provide for him. He has asked me to authorise you to spend whatever money will be required in order to provide pleasures in abundance. But he has warned that he will be displeased if revels put on under your direction do not produce the desired outcome.'

She nodded and winked, so as to leave me in no doubt as to what outcome she had in mind. I bowed, and promised that I knew how to bring about a satisfactory result, provided I were allowed both the time and the money that I needed.

This request was granted, and I proceeded with my task of that day.

Twenty-Seven

'You may have guessed, my dear friend, that my meeting with Nathan Roundhorn formed the genesis of the establishment in which you sit at the present moment; the establishment that has refined sensuality to the highest degree, creating pleasure of a variety never seen before.'

'Madame,' I responded, *'your tale has now reached a point at which it begins to turn back upon itself. I await the final episodes with anticipation!'*

'I am glad that you find my personal experiences of such interest, dear friend. I see that you have worn out many quills and consumed much ink in the course of my personal ramblings. But I am very tired, our narration having continued at great length today. Indeed, my exhaustion is so great that I must beg you not to expect any favours from me tonight, although tomorrow you may find much to delight you.'

The next morning she was at her usual place, awaiting my arrival, eager to launch into what was to be the final day's narration.

I understood what afflicted my new friend and future protector, Nathan Roundhorn. He had commenced his adventures in lust, being pricked onwards by the burden of shame and guilt that he had acquired with his upbringing. As a result of his shame, the adventures which he took part in during those early years acquired a special delight. Later, when his feelings had become more coarsened, that element of his joys no longer spurred him on, and the monotonous and unrefined nature of the sensual pleasures that were at that time available in London left him with little to maintain his senses at the pitch which ensures pleasures and joys in abundance.

I compared Nathan's experience with my own life, in which early guilts, fears and joys commingled, making what pleasures I snatched the more piquant for being illicit. Then I saw my fears and guilts fall away, and at the same time I entered an antipodean world in which sensuality was more developed than in this cold England of ours, and my loss of guilt and fear was accompanied by a deepening, not simply a broadening, of my sensual practices. As a consequence, I never experienced that tedium in my intimate relations which leads to dissatisfaction, loss of interest and, finally, to inaction.

I resolved, therefore, that I should strive to reawaken Nathan Roundhorn's dormant passions by staging a series of masques upon the theme of my life. While based upon the true account of my fortunes, adventures and mischances, my entertainment would fix upon those aspects of my sensual experiences which would most tickle the fancy of a jaded libertine.

The following days were spent in a flurry of activity, preparing the great chamber in Phoebe Grey's residence for the first masque. I required the services of carpenters, scene painters from the theatre, furniture merchants and dressmakers in order to produce the stage set I wanted. But the most important element in my masque would be the players, for in the first evening's entertainment I would make a sort of dumb show out of the early years of my experience as a lady destined to be skilled in the more intimate pleasures.

Accordingly I took to haunting the Docks of London, near, indeed, to where I had originally lived when I was in the home of Mr and Mrs Denver. There, as I became more familiar with the street life of the district – something I had been unable to do in my early years – I sought out the types of men and women that I required as actors in my masque. With the apparently limitless purse placed at my disposal, it proved not to be difficult to recruit to my forthcoming theatrical performance people willing and able to perform the roles that I had planned for the delight of Nathan Roundhorn.

Miss Grey's establishment was busy in the following days with the sound of hammering and sawing, and with deliveries of materials and effects. But the main labour was performed by me and my new-found fellow workers in the sensual arts as we practised together the masques that I had planned for the coming entertainments.

I do not wish to bore you, my dear friend Balthazar, with an account of the worries, the crises, the triumphs of planning and organisation that led up to the great day. Let us progress to that evening, as we near the end of our tale, my dear. I hope that you are not by now quite surfeited by my multiplicity of trivial anecdotes and memories which I have imposed upon you at such length over the past days.

I bowed respectfully to Miss Chaunce. 'Madame, your every word has been heard, appreciated, enjoyed, noted down by my trusty quill pen, and later transcribed for the benefit of posterity.'

Miss Chaunce laughed, and continued her narration.

Upon the appointed night Nathan Roundhorn arrived at our establishment alone, as had been agreed. Phoebe Grey absented herself from the proceedings, and it was I who opened the heavy oak front door. I was dressed for the occasion in a grey shapeless Puritan dress, of the type which was so familiar to me in my early days in London, and my hair was quite concealed in the linen cap which Puritan girls invariably wore upon their heads. I held in one hand a copy of *The Pilgrim's Progress*, bound in black leather. I started with surprise when I saw Mr Roundhorn standing in the doorway, accompanied only by his manservant, who carried a burning flambeau to light his way through the dark streets.

'Oh, Mr Roundhorn,' I said, raising my hand to my face in discomposure, 'you quite startled me. Once I begin

237

reading the words of John Bunyan,' and here I tapped my book affectionately, 'I quite lose any sense of where I am!'

Mr Roundhorn looked surprised at my words, for he had been expecting a quite different reception, but in a moment he seemed to understand the drift of our game, and fell into the fiction without demur. First I led him to a small dressing-room, where a suit of black clothes awaited him.

'Mr Roundhorn,' I said warmly, 'you are most welcome in our simple house, and I place you upon your honour not to take advantage of the hidden charms of me, your female companion. I am sure that you perceive me, not as a warm and passionate woman whose senses can be stirred up by the lightest caress, but as a chaste and pure friend. Please remove these garments,' I said, gesturing to his fine embroidered and laced suit, 'which are redolent only of pleasure, licentiousness, and sins of the flesh – pleasant though such vice may be – and put on this more sober set of clothes.'

At this, I left the dressing-room leaving him to change his clothing. When he came out he was quite transformed.

'It is so much better, is it not,' I said, 'that we should try through our dress not to draw attention to our physical charms?' I sighed deeply, pressed my hands against my bosom, rubbing them up and down in the space between each full and shapely breast, in so doing drawing attention to their volume and shapeliness.

The great chamber of the house had been partitioned with a screen, in which a window gave the appearance that one was in a small room. In this small space there was only a single candle burning in the darkness, but through the window in the other part of the room, it was well lit, with blazing chandeliers and candlesticks ranged all around.

I settled Nathan upon an easy chair beside the window, brought up a chair beside his, and looked surreptitiously at him as he stared through the window into the chamber. He was staring with keen expectant interest into a spare and simple room, with one pointed window in the Gothic style and furnished merely with church pews in oak. The whitewashed wall was decorated with an inscription containing the Ten Commandments, and, written in gold paint upon black, the Sixth Commandment, 'Thou shalt not commit Adultery' was picked out in large letters, so that it stood out amongst the rest. An altar table was placed at one side of the room. Upon it, surprisingly out of place, stood a vase of flowers, where white orchids and lilies were intermingled with daisies and daffodils. A powerful scent of incense mixed with musk and burning sulphur wafted out of this private space and into our antechamber, exciting our senses with contradictory hints of purity and corruption.

Nathan's face expressed strong but repressed emotions while he stared at all this, and his nostrils quivered as the scents set up notions and feelings yet more mixed, or so it seemed to me. He sat down and I, beside him, took up my volume of *Pilgrim's Progress*. Bringing the lamp near to the page, I began to talk to him again.

'Do not think, Mr Roundhorn, that devout ladies are unpricked by the desires that you have given such rein to in your riotous life. Indeed, it could be true to say that women such as I feel the physical passions with even more force. Suppressed feelings, once they spring forth out of confinement, have greater power than those which flow ever unchecked.' I stared into his eyes as I spoke, and rubbed my hands up and down my thighs, simultaneously drawing his gaze to my lower parts.

Then I commenced to read from the book, often while I read inclining my body towards his, and turning to him, staring in his eyes, touching and stroking my parts while I did so. I could tell by Nathan's eyes that he was not indifferent to my provoking behaviour. Then a church organ started to play, and a door opened on to the supposed chaste interior, and three young girls filed in, dressed as I was. They were about twenty years of age, buxom and fair, with rosy cheeks. Behind them came a manservant, of the African race, the same age as them, dressed in the Puritan manner all in black and carrying a pile of hymn books and Bibles in his arms.

Once at their places upon the pews, they took their hymn books from the manservant and, opening them, waited for the appropriate hymn music to strike up. They stood in a row facing our window, and sang as though their lives depended upon it, each expressing a sort of passion as they put all of their heart and soul into the task.

I whispered into Nathan's ear as he watched the show.

'You see, Mr Roundhorn, three innocent young people are pouring all of their youth into the worship of their Faith! You should feel proud and privileged to watch such pure and faultless pastimes!' At the same time I brushed my body against his, and took my dress between my hands and shook it. 'But Mr Roundhorn, do you not feel the excessive warmth of the air? It makes my senses feel quite unnaturally alive!'

Then I noticed Nathan start in surprise, and I turned my head to stare again through the window. The manservant had moved close to one of the singing girls – the one on the left, more buxom than the others, with big eyes that sparkled with passion. The proximity of his body to hers attracted her attention, and, still singing lustily, she turned somewhat to him, looking him in the eye, holding up the hymn book to him and encouraging him to join in the singing.

But it was clear that the male servant had amorous intentions, at least to the eyes of me and my companion, for he moved his body insinuatingly against hers, while she reddened with surprise, glanced in the direction of her two girl peers and ignored his provocation.

I moved my chair closer to Nathan's, and touched his knee, pressing my fingernails into his inner thigh. 'See what that lusty rogue does to his mistress, and in such a place, too! It is lucky for us, Nathan – you will allow me to address you with such familiarity, I trust – that his mistress is a girl of pure thoughts, and has little notion of what the boy has in his mind!' The girl was now smiling into the manservant's eyes quite unabashed. 'Yes, see how innocently she returns his bold stare!' I touched Nathan again upon his thigh, but closer to those parts where his masculine organs lay limp, waiting for my sensual gifts to make them spring into passionate and erect arousal.

I glanced in Nathan's direction. He was, as before, staring at the girl and her servant. The boy, in turn, had by now placed both hands shamelessly upon her full and sensuous body, cupping her breasts in each hand as if feeling their firm weight, exploring the swell of her hips, the slimness of her waist, the delicious curves of her thighs. The girl was by now clearly stirred in her sensual passions, for she had forgotten herself so much as to cease her hymn-singing momentarily, her features showing all the familiar signs of sensuous excitation. Her hands went to his, pulling at them to tear them off her body, but when he resisted she guided them to whatever place caused her the greatest degree of pleasure – between her legs or the inside of her thighs.

'Oh, Mr Roundhorn!' I whispered to my companion. 'I am ashamed at what I have brought you here to witness. Such shame upon our house!' By now the girl had pulled the laces of her garment open and guided the manservant's hands inside her clothing, and in a trice her breasts were bare, and revealed in their naked magnificence to our excited eyes.

'But really, such behaviour!' I went on to Nathan. 'I can scarcely believe that she can allow him to take such liberties! Yet looking at what they are doing together, openly to us (but of course, they believe that they are unseen), quite stirs my own feelings!' I placed my hand upon his breeches, and, to my great satisfaction, discovered that his male staff was beginning to show those signs of excitation that indicate that the sensual passions are beginning to take hold.

Now the two young people threw aside the normal constraints of decency, and in the midst of the hymn-singing the girl's skirts were thrown aside and the boy's hands were upon the golden bush that adorned the lower part of her belly.

Then the other two girls saw what was happening beside them, in the midst of their devout song. They held their hands up to their heads in horror and surprise, and made as if to pull their friend away from the clutches of the manservant. The girl was overcome with remorse at being discovered, and cried out to the manservant again and again that he should desist, that he should leave her purity alone, and suchlike. But by now, in truth his passions were risen to such a degree that he would brook no interference to their pleasures, and with many cries of disgust and anger the two chaste girls ran off to seek assistance.

Twenty-Eight

Now the manservant had pushed his lover forward until she was against the table upon which the orchids, lilies, daisies and daffodils were intermingled. His breeches were now loosened, so that his masculine member thrust outwards, hard and straining, towards its delightful goal. His body was lithe, golden in hue, finely muscled, and he tumbled the girl's skirts above her waist, so that all her most attractive and sensuous womanly parts were revealed in their full allure. Her fullness, his slenderness, the lightness of her fair complexion against the swarthy quality of his, the power and agility with which he lifted her, entered her, pulled her joyfully to and fro as both of them became overwhelmed with the irresistible force of the so-called tender passion – all these served to increase the piquancy of the scene to which Nathan and I were witnesses. I judged the time was right for me to advance further upon the game.

'So, you see', I commenced, 'how, despite her good intentions, despite her present protestations', for the girl was still mingling reproaches to her manservant for having taken her virtue in such humiliating circumstances, 'even she has been carried away by her passions, and why not? You see clearly the beauties of her parts, so why should not she share them with another? And, my dear Nathan – I hope you do not object to my placing my hand lightly upon such an intimate' organ – if you were to seize the present opportunity of using me in the same way, I am in no doubt that you would find my womanly parts as fine as that girl's.'

He responded to my provocations as I had hoped, by

243

caresses and touches upon my own parts, but I held him back, wishing further to increase his desire before satisfying it.

'Calm, my dear Nathan! See what happens on the other side of the window! Let us see if the minister will be able to turn this shameless couple from their evil ways.'

For now the clergyman had returned, running, accompanied by one of the chaste girls, and he and she knelt before the shameless couple, still engaged in their loud and exuberant love-making.

'Have shame, I pray you both, have shame! Do not defile our premises with such lewdness; in front of me, and in front of my dear sister in religion, Jane.' Here he gestured to his attractive young companion. She threw her arms around him, telling him between sobs how terrible it felt to see such Godless behaviour, and asking him to protect her from the shame that such a scene brought upon her.

But we saw little more of that masque, for Nathan Roundhorn's passions had risen to such a degree that I was no longer strong enough to keep away his importunities. He forced me down to the floor, and with only a carpet to temper the hardness of the wooden planks, he tumbled my skirts high above my waist, pulled the fabric around my bust away so that the full magnificence of my breasts was revealed to him. I responded by pulling his breeches down, revealing that he was endowed with a magnificently proportioned masculine organ, fully engorged and ready for its task.

But I urged him on by still maintaining the fiction that I was shocked and afraid of what he revealed to me. 'Oh Mr Nathan Roundhorn! You do not understand that I am not experienced in the arts of love. You shock me with your behaviour. Such a thick and weighty member cannot enter into me. I cannot take it inside me, please believe me!' And I said much more in a similar vein. The effect of my words was as I had hoped, for his passions ran higher and higher, until we were both swept away upon a veritable storm of love.

* * *

'And so, my dear Balthazar, commenced my career as an impresario, a creator of extravagances that serve to increase the desires of those who wish to make use of my services. Nathan Roundhorn was enraptured by the pleasures that I procured for him that night, and indeed, if truth be told, made use of the services of the girl who had been the instigator of the whole affair in the masque. Such was his pleasure in what I had achieved that he set me up in this establishment, giving me the wherewithal to run it myself in the manner which seemed most profitable to me, insisting only that I provide whatever services he requires.'

I bowed my head to Miss Chaunce. 'Truly, madame, a most remarkable tale. I believe, then, that your latest episode has brought us to the present day?'

'Indeed it has, and as a token of my appreciation for the many dull hours you must have spent listening to my inconsequential ramblings, transcribing in your own time from the cunning system of notation that you have employed, I should like to present you with a simple masque which I believe you will find to be of interest, as it illustrates the joys of true nakedness and variety.' At this, she rang her bell and extinguished the candles in the room, leaving only the light of the burning wood in the fireplace to save us from utter darkness.

After a few minutes, the curtains at the far end of the chamber opened. I gasped in surprise at what I saw, but Miss Chaunce put her finger to her lips, enjoining silence. The entire area had been transformed into what looked like the veranda of a house in a tropical region. I had little doubt that it represented a scene in the Brazil to which Miss Chaunce had so often alluded in her narrative.

Between two of the veranda's posts, supporting the roof of the supposed edifice, swung a hammock of the sort that Miss Chaunce had referred to in her tale. And in the hammock lay a young lady, like Miss Chaunce, of fair complexion, slender, perhaps the image of what Miss Chaunce herself had been in her earlier years. Candles had been cunningly used to suggest the rays of the setting sun. She held in her hand a fan, which she used constantly as if to cool herself, thus creating the illusion that it was the hour of sunset on a day of great heat. Her clothing was loose and voluminous, and the white cotton was of such a light texture that, wherever it clung to her body, it picked out her appealing form quite clearly.

As she shook her fan, she spoke to herself continually, complaining of the extreme warmth.

'Oh, but it is so unbearable to be in such heat, even in the lightest clothing. Even eschewing the scantiest underclothing, it is impossible to find comfort. The slightest movement only increases the discomfort. I quite envy the freedoms of those lower-class women who go about apparently without any trace of embarrassment, clad only in the briefest of short skirts, and no trace of any other garment upon their upper parts!'

At this, she recommenced fanning herself with redoubled vigour, and continued talking. 'But the discomfort is not the only problem in these hot days. The excessive warmth stirs up the passions also, and if one is not in a position to satisfy them, one becomes quite languid with desire!'

She commenced touching her own breasts, at first with light palpitations upon the outside of her dress, then with her hand inside the fabric, so that, as we supposed, her hand would be in direct contact with the rosy nipples themselves. Then, as the woman's passions were further set alight, the loose material was pulled down so that her breasts were quite bare, and her fingers were seen to be working upon the small and upstanding nipples.

But such pleasures obviously did not satisfy the woman, and in a moment her hands were inside her skirts. Her hands caressed thighs and the silken and golden bush which came into my delighted gaze, until they were wide parted and the very lips of her desire were being opened and manipulated by her busy fingers.

This delightful sight excited my own masculine senses, as you can imagine, and I asked myself whether I was to be invited to join in the fray. Miss Chaunce, perhaps divining my thoughts, placed a finger upon her lips, enjoining

patience. *At this moment, just when the woman had commenced uttering little sighs and gasps of pleasure, a person
that I took to be a menial entered the stage. She was of that
mixed race that one sometimes sees here in London, having
arrived from foreign parts, perhaps a mixture of Brazilian
Indian and African, with a golden skin and fine figure, taut
and slender, but with full upstanding breasts. She was of
course dressed in the fashion of her native country, bare to
the waist. When she saw the occupant of the hammock she
started in surprise, but her mistress showed little shame.*

'Really, Leonie, you should not come upon me un-
announced. You know how this hot weather affects me.' *She
spoke languidly.*

'But the mistress should not wear so many clothes. Look!'
*And Leonie (whom I supposed to be the image of the servant
that Teresa Chaunce had been close to many years ago) in
a moment untied a cord at the back of her skirt, and allowed
it to fall on to the floor around her, standing thus in front of
her mistress quite naked and unashamed. I could not keep my
eyes from the triangular, black and tangled bush that
adorned her lower belly, but then she knelt down in front of
her mistress, and commenced loosening the clothing that
clung around the white woman's body.*

*Then they were both naked, and they shared the hammock,
the darker woman's hands playing over all parts of her mistress's golden and white body. Miss Chaunce whispered in
my ear,* 'You can only enter into their game if you remove
every garment and go to them without shame.'

And so it was.

247

NEW BOOKS

Coming up from Nexus and Black Lace

A Matter of Possession by G. C. Scott
September 1995   Price: £4.99   ISBN: 0 352 33027 9
Barbara Hilson is looking for a special kind of man; a man who can impose himself upon her so strongly that her will dissolves into his. In the meantime, she has other options – like an extensive collection of bondage equipment, and her glamorous and obliging friend Sarah.

Teresa's Voyage by Romany Vargas
September 1995   Price: £4.99   ISBN: 0 352 33034 1
Strict Puritan parents prevented Teresa from enjoying the delights of uninhibited sex for most of her young life. But now that they are gone, she is free to indulge her most outlandish desires. What better place to start learning than a naval vessel full of frustrated sailors?

The Spanish Sensualist by Josephine Arno
October 1995   Price: £4.99   ISBN: 0 352 33035 X
Julia's seemingly impossible task is to persuade the stubborn Don Lorenzo Alvarez de Quitana to lend some of his fabulous pieces to a London art exhibition. Don Lorenzo accepts, but on one condition: that she joins his exclusive group of Hedonists. And in order to do that, she must pass five arduous tests of her sensuality.

The Ice Queen by Stephen Ferris
October 1995   Price: £4.99   ISBN: 0 352 33039 2
She strides through the corridors of the Institute of Corrective Education with a whip in her hand and a sneer on her face. Her gaze strikes terror into any man or woman unlucky enough to be placed in her care. She takes no excuses and gives no quarter. She is Matrilla, the Ice Queen; and she has just received a new batch of sinners to correct.

Conquered by Fleur Reynolds
September 1995   Price: £4.99   ISBN: 0 352 33025 2
16th-century Peru, and the Inca women are at the mercy of the
marauding conquistadors. Princess Inez eludes their clutches and
sets out to find her missing lover, only to be taken prisoner by an
Amazonian tribe. But her quest is soon forgotten when she is
initiated into some very strange and very sensual rites.

Dark Obsession by Fredrica Alleyn
September 1995   Price: £4.99   ISBN: 0 352 33026 0
Annabel Moss had never thought interior design a particularly
raunchy profession – until she was engaged at Leyton Hall. The
Lord and Lady, their eccentric family and the highly disciplined
staff all behave impeccably in company, but at night, the oaken
doors conceal some decidedly kinky activities.

Led on by Compulsion by Leila James
October 1995   Price: £4.99   ISBN: 0 352 33032 5
A chance visit to a country pub on the east coast turns into an
orgy of revelry when Karen becomes ensnared in Andreas's world
of luxury and fast living. With the help of the devine Marieka and
a multitude of willing and beautiful slaves, he throws the best and
most depraved parties in town.

Opal Darkness by Cleo Cordell
October 1995   Price: £4.99   ISBN: 0 352 33033 3
Twins Sidonie and Francis share everything: clothes, friends, a
love of the arts – and a rapacious appetite for sex. They set out
together on a grand tour of Europe with the intention of discovering new pleasures. But in the hypnotic Count Constantin and
his gorgeous friend Razvania, they may have taken on more than
they bargained for.

THE 1996 NEXUS CALENDAR

The 1996 Nexus calendar contains photographs of thirteen of the most delectable models who have graced the covers of Nexus books. And we've been able to select pictures that are just a bit more exciting than those we're allowed to use on book covers.

With its restrained design and beautifully reproduced duo-tone photographs, the Nexus calendar will appeal to lovers of sophisticated erotica.

And the Nexus calendar costs only £5.50 including postage and packing (in the traditional plain brown envelope!). Stocks are limited, so be sure of your copy by ordering today. The order form is overleaf.

Send your order to: Cash Sales Department
Nexus Books
332 Ladbroke Grove
London
W10 5AH

Please allow 28 days for delivery.

Please send me ____ copies of the 1996 Nexus calendar @ £5.50 (US$9.00) each including postage and packing.

Name: _____

Address: _____

_____

_____

_____

☐ I enclose a cheque or postal order made out to Nexus Books

☐ Please debit my Visa/Access/Mastercard account (delete as applicable)

My credit card number is:

‒ ‒ ‒ ‒   ‒ ‒ ‒ ‒   ‒ ‒ ‒ ‒   ‒ ‒ ‒ ‒

Expiry date: _____

FILL OUT YOUR ORDER AND SEND IT TODAY!